# THE
# KILLING CREW

Also by Murray Bailey

Singapore series:
Singapore 52
Singapore Girl
Singapore Boxer
Singapore Ghost
Singapore Killer
Singapore Fire

Ash Carter Near-East series:
Cyprus Kiss

Egyptian Series:
Map of the Dead
Sign of the Dead★

The Lost Pharaoh

Dare You series:
I Dare You
Dare You Twice

Black Creek White Lies

★ previously entitled Secrets of the Dead

# THE
# KILLING CREW

Murray Bailey

Heritage Books

Heritage Books, Truro, Cornwall

For my wife, Kerry, my everything

# Author's Note

The large-scale desertion towards the end of the British Mandate for Palestine appears unique in British colonial history. The number of soldiers and police deserting hasn't been widely reported and figures vary by source.

I am immensely grateful for research by Mssrs. C Caden and N Arielli and their article entitled *British Army and Palestine Police Deserters and the Arab Israeli War of 1948*. They identified seventeen pro-Jews although the number may have been twenty. The number of pro-Arab deserters may have been between 80 to 200. It is also unclear how many of the deserters were from the army and how many from the police.

I found *Major Farran's Hat* by Dr David Cesarani an insightful read. In addition to painting a clear historical picture and the challenges faced by the British military and police, it explains the unofficial units known as the Special Squads. Since they were denied by the British authorities, it is difficult to find much about them although I should point out that they should not be confused with the official Special Night Squads. The former were staffed by ex-commandos and SAS personnel and targeted Jewish terrorists. The official unit operated until 1938 with British infantry and Jewish Haganah commandos against Arab insurgents.

Until the end of the British Mandate, some street names were different. For example Allenby Street was originally designated as Allenby Road. The official spelling of Jewish streets also varied. British cartographers spelt Hovevei Tsion Street as Hoveve Ziyon Street. To avoid confusion, I have used current accepted spellings and names.

Figures and dates of attacks, deaths and responsibility vary by source. I have generally relied on *The Routledge Atlas of the Arab-Israeli Conflict* by Martin Gilbert which is widely respected and accepted.

All places mentioned in the book existed except for the farm I called 'Shuldik'. I have also taken the liberty of moving Sarafand Garrison a few miles south of its true location.

A number of groups existed alongside as pro-Arab militia. However the Killing Crew and their actions are fictitious.

# PROLOGUE

Despite the early hour, flies had already discovered the body. They buzzed around the man's head rather than the heavily charred lower half.

Dawn light cut through the burnt-out roof of the farmhouse, providing a surreal frame to the scene. The detective ran his hand through his hair, thinking.

Why would someone kill themselves this way? Was this the mysterious Engineer? Was this whole sordid episode over?

SIB officer Ash Carter stood in the courtyard below, looking up at him. Carter had been in the loft and then hurried down, leaving the detective alone with the body.

They exchanged nods as though they knew what was going on. He hoped that Carter did, because so far this raised more questions than it answered.

In the distance, he saw a car moving fast, dust spilling through the air in its wake.

Had Carter seen the car? He was now walking away from the farm down the track towards it.

The car braked hard as it reached Carter. Who was driving? The detective couldn't make them out, but they handed something to Carter, who then became animated.

When the detective got outside, the car was driving away as Carter jogged back to the farm.

"What is it?" the detective asked, hurrying to join the SIB man.

"It's all an elaborate trick. Clever, but he made mistakes. Like you said, that's not the Engineer up there."

The detective took a breath.

Carter had a newspaper clipping. He handed it over and pointed.

"What am I looking for?" the detective asked, puzzled.

But Carter was already moving towards his Land Rover. "Let's go," he said. "You drive, and I'll explain on the way."

The detective barked instructions to his team, jumped behind the wheel. He started to drive out of the farm but Carter pointed in a different direction.

"Over there?" the detective said, surprised there was another route.

"There must be another track, and it'll confirm my theory."

"So who is it?"

"We've time," Carter said. "I need to start at the beginning. Then I'll point out the clues."

# ONE

It was the end of June, 1948. The new state of Israel was at war, although there had been a threadbare ceasefire for the last two weeks.

However, the war wasn't my concern and neither was the man I saw on King Feisal Street.

There are two types of debt collector, those who are smooth operators, and those who are thugs. I prefer the latter because you know exactly where you are with them. There's no pretence.

The man I saw working the housing block was of the former type. He had a fake smile and swagger and I took an instant dislike to him.

I jogged past him down to the old port of Jaffa, where the buildings were even more tightly packed on a hill spiked with church towers.

The few faces I saw around me were mostly Jewish. They'd been predominantly Arabic only months ago. And the once-thriving port area, with its crammed shops, arcades and warehouses, was eerily different.

There were boats in the harbour, and I counted five, whereas the last time I'd been here I'd seen a mass of hulls and sails. Too many boats to count. It was a thriving bustling port that had suddenly lost its vibrancy. There was no background noise—the clatter and voices. There was no smell of fruit or spice. No sign of the famous Jaffa oranges.

There was just the sea.

It was as though some terrible disease—the bubonic plague or Spanish flu—had struck the area and left it bereft of life. I guess the aftermath of war is pretty much the same thing.

I saw beggars, notices of eviction and planned demolition. I saw despair and decay, and I turned around, wanting to leave this place and find the positive vibe that I knew had flooded through most of the newly established state of Israel.

Past the bombed-out remains of the old British Army Arab Soldiers' Club, I came to the Gaza bus station. Again, this had previously been crammed with people and vehicles. Now it was deserted except for a solitary woman pushing a pram.

I heard her baby cry.

And then she collapsed.

When I reached her I could see that she'd also been crying. She sat on the floor, one hand still holding the pram.

"Are you all right?" I asked awkwardly, keeping a respectable distance because I felt like I was intruding upon her grief.

She blinked with bloodshot eyes and looked away.

"Madam?"

She tried to stand, and I reached over and helped her up.

"Thank you." She cleared her throat before speaking less quietly. "You are English, no?"

"I am."

"You shouldn't be here."

She was right. The British had left suddenly and the state of Israel had been born. We were despised and unwelcome. Seen by many as the enemy.

I glanced at the crying baby as she said soothing words to it.

"He's hungry," she said. Her jaw tensed and her face reflected discomfort before she spoke again. "He needs milk and I have run dry."

"Is that why you were crying?"

She pulled a small baby-bottle from under the baby's blanket. The liquid inside was clear. The child drank a little and seemed to settle.

"It will keep him quiet for a short while. He wants milk." She forced a smile and started walking away.

I had some paper money in my pocket and pulled it out.

She stopped and shook her head. "No, but thank you. I'm no beggar. I won't take your money."

However, I saw the way she looked at the money in my hand. She was tempted but perhaps thought the cash came at a price.

After a moment I said, "I was just about to buy myself a bottle of milk. I'll gladly share with you and your child. Stay here."

Without waiting for a reply, I jogged to the end of the street. I wasn't far from the bustling Jaffa–Tel Aviv Road, where I knew I'd find a shop.

All food shops had queues these days, and I waited with nine others lined along the street. Once inside, I asked for two bottles of milk but was restricted to one.

"Rationed," the lady shop owner said in heavily accented English that I couldn't place. Many immigrants couldn't speak Hebrew so, despite it being the official language of the new state, the lingua franca was still English.

In addition to the milk, I bought lemonade, as well as rationed provisions of a loaf of bread, a few ounces of butter and a package of lamb meat.

It had taken me twenty minutes, and the sun had just dipped below the horizon by the time I returned to the bus station.

The young woman watched me approach. Her tearful face had transformed into one of curiosity.

I put my bottle of milk and small bundle of provisions on the ground then opened the lemonade bottle and drank.

"That's enough for me," I said. "It looks like I don't need the milk after all. I guess I'll just leave it here."

As though I'd fired a starter's pistol, the girl snatched up the milk, emptied the baby's bottle of water and refilled it with milk. Seconds later, the baby was drinking hungrily.

"Thank you," she said with a sigh. "I can't repay you."

"No payment required," I said. "And take the other food as well."

She began to cry, although this time it was with relief rather than despair. A minute later, she began to talk. She told me her name was Hannah Münz, from a place in Hungary that I'd never heard of. She and her husband, Jacob, had been refugees, moving from town to town, never settling, always afraid of the Nazis. And then, after the war, they had decided to travel to Eretz Israel but they'd become separated after a riot in Piraeus. They'd made contingency plans early on that they would meet in Tel Aviv, and so she'd boarded a refugee ship and arrived off Majdal without him.

"I was one of the thousands of *mapillim*," she said, referring to illegal Jewish immigrants. "We were smuggled ashore, and at first everyone was so kind and

helpful. But somehow I was handled by the wrong people, and when I was brought to Tel Aviv I owed them money. Of course, I couldn't afford to live in Tel Aviv itself, so I was put up in a house on King Feisal Street here in Jaffa. And then our son, Adam, was born. Jacob hasn't even seen him yet!"

Her breathing shuddered and I realized she'd travelled pregnant and been raising her son alone.

I said I'd walk her back to her house, and that's when she told me of her fear. She was hiding at the bus station because the debt collector was coming.

# TWO

The man I'd seen earlier in the day stepped straight into Hannah's home as she opened the door. It was really a single room but a curtain separated the living area from the bedroom. Three months old, baby Adam was asleep in a crib, and I was standing behind the curtain, peering through.

As I'd walked Hannah back to her home, she'd told me that she had to pay the debt collector twenty *mils* a week. It wasn't much but she hadn't paid for three weeks.

"How much do you owe overall?"

"Three pounds," she'd said. "Originally it was one pound, but they call it interest, and the amount keeps rising."

She'd told me that the debt collector had been charming, but two days ago he'd threatened her if she didn't pay today. She thought he'd be back after eight o'clock, so I left her with the promise that I'd return soon.

I went to my lodgings on Gordon Street, changed, picked up some more cash, and returned to Hannah's house.

I'd only been there a few minutes when the debt collector knocked on the door.

He glanced around the room as he entered, probably gauging whether there was anything of value to be taken in place of the arrears. Hannah kept the room clean and tidy despite the dilapidated state of the building, but she had nothing worth taking.

"You know why I'm here," he said in English with an eastern European accent and a smile that didn't reach his eyes. Hannah had told me he was Slovakian.

"I have the money," she said.

He looked surprised. "How much?"

"Sixty mils."

He glanced around the room again, although this time I realized it was a delaying tactic.

When his eyes returned to Hannah, he said, "It's more because you didn't pay. I told you that two days ago—and you weren't in earlier so I wasted a trip."

She said nothing, and I thought I could hear her nervous breathing.

He said, "One hundred mils."

She put her hand in her skirt pocket.

The man stepped closer. "Or we could forget the debt this time, Hannah." His voice had an oily edge to it that made my skin crawl.

I gripped the curtain ready to step out, but she'd asked me not to intervene. She'd pointed out that I couldn't be here every time the debt collector called. So I waited for the signal she'd give me if I was needed.

The man's hand reached out and touched Hannah's shoulder. "You're a pretty woman."

She shrank away from his touch.

"We could come to an arrangement." He reached again and this time she gave me the signal.

"Enough!"

I stepped through the curtain and the debt collector briefly looked like he'd have a heart attack. He froze, mid-reach, his eyes bulging.

"Who are you?" he asked.

"I'm the man taking over this debt."

He cocked his head to one side and studied me as he regained his composure.

"*Deutsch*?" he asked, because I'd spoken German. "I don't know any German debt collectors."

"You do now," I replied, continuing the pretence.

His head cocked to the other side, and when he smiled this time, it did crease around his eyes.

"You don't look Jewish."

"And you, *mein freund*, don't look like an idiot."

He stopped smiling.

"How much is the debt?" I asked.

"Five Palestinian pounds."

"This lady told me it was three."

He shrugged. "If you're a debt collector then you know how this works. Call it inflation."

I shook my head. "I'll pay you four and the debt is mine."

He shrugged again but I could see he was considering the deal. I may have interrupted his planned fun with Hannah, but he would be making a reasonable return.

"How much for all the debt in the house?" I asked.

Hannah had told me that there were twelve families here and that many of them owed this man money, although none had originally borrowed from him. He'd bought the debt from the gang who had brought them here. And now a competitor was offering to buy the business from him.

"Fifty pounds," he said. The way he raised his chin as he delivered the figure told me it was a huge exaggeration.

I said nothing as though considering the sum.

He said, "That includes a premium for future lost business." He had his right hand in his pocket now and I wondered what he had in there. His money perhaps.

I nodded. "Thirty pounds is fair."

"Forty-five."

"Thirty-five."

I expected him to compromise on forty, but he said, "Good. Let's finalize the deal outside. I'll give you the documentation."

Documentation? I seriously doubted there would be any paperwork.

Hannah looked at me with concern, but I just inclined my head and told her I would be back to agree repayments.

The debt collector let himself out and I followed him into the corridor and then out onto the street. It was dark. The nearest street light was fifty yards away but there was enough light from windows to see as he pulled his hand from his pocket and showed me a seven-inch cosh.

"No need for that," I said, raising my hands and patting the air. "We are businessmen, am I right? I will pay you fifty pounds for the business."

"Berek!" the debt collector shouted.

I said, "*Bitte*?" Pardon me?

A door opened two buildings along the street and a block of a man stepped out. He was the second type of debt collector with an ugly square face and small nose.

Again I patted the air. "I don't want trouble."

The man with the cosh said, "Of course, we don't want trouble either."

The second man closed in. Both were ten feet from me and six feet apart.

Berek spoke in what I guessed to be Slovak. The way he looked towards me made me think it was a question like, "Who is this, Hersch?"

"Someone we need to deal with," the first man said in German.

I said, "I want to buy your business for this house."

Berek's frown suggested he was less intelligent than Hersch and didn't follow or know how to handle the situation without instructions.

Hersch spoke to his colleague in Slovak. I didn't understand.

I said, "Let's not do this deal on the street. I've been using the old tanner's place at the docks." I'd seen it was closed up when I'd run past earlier. And on my way back to Hannah's I'd paid a quick visit, just in case. "Let's do the deal there."

Hersch spoke and then both men grinned before the smooth, confident one smiled at me.

"Lead the way, my German friend."

Two minutes later, I was pulling open the doors to the tannery and gagging at the smell of rotten flesh and the shit used to treat animal skins.

There was a light on the dock and it shone, grey through a window. It showed the concrete floor and vats and numerous piles, which I guessed were animal hides.

After five paces, I turned.

The Slovaks stayed in the doorway, presumably assessing the scene. Then the smarter one nodded and they stepped forward.

"How much money do you have on you?" Hersch asked.

"Enough to buy the business," I said.

"How much?" the square-faced one asked.

"Fifty pounds."

I dipped into my pocket and pulled out a purple Palestinian note. Then let it flutter to the ground between us.

Berek crouched and picked it up, studied it and then grunted. The five hundred *mil* banknote was similar to the fifty-pound note, and they weren't fooled despite the poor light.

"What?" Hersch said. "You're being funny." He stepped closer. Berek pulled a knife.

These were hard men, used to violence, and they knew the rule: strike first and strike fast. But I knew it too.

The square man lunged and I sidestepped further than necessary. It was deliberate. There was an upright support and against it I'd left an iron rod.

One second I was moving away and the next I was swinging the weapon at Berek. He'd been lunging after me with his knife. Maybe he thought I would run. Or maybe he didn't think at all. As the rod smacked into his head, I figured he wouldn't do much thinking again.

The big man went down, jerked and lay still.

I'd expected the other one to attack immediately, but he stepped back and paced like a caged tiger.

"That was cowardly," he said in English rather than the German we'd been speaking.

I said, "He had a knife."

"I don't." He dropped his hands. "We could still do the deal."

I said nothing.

He said, "Thirty pounds."

I said, "Tempting."

He took a breath and tried to sound relaxed. "You aren't German, you are English. Your German is good but not natural."

It was schoolboy German and supported by my mother's teaching, but I'd never visited the country, so I guessed he was right.

He said, "There is no German gang here, it is just you, Englishman."

I said nothing. This was taking too long. I wanted to get away from this hellish stench. In the quiet moments when we weren't speaking, I could hear flies and rats feasting on the uncured hides.

He said, "Put down your weapon and deal. We can both win today. Otherwise, you will be forever looking over your shoulder for my Slovak friends. You are alone, we are not."

I looked at his colleague, who was clearly dead. "What about Berek?"

"No hard feelings. He was an idiot. He attacked you and you defended yourself."

"Thirty pounds?"

"Yes."

I let the iron rod clatter to the concrete floor. The sudden noise must have scared the rats because for a second there was absolute silence.

I don't know whether he had his own knife or had secretly picked up Berek's but there was suddenly the flash of steel in his hand.

His friend had lunged whereas Hersch flicked in a short slashing motion. He drove me back and I watched his knife-hand and his rhythm.

I backed up. He closed in.

Slash right to left. Back-slash left to right.

I stepped until I reached the hides. The stench made me breathe through my mouth.

Slash right to left. Back-slash left to right.

Only he didn't finish the move that time.

I'm left-handed, and as soon as he started the back-slash, I'd stepped inside and driven my fist through his face.

He went down, and to my surprise, bounced straight back. Impressive, but he was just giving me another target and so I hit him again.

I was shouting. I don't know what, but the adrenaline had gotten the better of me. Whether it was the knife or the smell or the hatred for these two men who preyed on the misfortune of others, I lost control for the first time in a fight. I had the man's face pressed hard into the stinking pile of animal skins and it wasn't until he stopped kicking that I let go.

# THREE

"You're late and you smell awful!" Erika Arnold stood outside her kitchen with hands on her hips. She was my landlady on Gordon Street and she was right. I not only smelled of putrescence from the old tannery, but I probably also smelled of sick.

After the fight with the Slovak debt collectors, I'd rushed outside and thrown up. My old boxing coach from Manchester had taught me to stay calm. Anger clouded the brain. Anger led to mistakes. So despite winning the fight, I was disappointed with myself.

"Take a bath and I'll fix your dinner," she said. Erika had a matronly manner, although she wasn't much older than me. Perhaps late twenties, possibly thirty.

A good-looking woman, she was originally from Southern Germany, although from her appearance I would have guessed Persian blood rather than Germanic. But then again she was a Jewess. She might have been a film star if she'd only smile.

On the first evening we'd talked I made the mistake of asking, "Why so serious, Erika?" and she'd replied, "Because life is serious."

She was still looking at me with her usual disapproval.

"Thank you, that's kind," I said, because it wasn't one of my two allocated bath nights.

"Don't thank me," she said. "You aren't coming into my kitchen looking and smelling like that. And I'll add the cost to your bill."

It was a communal, hall-bath, and I sat in tepid water and splashed it up and over my body. She'd added rose essence and I guessed it was preferable to my previous body odour.

I towelled dry in my room, and when I entered the kitchen, I could have sworn she gave me a brief approving glance. However, her tone contradicted that view.

"Matzo ball soup," she said, putting a bowl on the kitchen table as I pulled up a chair. She raised a finger, like a teacher giving me a lesson. "Don't expect this every time, Mr Carter. You know that dinner is at eight every day. It's included in the price, but not earlier and not later."

"Understood."

"This is a one-time thing." She narrowed her big dark eyes. "I don't approve of tardiness so don't expect this again."

"I won't," I said, trying not to smile at being told off. However, after a beat, I countered with: "You have exceptionally long eyelashes, Erika."

She huffed and turned away, but I was sure she liked the flattery. Who doesn't?

The chicken soup was as delicious as always. My landlady didn't have a wide repertoire but what she did cook was exceptional.

"Could I have more?" I asked, scraping the last juice from my bowl.

"No."

I didn't expect any and then received a lecture about food rationing and having to be careful with portions. However, I knew that Erika was reasonably well off and could afford to buy black market goods. Unlike Hannah Münz, who had nothing.

After the fight, I'd returned to the house on King Feisal Street and told Hannah that the debt collector wouldn't be coming back. I told her that her debt and the debt of the other tenants had been paid off.

She'd cried then, but it hadn't been with relief. I'd never needed to borrow money and I didn't understand. These people paid money back so that the money lenders would give them more. It was a spiralling debt problem that could only benefit the lenders. And if a young woman couldn't pay then they would take payment in other ways.

I struggled to understand her tears.

"But the slate is at least clean," I said. "And you and Adam are safe."

I couldn't help the other tenants but told Hannah that if she could find a job then I would help with her rent in Tel Aviv.

She'd blinked at me through her tears. "Really?"

"For a short time. A few weeks, until you find your feet—and hopefully your husband."

After dinner, Erika poured herself a brandy and we sat in her living room. It was the best room in the house, with curtains and a plush rug. The armchairs were leather and I tried not to think of the rotting animal skins I'd inhaled earlier. Between us was a card table upon which Erika dealt our hands for a game of gin rummy.

My game of choice was poker, more for the camaraderie than the betting. It also helped me hone my

18

skill of reading people and their tells. However, rummy with my attractive, if miserable, landlady was a good way to spend the evenings.

I'd been in Israel for nine days. Major Bill Wolfe and I had left Mandatory Palestine with the other seventy-odd thousand British military and police personnel in May. The two of us had gone to Cyprus awaiting instructions, and five weeks after that, I was back. Only it was the new state of Israel now, and different in many ways, not least because the patrolling military were Israelis and nearly everyone was Jewish.

Bill Wolfe had met me from the boat in Haifa and driven me to Tel Aviv. His car was a black Bentley, with a smoother ride than the Land Rovers we were used to. It had belonged to someone high up in the Colonial Office before what was loosely called 'the handover' to the Israelis.

The car was big and obvious and not at all what I expected. I thought our mission was to be clandestine, but I soon realized it couldn't be. There were military checkpoints everywhere—just like there had been in the twilight of the British rule. We'd been worried about Jewish terrorists. Now they were at war with the Arab states and were concerned about anyone who wasn't a Jew.

The British were hated by many, and at each checkpoint we had guns thrust in our faces. But Wolfe stayed calm. We had legal papers. We had authority from the Israeli government with travel passes, because we were on a mission.

It was sixty-three miles from Haifa, and in pre-Israel times, I'd done it in under ninety minutes. When Wolfe drove me in the Bentley it took more than twice that time because of all the stops and interrogations.

We saw military jeeps and trucks, commercial lorries, buses, but only a handful of private cars. There were so few on the roads that you tended to remember them. I was sure no one would forget the Bentley. Indeed, on the outskirts of Tel Aviv, we were recognized by soldiers at a checkpoint and sailed through. It was a shame this didn't happen every time.

Wolfe showed me our office on Nahmani Street. It had been used by the SIB but was part of a larger building. The place was a wreck, abandoned in a hurry and subsequently ransacked. Wolfe had cleaned one of the ground-floor rooms and set up four desks and a noticeboard. We also had filing cabinets and a safe, although they were all currently empty.

There was also a telephone, although he told me not to use it.

After handing me keys and telling me I was to obtain two years' worth of the *Palestine Post*, he took me to my new lodgings and introduced me to Erika Arnold. Then he'd left. All he said was that he was making contact with his old Arab informer, which would mean crossing over into occupied territory. He also took the Bentley.

"You're distracted tonight," Erika said after declaring 'Gin' and adding an extra twenty-five points to her score. She studied me in the orange glow of the table lamp behind her.

"Am I?"

"You know you are."

I picked up the cards and shuffled them.

She said, "Since you've been here, you've gone out running and walking and have seemed generally bored."

She was right.

"But something happened tonight," she said, raising one of her neat eyebrows. "But I don't expect you to tell me what."

"Today I learned that my German isn't as good as I thought."

Surprise lit her eyes. "You speak German?"

In the foreign language, I said, "My mother had family in Dresden. She liked me to speak German, although I never visited. And then of course the war happened." We chatted for a few minutes and she finally nodded, her lips pursed.

"What?"

"Your accent is all over the place, and Germans usually hold up a finger and thumb for two. Unconsciously, you held up two fingers, like your Winston Churchill's victory sign."

I dealt the cards for another round and she watched me closely.

"But that's not it," she said. "That's not what has been bothering you."

"No. I suppose I'm wondering what I'm doing here." Of course, it was a lie, but she accepted it.

"Me too," she said.

After a few nights at Erika Arnold's house, she'd invited me into her private living room to play cards. Which made me ask her why.

"Because I rent out four rooms," she'd said, "and you are the only single person. I think you call it Hobson's Choice."

So I'd played cards with her each evening and gradually learned her story. At eighteen, with her new husband, Horace, they'd fled Nazi Germany. They'd guessed persecution was coming but hadn't predicted the extent of the horror that would follow.

They'd settled in Tel Aviv, and although they'd never had children, they'd been happy. They'd planned to start a hotel, but Horace first joined the police and then later the Jewish Haganah. He hadn't been a terrorist and yet he'd been shot by a British bullet only months after the war with Germany had ended.

"The imperial British imposed military law here. They treated us all like criminals. They were anti-Semites and no better than the Nazis," she'd said with passion.

"And yet you have accepted me as a guest."

"Paying guest," she'd corrected me. "I am a businesswoman, Mr Carter. However, if you do anything to upset me, I will not hesitate to throw you out."

I didn't doubt it. I was on a knife-edge and she liked the money more than she hated the British.

That evening, I decided to tell her why we were here. I thought it might make her view me—and my countrymen—with less animosity.

I said, "I'll tell you something, but I'd like you to be honest with me."

She nodded, curious, and then took a sip of her brandy.

"Do you remember the bombings and killings during the conflict in Mandatory Palestine?"

"Of course." She swallowed, and I wondered if she was thinking of her husband.

I said, "There were some unexplained ones—some that allegedly involved British soldiers and equipment."

"Arabs and their supporters," she said.

"Yes. They were known as the Killing Crew."

"They were working for your lot!" She almost spat the words.

"No! No!" I said, trying to calm the rising tension and now regretting my whole approach. I'd handled this badly from the start.

She took a larger mouthful of her drink and studied me with her dark eyes.

I said, "They were definitely not acting with British approval. My colleague and I are here to bring those men to justice. And we are here with the approval of your government." I hadn't needed to add the latter. Without their approval, we would have been ejected from the country. While I'd been in Cyprus, Wolfe had been here acting undercover, gaining intelligence, but it couldn't have lasted. Eventually he'd have been arrested as a spy and undoubtedly executed. That was my opinion. He, on the other hand, had been more sanguine about the prospect. I suspected his relaxed attitude had been due to returning to the arms of his girlfriend in Jerusalem.

"Good," Erika finally said. "I feel less bad about having an Englishman in my house."

She picked up her cards and we began to play another hand. She carried on winning.

When she'd reached five hundred points, she drained her glass and stood. There was the faintest hint of a smile on her lips, which was probably because she'd beaten me again.

But she surprised me. "Before I go to bed," she said, and then paused, "I've been waiting for your question. You asked me to be honest with you."

"Why are you really happy to have me as a guest, Erika?"

"I already told you, Mr Carter. It's because you are paying me."

I nodded and smiled. "But that doesn't truly explain it."

"Oh yes it does, Mr Carter. You might like to think it's your good company, but I could never forgive the British."

"Then it must be my ability with cards."

"Yes, it must be that. Now goodnight, Mr Carter."

23

I found that the game and conversation with my landlady had taken my mind off the incident with the Slovaks.

However, in the early hours, I woke with a start. Someone was banging on my door.

Dressed only in my pyjama bottoms, I opened the door and was immediately grabbed by two men with guns.

# FOUR

"Where were you yesterday evening?"

I was in a police cell, still in my pyjamas, handcuffed to the bars. I'd been manhandled out of Erika's house, watched by all the residents, and bundled into a police car. One of the policemen had forced my head into the seat and put his whole weight on me.

The urge had been to fight. But they were police and they were armed. I was not. So I just accepted the discomfort and was grateful that it only lasted a few minutes before I was pushed and hit until I was inside the cell.

No one had spoken to me for half an hour before a detective walked in and asked me the question.

"I was playing cards with my landlady," I replied.

"Before that!"

I thought about it. "I took a walk."

"Where did you walk?"

"Oh, I don't know. I strolled up and down the seafront mainly."

"Where else?"

"I got some food—bread, butter, milk, that sort of thing—from a grocer's on Ajami Road, off the Jaffa–Tel—"

"I know where Ajami Road is!" He raised his eyebrows. "And the important fact is that you admit you were in Jaffa this evening."

"I went to a shop."

"What time?"

"Sevenish."

"What about later?"

"I walked about a bit more and went back to my lodgings on Gordon Street."

"What about the port at Jaffa?"

I shook my head.

"You were seen going into an empty building at the port."

Ah, an old interrogator's trick: make it sound like you know more than you do. Imply you have a witness and hope for the first admission. Then work with that until you get a full confession.

I shook my head. "Not me. Look, what's this all about? I have official papers. I'm allowed to be here."

He said, "Tell me about the Slovaks."

"What Slovaks?"

He had a swagger stick and whacked the bars, hoping to intimidate. "I don't believe you!"

I said nothing.

He growled, "What are you doing in Tel Aviv?"

"Your HQ knows all about my mission."

"And where do the Slovak debt collectors fit in?"

I shook my head. "I don't know anything about debt collectors."

He grunted, spun on his heel and marched away.

Thirty minutes later and the cell was starting to get uncomfortably warm. I called for water but got no response.

I was there for two hours before the door opened and someone I knew walked towards my cell.

"Dave Rose!"

The young man, about my age, had a grin on his face. Since I'd last seen him, he'd let his once trim beard fill out. But he had the same blue eyes that sparkled with intelligence, and sandy hair that we liked to joke was red.

"Ash Carter!" he said. "I heard you'd returned. He opened the cell door and started unlocking my handcuffs. "Sorry about the misunderstanding."

"An Englishman in Israel," I said. "I expected the rough treatment."

He nodded and tucked the cuffs away.

I said, "But you? How come you're still here?"

He chuckled. "You didn't know?"

"Know what?"

"I'm Jewish."

Of course I hadn't known. I was his friend and he'd never once hinted at his religion. I must have stared open-mouthed, because he chuckled again.

"I'm known as David Rosen these days. I was always Jewish, just never broadcast it. Tea?"

He didn't wait for a response and called for someone to bring us tea. We were walking out of the room and he led me to an office with comfortable chairs.

"Put something on," he said with a chuckle in his voice as he threw me a shirt. The colour was off-white, but it seemed clean enough. I put it on.

"Dave Rose." I shook my head as I took a seat.

"Rosen," he corrected me.

We'd been friends for the two years I'd been in Mandatory Palestine. We'd both been based in Haifa at the end, me in the Royal Military Police and him in the Palestine Police Force.

During the war, Rosen had been first assigned to the Home Guard due to health issues and then the police.

After the war, the PPF was expanded, more than doubling to 4,000 British members. Most of these were ex-British servicemen, demobbed from the army. Because of his police experience, Dave Rosen stood out and gained rapid promotion to captain of his division in Haifa. He was now a sub-inspector earning considerably more than during British rule.

I'd met him at the Camel Club for officers when he'd joined our poker game.

At five ten, he was smaller than my military police buddies. But what he lacked in stature, he made up for in personality.

When I'd taken my furlough and visited Egypt with three others, Rosen had cajoled his way into the group. We'd flown to Cairo and stayed at the Mena House Hotel, a short walk from the pyramids. Three days there and then three more in Ismalia and a crazy time at the famous Blue Kettle Club. The discovery that he'd lost his mother a few years ago, and, like me, hated his father, had cemented our friendship.

"Sorry about the over-zealous lieutenant who arrested you," he said as sweet tea was delivered. "These are difficult times and... well, you're British. Assumed guilty until proven innocent." He laughed.

"What's innocent?"

"Becoming a Jew." He continued laughing, like we were in a club having a great time.

"Seriously, Dave," I said. "What was it all about? All your lieutenant kept saying was something about Slovaks—debt collectors, I think he called them."

He cleared his throat and nodded, suddenly serious. "Two bodies were found in the early hours of this morning—Slovak Jews."

"Bodies? Murders?" I said, feigning innocence.

"Yes." His eyes narrowed. "And you know nothing?"

"No, why…?"

"Because you were seen in the area."

"Earlier," I said. "I'd been walking through and went to a grocery shop in Jaffa."

"Of course," he said as though it explained everything.

"So what happened?"

"It was in an Arab tannery. One with his head bashed in and another suffocated in a pile of stinking animal skins."

I pulled a face. "Who were they? I presume you knew them."

"Like you said, debt collectors. That's what they call themselves, but they prey on the misfortune of refugees." He shook his head but his eyes stayed on me, assessing. "Whoever killed them did us a favour."

I doubted he would try and trick me, but just in case, I stuck to my story of innocence.

"Anything else?"

"They were robbed," he said quickly. "Their money belts were cut off." Then: "What?"

*Damn!* He was a good people-reader. My face must have given away my surprise at the last piece of news. Someone had discovered the bodies and taken their money. Not me.

I said, "The killer or… you know?"

He frowned at me.

"Could the police have taken them?" I shrugged. "It happens a lot, Dave. First copper on the scene checks for money and no one's the wiser. A simple murder becomes murder and theft."

He seemed to buy my response and looked thoughtful. "So, we look for the wrong motive. Not about money?"

"It's possible."

He finished his tea. "All right, Ash. You know the score. I have to write a report. Tell me you were not wearing a hat."

"I was not."

"Good. Someone was seen entering the premises with a hat, so it'll be easy to explain your release. That and the fact you didn't do it, right?"

"Right."

He pumped my hand. "It's good to see you, Fred."

"You too, Ginge."

His nickname had been coined partly because of his name but mostly because he hated to be called a redhead. Ginge short for Ginger. I knew he wasn't, but it was fun to wind him up. He scowled at my humour then laughed because he must have expected it.

"We should go back to the Blue Kettle Club one weekend," he said.

We'd picked up the names Fred and Ginger after our furlough in Egypt. We'd been a bit of a double act with the ladies, and my poor skill on the dance floor made the association with Fred Astaire more amusing.

We reminisced as he walked me outside, both reflecting that he was unlikely to be allowed into Egypt any time soon.

"One more thing, Ash," he said, stopping on the doorstep.

I waited.

He said, "Your mission here is approved, I know that."

"Right."

"And you've got permits to make sure no one—the police, the army… anyone, gets the wrong idea."

"Right." I wondered what was coming.

He said, "Why four? You and Bill Wolfe, I get, but who are the other two?"

# FIVE

"Who are the other two?" I asked Bill Wolfe. He'd pulled up in his conspicuous Bentley just minutes after I'd finally taken delivery of the old newspapers he'd asked for.

His normally expressionless face appeared to beam, his eyes bright above a full beard. When I'd last seen Wolfe, he'd had a serious moustache and stubble on his chin. The new beard was brown and curly like his hair, and, if it weren't for the clothes, he could have passed as a local.

"Samuel Macintyre and Albert Finney," he said answering my question when we were inside and out of the intense sunshine. "There will be four of us on this assignment. How did you find out?"

"Dave Rose. I bumped into him. Only he's calling himself Rosen these days."

"Jewish?" he said.

"Apparently so."

"Doesn't surprise me," he said without explanation. "When you say 'bumped into', what happened exactly?"

And so I told him about the incident last evening, about the young woman, Hannah Münz and her baby, who needed help, about the debt collectors and our fight. I probably gave him too much detail but he didn't interrupt me.

"You know your problem, Ash?" he said, scowling at me when I'd finished telling him about the conversation with Rosen in the police station. "You have the *kisa syndrome*. That's your fuckin' problem."

His Yorkshire accent came to the fore, so I knew he was annoyed.

"Kiss-her? I told you," I said indignantly, "that's not—"

"K-I-S-A," he said. "It stands for Knight In Shining fuckin' Armour. The F is silent." He grinned, and I relaxed. "You see a damsel in distress and have to go charging in. You've done it before and no doubt you'll do it again, but you need to be careful. We're in a country where being English is almost as bad as being a Nazi German. You go charging in and one of these days you'll come a cropper."

"What do you suggest?"

"Stop trying to solve everyone else's problems—especially pretty girls'. No"—he raised his index finger—"let me be more specific: stop rushing to help any damsel in distress, no matter how bed-able she is. Understood? Just like in military strategy, you learn to pick your fights. Use that same discretion when someone needs help. And remember, it's not your problem and you don't have to be the one to step in."

I nodded. This was the longest speech I'd heard Wolfe make and was sure it was sage advice. However, it's near impossible to fight your natural instincts. I knew, no matter what, I couldn't walk on by.

I'd always been like it. The first time had been at school. I'd been about nine when, on the way home, I'd seen a bigger boy picking on a girl. I had no idea why, but when I saw him pull her hair, I charged in. He was two years older and gave me a sound beating, for which the girl never thanked me. She'd disappeared by the time I got up off the floor, battered and dirty. My shirt got ripped too. I was scolded by my father for being in such a state when I returned home. Which was ironic since it was a principle he'd mentioned. And I'd heard it in church.

It took me a week reading the Bible before I found the section in Proverbs: *Open your mouth, judge righteously, defend the rights of the poor and needy.*

Admittedly, this didn't talk of violence, whether by the fist or the gun, but speaking out rarely has the desired effect. I'd tried to reason with the debt collectors and they'd thought me weak.

Despite Wolfe's lecture, would I do it again? Would I defend Hannah Münz? Of course I would. If I could go back and advise the nine-year-old Ash Carter, I couldn't stop him from defending the girl. Although I would teach him how to fight better.

Wolfe was shaking his head and I had no doubt he guessed what I was thinking.

"You'd better have one of these," he said, his voice heavily laden with disappointment. Raising his leg, he thumped the foot onto a table and pulled up the trousers.

My mouth dropped open. Around his ankle was a holster.

He unclipped it and pulled out a Beretta.

"You have a gun!" I immediately felt foolish for stating the obvious and he responded by clearing his throat. I was a constant disappointment to the major. Two of us on an important, sensitive mission and he'd been lumbered with me. So far all I'd been was a liability, first in Cyprus and now here.

I tried to cover my embarrassment by saying: "Our approval here specifically excluded the carrying of arms."

He replaced the gun, took his leg off the table and gave it a shake, presumably adjusting the fit.

"So you don't want one?"

He waited a beat before opening a shoebox he'd brought in from the car. From it, he pulled out another gun and ankle holster. He slid it across the table towards me and I took it.

"Where did you get them?"

"My Arab toad."

Toad was slang for an informant, someone who would betray their fellow countrymen. An undercover operative who was motivated by money rather than loyalty to the British.

Wolfe had found his man and been given the guns. I wondered how much they had cost.

I attached the holster to my left ankle, covered it with the trouser leg and walked around the room. It felt heavy, awkward and obvious.

"You'll get used to it quickly," Wolfe said.

I shook my leg like he had seconds before and felt the weight settle above my ankle, then nodded. "Tell me about your toad."

"He's angry and bitter."

I nodded. The British had fled. The UN's Partition Plan hadn't been acceptable to the Arabs, and Britain had not only abstained from the vote but rushed to leave the country afterwards. For thirty years, the Palestinian Arabs had been our friends and we'd abandoned them in their hour of need.

"What did he say about the deserters?" I asked.

"That we fuckin' deserved it! But he doesn't know who the Killing Crew was."

"Where did you find him—your toad?"

"In Jerusalem, where I expected. The city is still under martial law, only it's theirs now. There's still an Arab and Christian quarter, although the Arab sector is barricaded off."

"And Beth?" Beth had been Wolfe's Coptic Christian girlfriend.

He eyed me suspiciously before allowing a grin to appear. "Oh yes, Beth's still there. Why do you think it took me so long?"

I was disappointed. I knew Wolfe's reputation as a bit of a rogue, but we were on a serious mission and he also had a reputation as a good investigator and soldier.

"What's up?" He eyed me suspiciously.

"I'm surprised, that's all," I said. "We've a job to do—"

"And we'll do it, Ash! This won't be easy and we've got to wait for the rest of the team."

"Who are these Macintyre and Finney chaps? You haven't explained."

"Because I'm not sure." He shrugged. "We're getting all the files of the deserters. They're being shipped back from England. Tomorrow we go back to Haifa and meet the boat from Liverpool. That, I predict, is when all will be revealed."

# SIX

Wolfe and I were discussing the little we knew about the Killing Crew when there was a knock on our improvised office door.

The man who entered introduced himself as an official from the Israeli Security Council. He wore a severe black suit and matching trilby.

"You are here with our approval," he began.

It was an unnecessary statement, and since there had been no preamble, served to tell us this was a formal visit.

"Major Bill Wolfe," Wolfe said. "And this is Captain Ash Carter." We'd both been recently promoted, and since Wolfe and I were on first-name terms, I hadn't become used to my new rank.

The Security Council official didn't give us his name. Instead, he opened a briefcase and pulled out four sheets of paper.

"There are four warrants," he said. "Who are the other two members of your team?"

"Albert Finney and Samuel Macintyre," Wolfe said.

"I can read that! Who are they?"

Wolfe didn't react to the official's rude outburst. Instead, he calmly replied, "The British War Office applied for the permissions. All I know is that our colleagues are yet to arrive."

"Fine." The official tapped the warrants. "You have a single mission here. You will identify and apprehend the gang known as the Killing Crew." He paused and pulled his dry top lip with his bottom teeth. "Then you will hand the criminals over to the IDF for prosecution."

"No," Wolfe said calmly. "We will take the criminals back to Britain for prosecution. They are army deserters and will be treated as such."

The Security Council official said nothing for a minute. He looked around our makeshift office as though assessing our ability to perform the task at hand.

"There were many deserters," he said, turning his focus back to Wolfe. "Some of them are heroes."

He was referring to the deserters who had been pro-Jew and joined the IDF.

"We have no interest in those men," Wolfe said.

The other man nodded. "Good."

"Just like we have no interest in the other pro-Arab deserters."

The official breathed out, a growl under his breath, like a smoker's wheeze. "I want information on any of our enemy you identify."

"That isn't part of our orders, sir," Wolfe said, with a deference that surprised me.

The Security Council man waited. He did the thing with his lip and lower teeth again. In the awkward silence, I felt sweat trickle down my back.

Finally he said, "Any help would be greatly appreciated."

Wolfe said, "We'll do what we can."

"Good. And I will help by providing you with secretarial assistance. She's called Miss Rom and will be joining you this afternoon."

With that, the unfriendly black-suited official spun on his heel and left us.

"You can't be serious!" I blurted as soon as we were alone.

"Which bit?" Wolfe said, perching on a desk.

"The bit about helping them with pro-Arab deserters."

"Whatever gave you that idea? Of course not. We do our job and only our job. And this fuckin' secretary—this Rom girl—"

"Yes?"

"Be careful. I don't want you to have a romantic liaison with her. Understood?"

I did. My last girlfriend had been our secretary in Cyprus, and that hadn't ended too well. Bill Wolfe might well be enjoying sexual relations in Israel, but I was steering well clear of the opposite sex.

Miss Rom was nineteen and strangely good-looking. She had cropped mousy-brown hair but it somehow worked on her chiselled features. Deep brown eyes with long lashes helped.

However, she wore no make-up and turned up with a typewriter and an expression of a new employee, nervous and unassuming.

She introduced herself before apologizing.

"Why are you sorry?" I asked.

"Because I've been forced on you," she said. "That's not nice. For you or me."

Wolfe told her to take one of the desks and gave a shrug that seemed to say, what are you going to do?

She set up her typewriter and discovered we had no appropriate paper for it.

"I'll get some for tomorrow—and carbons."

We watched her.

She said, "So how far have you got? Would you bring me up to speed, please?"

Wolfe said, "With what, Miss Rom?"

"Call me Sylvia. Please." She flashed a smile, and I started to think her initial meekness had been an act. "The Killing Crew," she clarified. "That's who you're after."

"What do you know about them?" I asked her.

"British soldiers acting on behalf of the Arabs," she said confidently. "Either deserted before independence or deserted when the British left—which would imply a degree of complicity."

"Meaning?"

"That they were acting with the approval of their commanders."

"Not a fuckin' chance," Wolfe said, and Rom looked surprised by his vehemence and language.

"All right," she said defiantly. "What about the Ben Yehuda Street bombing on the twenty-second of February, eh? You aren't going to pretend that the British didn't do it, are you?"

Wolfe and I knew all about the infamous car bomb in Jerusalem that killed fifty-five. We'd discussed it because Wolfe had been the investigating officer. Three misguided British deserters had been involved and Wolfe had brought two to justice. One of the men had been a corporal from our own military police unit. It had been an embarrassment to us, but even more so to the men themselves. They'd worked with radical Arabs who turned out to be anti-British as well as anti-Jew.

We knew this because the Arabs set them up. The deserters were used as drivers and fall guys. The third man had escaped and fled to Egypt, where the Islamic extremist Husseini gave him no support. Rejected and dejected, he handed himself in.

Wolfe said, "That wasn't them. We're a hundred per cent sure of that."

"Why?"

"Because we got them and they didn't have the brains." Wolfe looked at me and gave me a signal to say nothing, before turning back to Rom. "You can help by going through the papers and noting down all the attacks and any reference to the Killing Crew. See if that provides clues as to who they are."

"And you?" she asked innocently, "What will you do, Major?"

"We, Miss Rom, are going to get the personal files on all of the deserters. We're meeting a boat in Haifa."

\* \* \*

A man with a limp stood at an upstairs window inside the little Orah Cinema on Nahmani Street. Almost directly opposite was the building that the British SIB had used. They were in there now having cleaned up the downstairs office. Major Wolfe and Captain Carter. British Military Policemen in Israel.

He'd seen the Security Council official visit. Wolfe and Carter were here with the government's approval. They were here to hunt for the Killing Crew.

They would be dealt with if they got too close.

\* \* \*

A fourteen-year-old boy came out of the alley grinning. His excitement ended when he saw the man and remembered the menace. It wasn't that the man had

41

said anything frightening, it was just his tone and the look in his cold eyes.

The teenager started speaking but the man held up a hand and beckoned him into a doorway.

"What have you learned?" the man asked quietly.

The boy swallowed hard. He didn't like being alone in the dark with this man. "It all works, sir. I can hear everything and can pretty much see the whole room."

The man wasn't interested. "I asked what you'd learned?"

"They were talking about attacks. They have the secretary going through old newspapers."

"Have they worked anything out about the Killing Crew?"

"I don't think so."

"Anything else?" the man said, sounding annoyed at the limited information. But how was he supposed to know what was important, and the man scared him. It was hard to think.

"They're going to Haifa," the boy blurted.

"Why?"

"Erm... they're getting the files on the army deserters."

The man said nothing. His eyes narrowed, and for a horrible moment the boy thought he'd done something wrong. But then the man with the cold eyes handed him some money.

"Pay more attention tomorrow. I need to know precisely what they know, understand?"

"Yes... sir."

"I need to know who they suspect."

# SEVEN

We weren't meeting the boat in Haifa until the morning, but we didn't explain that to Sylvia Rom when we left the office. Instead, we went to the cinema on Allenby Street. There were twelve cinemas in Tel Aviv, including one opposite the office. They were exclusively Jewish, except for Allenby Cinema, which still showed the Pathé News. It was our best way of getting world news under the new regime.

There was a film afterwards, but we didn't stay for the entertainment. Instead, Wolfe said we should find a safe place to talk. This turned out to be the quiet corner of a bar. Patrons glanced at us with suspicion, undoubtedly recognizing us as Brits, but we were left alone.

"Sylvia is a spy," I said.

"Of course."

"How do we handle her?"

"Involve her but only so far," Wolfe said. "Feed her enough to make her report that she's involved. But I'll be damned if I'm going to help them unnecessarily."

I nodded.

"What are you drinking?"

"Water."

"Let's wind down and have a beer. We deserve it."

"I don't drink."

"What?" Now he looked at me like I had two heads. "Why the fuckin' hell not, for Christ's sake?"

I wondered how his Christian girlfriend accepted his colourful language. Maybe he had it under control when he was with her.

"Health reasons, fitness," I said. "Never needed it or enjoyed it. Take your pick of the reasons."

"And how did I not know this? What about on the boat to Cyprus. You had a beer then, right?"

Wolfe and I had spent hardly any time together. I'd not worked with him before this assignment, and since then, he'd been in Israel while I was in Cyprus.

"How have you been spending your time while waiting for me?"

"I run, and I found a gymnasium at the end of Ahad Ha'am Street. You should come along."

"Why?"

"To keep fit. Be healthy."

Wolfe gave me a cockeyed smile. "I'm naturally fit. I don't need to punch bags, lift medicine balls and run on the spot to prove it."

After I shook my head, he grunted. "Anyway, my point is, you can't trust a man who doesn't let himself get drunk."

He got up and fetched a beer for himself and a glass of water for me.

"Interesting," I said as he sat back down. "You have an example of someone you couldn't trust?"

He took a mouthful of beer. "Madison, the corporal involved in the Ben Yehuda Street bombing."

"Really?"

"I expect so!"

We talked about the case and confirmed his belief that they weren't smart enough to be our targets. They'd referred to themselves as a detonation squad. Our belief was that they would have said Killing Crew for the glory if it had been true.

I hadn't been involved in the case. In the last few months it had become crazy and I'd been investigating stolen goods rather than AWOL soldiers. As soon as the British declared we were withdrawing, the black market for army and police surplus goods exploded. We were used to small items disappearing, but Arab and Jewish forces alike were bidding for our equipment. The heavy goods were being left behind and had to be destroyed, but the money being offered was astronomical. Treacherous privateering is what Command called it, and I witnessed it first-hand when I apprehended a sergeant in the process of selling a Sherman tank for two thousand pounds. Cromwell tanks could fetch as much as three thousand.

Someone even tried to sell an RAF Spitfire for eight thousand. That one, I witnessed being dismantled, so I was sure it hadn't fallen into enemy hands. Land Rovers and Bedford trucks on the other hand were more easily stolen, and we knew that most of the deserters in the final weeks disappeared with vehicles.

Wolfe said, "I heard that a deserter could guarantee a salary of twenty *thou* plus money for his Landie if he joined the Jewish fighters. As you know, the Arabs were offering a hundred pounds a day for a man with a Bren gun."

I thought of my friend Dave Rosen. He'd been promoted and given a significant pay rise. Could he have boosted his income by providing goods? He didn't seem the type, but you never know, do you?

Wolfe and I had been at the Haifa Port on the last day. All but a handful of British civilians remained, most of them being evacuated on the *Franconia* weeks earlier. The Haganah, the army that was to become the IDF, had taken the city and penned us in at Peninsula Barracks.

The police had been holding the Tegart Fortress in Haifa, but they were shipping out with the rest of us, and, after the Battle of Haifa, had withdrawn to the docks as well. I thought back to that chaotic time with too many people crammed in and waiting to ship out. I hadn't spotted Rosen and had assumed he'd caught one of the early boats out. Now I knew otherwise.

# EIGHT

That night, Erika Arnold waited until we were alone in her living room playing cards before she asked me about the police.

"Mistaken identity," I said.

"About what?"

"Wrong place, wrong time," I said.

She put down her cards and fixed me with an inquisitive eye. "I'm not an idiot. Either you talk to me or you can go to your room and forget our evening game of cards."

I said nothing.

She said, "And perhaps I'll put your rent up."

I said nothing, thinking of how much I valued her company in the evenings.

She took a long breath then a slug of brandy. "You can trust me, Mr Carter."

"Can I?"

"Jews and Brits can be friends."

I thought about Dave Rosen and nodded. It was true. Of course it was true. Many of the soldiers and police had hated the Jews in the end. The constant fear of terrorism can do that to a man, irrespective of rationality. But not all Jews were terrorists.

I said, "Most Brits aren't anti-Semite."

"Are you?"

"No."

She seemed to accept that.

I said, "I helped a young Jewess and her baby yesterday. I bought her food... for nothing in return."

"Very altruistic, Mr Carter. A Good Samaritan."

"I was raised as a Christian," I said.

"We all have our load to bear." It was one of the rare occasions that she smiled. "But how does that explain the police?"

"She owed money to two men and they were found dead last night. The police put two and two together and wondered if I'd been involved."

She was reading my eyes.

I said, "I convinced them that I had nothing to do with it."

After a pause, she asked: "Was the girl a *mapillim*?"

"Arrived illegally? Yes."

She frowned. "Then wasn't she taken care of? The Irgun—"

"At first," I said. "Then she was handed off until she was with a group who wanted money."

We talked some more about Hannah Münz's experience and I could see it distressed my host. Erika struggled to understand how her own people—as she described them—could take advantage of new immigrants.

I said there was always someone willing to take advantage of those in need.

We returned to our card game and the conversation turned to Jaffa and the destruction I'd seen.

"Don't be all high and mighty," she scolded me. "The British destroyed swathes of Jaffa in the twenties.

Without much notice or compensation, they turfed out residents to build the wide roads into the port."

"That was for business," I said defensively. "As I understand it, the port was growing and the old roads couldn't cope with modern traffic. It's progress."

She snorted derision as she took a drink.

I said, "The Irgun attacked innocent people. They forced evacuation. They murdered."

She glared at me. "They were fighting for a righteous cause, fighting for our homeland."

I shook my head. I'd heard the same argument in Ireland. Terrorists often claimed the moral high ground. "Killing innocents is never justified."

"Have you ever killed a so-called innocent?"

I thought about the people I'd killed. I thought especially about the two Slovaks in the tannery. Were they innocent? No. They would have killed me if I'd not killed them.

Before I could answer, she said, "You hesitated. It's hard to know, isn't it?"

"I'm sorry about your husband."

Anger had been growing in her but now it subsided and was replaced by sadness.

I continued: "I'm sure his death was an accident."

"Play your cards," she said.

I played and she beat me.

It was another twenty minutes before either of us spoke again about anything other than the game. When she finally did speak, I suspected the slur in her voice was due to the brandy.

She said, "Tel Aviv was originally, briefly called *Ahuzat Bayit*, the Homestead. Did you know that?"

"No, I didn't."

"It's the Old New Land, the Biblical Tel Abib. It should be home to all Jews. No one should suffer coming here."

I said, "You're thinking about the girl and her baby?"

"But they must help themselves. We fought for this land. They must fight in a different way. She must fight rather than depend on charity."

I said, "Most of the housing in Jaffa is dilapidated."

She nodded. "Even we have slums, but there are plans."

I looked at her wondering what she meant.

"New, social housing. You must have noticed the slums in Manshiya." She must have seen my uncertainty and added: "In the south just before Jaffa. It was originally Arabic."

Then I remembered seeing building work. An area being cleared by bulldozers.

"That's where the new housing blocks will go," she said when I nodded. "I'm sure they will be functional rather than attractive, but it should help."

I nodded again and told her what I'd said to Hannah Münz. I'd returned to her house in Jaffa after the fight with the Slovaks and told her they wouldn't be coming back. She'd been concerned about where she could get money from and explained that debt collectors were also money lenders. They collected a bit and lent more later. It was one of the incentives to pay, although the borrower got further and further into debt with no way out.

She wanted to work but had a baby to care for.

I gave her a little money and said that if she could find a job I'd help solve the problem. Maybe I wouldn't need to if this social housing was available.

"You're a soft touch," Erika said.

I said, "I think you're warming to me, Mrs Arnold."

"Not really," she said. "It's late, past my bedtime, and I've had too much to drink."

# NINE

It had been raining during the last night of the Mandate, and when Wolfe and I boarded the boat for Cyprus in the morning, the sky was still pewter-grey. Water sloshed along the concrete and down rail tracks. It seemed like a fitting, inauspicious send-off.

This morning, the big sky held no clouds. The weather might have been different, but Haifa Port seemed hardly changed from six or so weeks ago. There was still the taste of oil in the air and the big *Haifa Shipping* sign was proudly emblazoned over the long warehouse block. The cranes at the eastern end looked on as impassively as ever, and the activity beneath them was as frenetic as before the handover.

The *Orduna* had docked at nine in the morning and had been unloading for an hour by the time we reached the front of the Port Office queue.

Wolfe showed his papers and explained that we were meeting a package from London. Whether it was our nationality or simply that the clerks were incredibly busy, we were made to wait outside for another thirty minutes.

Eventually, a young man in brown overalls, two sizes too big, waved some paperwork at us and said we should follow.

We trekked along the rail tracks, past Customs and then a parcel depot. Finally we stopped. Wolfe and I exchanged looks before he gestured confusion with open hands.

"Immigration," the boy said.

"No," Wolfe said with slow impatience, "we are collecting some parcels."

The boy raised an eyebrow then nodded towards the door in front of us. I assumed there was more bureaucracy ahead. It had probably been like this for civilians when we ran the port. A taste of our own medicine, I supposed.

Inside were rows of benches upon which people sat as though waiting for a bus that would never arrive.

"Parcels," Wolfe said again, but the boy ignored him. He spoke to a man behind a front desk, showed papers and then beckoned to us.

When we stepped towards the official at the desk he pointed into the crowd and bellowed, "Albert Finney!"

Immediately, a young man leapt to his feet and bounded towards us like an excited puppy.

He thrust out his hand, hesitated and then saluted.

"Sergeant Finney, reporting for duty, sir!"

The official behind us grunted, "You have his Israeli travel warrant?"

Wolfe blinked at Finney then thumbed through the pile of paperwork he was carrying. Fortunately, he had everything, including the authority for himself and McIntyre.

The official scrutinized the document before handing it back and announcing, "Mr Albert Finney, welcome to Israel."

Wolfe and I stared at Finney, who grinned foolishly.

"We were expecting parcels," Wolfe said.

"Oh, right, sir. Wait!" He scampered back to where he'd been sitting and started pulling a handcart back. I counted six boxes bound with string. A kitbag sat precariously on top.

When he returned, Finney said, "I'm the courier and have taken good care of them, sir. They never left my side."

*Until just now*, I thought but said nothing. The young man's enthusiasm was infectious and I immediately liked him. Wolfe on the other hand scowled.

"Right, follow us." Wolfe marched out of the building.

Finney hurried behind us with his trolley. I guess because he'd been travelling for two weeks, he was so excited to finally be here, he started talking at a hundred miles an hour.

"Stop talking!" Wolfe barked.

We continued in silence except for the clack of our shoes and the squeaking trolley wheels. It seemed a longer walk back, past the Port Office and then through two security gates.

The Bentley's boot took four of the boxes and Finney had to sit in the back with the remaining two plus his kitbag.

Wolfe started the engine and the big car rolled forward before he finally spoke again.

"Two rules," Wolfe said over his shoulder.

"Sir?"

"The first is that you don't call us sir. No reference to rank, understood, Finney?"

"Yes."

"You call me Wolfe and this is Carter."

I turned and winked at the kid. He smiled back. Despite Wolfe's gruffness, the young man's enthusiasm hadn't been dented.

"Second rule," Wolfe said, "is you don't talk too much."

"How do I know how much is too much, sir—I mean Mr Wolfe?"

"It's just Wolfe, and if in doubt, say nowt. Understood?"

"Yes."

We passed the old barracks and then Jalama Camp, which had been the refuge for British civilians before evacuating Palestine.

My thoughts were in the recent past, the fear and tension, when Finney disturbed them.

"Mind if I smoke?" he asked. "I'm dying for a fag and we weren't allowed to at the port."

"No smoking," Wolfe said. "In the car or in the office, understood?"

"Yes, sir."

"That's rule three."

Finney said nothing for a beat, then: "I thought there were only two rules."

That made me smile, but Wolfe said, "There are as many fuckin' rules as I say there are."

On the outskirts of the town we approached a barbed-wire checkpoint.

"Welcome to Israel," I said to Finney as we joined a queue of two trucks and three cars. "We have to go through three of these to get to Tel Aviv."

"They've got guns!" the young man said nervously.

"Just stay calm and we'll be fine," I said. "They're looking for Arab terrorists."

Wolfe said, "There's a truce at the moment, so it's not as bad as it has been."

The truck at the front was cleared and the next vehicle waved forward.

"Shit!" Wolfe grunted. The driver and passenger stepped out of the car. Previously, Wolfe had shown our paperwork and been waved on. We'd been challenged and verbally abused but not once had we been asked to step out of the car.

"Is there a problem?" Finney asked.

"No," I said, but I was thinking about the gun on my left ankle. We weren't supposed to be armed. If they found our pistols these soldiers might overreact.

The two got back into their car and were waived through. Then a truck was stopped and the driver questioned. I'd been holding my breath and let it out when they quickly waived him through.

"We'll be fine," Wolfe said calmly.

The next truck and then the car in front were soon through the checkpoint and my heart rate eased.

We were beckoned forward. Four soldiers, two on either side. Three rifles held threateningly. A sergeant, more relaxed, held his hand out.

"Papers?"

Wolfe passed our warrants through his window.

The two soldiers on my side looked at me hard, looked at the boxes and Finney on the back seat.

Then the nearest one pointed his gun at my head and yelled in my face.

# TEN

"Get out of the car!" the IDF sergeant screamed at us.

We complied, slowly.

"What's in the boxes?"

"Paperwork," Wolfe said.

The sergeant nodded to his men, and seconds later the boxes were opened, Finney's bag was tipped out and the boot popped.

I said, "We're hunting the pro-Arab deserters."

I'd hoped my comment would ease the tension. It didn't.

We waited in a line, two guns trained on us while the other two soldiers rifled through our documents. After a few long minutes they gave up and crawled through the car, checking under the seats and carpets. Then the sergeant told his men to search us.

A wet patch appeared on Finney's pants. I could see his hands shaking. Wolfe scratched at his beard and I hoped I looked as relaxed as him despite my pounding heart.

We were patted down, but they failed to check our ankles and we were soon back in the car with the IDF men acting as though nothing had happened.

"Are you all right, Albert?" I asked once we were beyond the checkpoint.

"No, not really," he said, his voice shaking as much as his hands had been. "I need to change my pants."

After a mile, Wolfe pulled over, and we waited while Finney put on dry trousers.

"I'm sorry. I'm sorry," he murmured once back in the car.

"Don't worry," I said. Wolfe grumbled under his breath but I ignored him and continued: "Where are you from, Albert?"

"Sandhurst."

I swivelled in my seat and stared at him. A sergeant who'd been at the officer training base?

Finney smiled. "It's actually a real village just down the road from the barracks at Camberley."

"But you *are* an MP?"

"Yes, sir, based in Aldershot."

"How old are you," Wolfe grumbled. "Nineteen?"

"Twenty, sir."

"Wolfe. Not sir!"

"Sorry, Wolfe," Finney said awkwardly.

Despite my dislike of cigarettes, I could see the young man was still distressed, so I told him to light up. After all, the windows were down because of the heat.

"Just keep it outside and blow the smoke outside too," I said.

Wolfe glanced at me with narrowed eyes and I shrugged in reply. I felt sorry for the kid.

However, I changed my mind after ten minutes because the cigarette not only relaxed him but loosened his lips. He bored us with tales of his boat journey here interspersed with snippets of his experience. He also insisted we call him Bert. Only his mother called him Albert, and that was when she was angry.

I eventually tuned him out and could see that Wolfe had done so a lot earlier.

By the time we reached the next checkpoint, Finney had stopped talking and fallen asleep. Which wasn't surprising since he'd told us he'd been up since four in the morning. The bouncing of the big car combined with the heat had finally taken its toll. He was curled up on the back seat, his head on the door, hugging his kitbag like it was a giant teddy bear.

We were recognized and waved through the checkpoint and had another two miles before our destination.

I took another look at Finney to make sure he really was asleep before speaking.

"Why are you so angry, Bill?"

"I was expecting our third man would be a sergeant."

"He is."

"Not really. I wanted a nose-to-the-grindstone type of chap. A good MP sergeant with twelve years' experience. Not some limey-arsed kid with less nous than a slice of buttered bread."

"You don't know that."

"I know that he has no experience. I know that he was only just promoted, probably because he was being sent out here."

Wolfe was right. The kid had limited experience. He was just a courier and keen to be here, presumably because he didn't appreciate the risk. He'd be limited use in investigating the identity of the Killing Crew and even less in bringing them to justice.

I said, "So who's the fourth man?"

Wolfe looked at me hard.

"You know who he is, don't you? Who is this Samuel Macintyre chap?"

"We'll see."

"What does that mean, Bill?" I asked, trying to suppress irritation. He might not have known about Finney but I was sure he knew the fourth man.

However, he said nothing more, looking straight ahead as we drove into Tel Aviv. The white modern buildings were in stark contrast to the sand-coloured, seemingly disorganized Arab villages we'd passed in the desert.

People called this the Hollywood of the East and it did have a certain air. It spoke of prospects and prosperity, of hope and a bright future. Of course, the palm trees and beach added to the allusion.

Finally, I decided to break the ice. "Earlier when you were talking about Finney, you used an expression. What does *limey-arsed* mean?"

"I don't know. Couldn't think of the word. I'm still angry."

We turned onto Nahmani Street.

He said, "I'll get that secretary to find a hotel that we can put Finney in. At least she can do something worthwhile."

However, when we arrived at our makeshift office we were astonished. Sylvia Rom hadn't just been through the pile of newspapers, she'd done something much more useful.

# ELEVEN

Our Jewish secretary had created a timeline. On the noticeboard she'd created three columns. The first had pieces of paper with dates. The second column had descriptions. The third had a number.

"I hope you don't mind," Sylvia Rom said as we stared.

"It's… it's excellent," I said.

She nodded curtly. "I did as asked. I read through the papers for references to the Killing Crew, but I already knew what I'd find."

"What?" Wolfe asked.

"There were seven mentions, but nothing specific. You see, we all knew they existed but they never claimed responsibility for their actions. Not like, say, the Irgun."

She was right. Whenever there was a Jewish attack, most of the time, the papers reported which group had been responsible. Either they had inside men or were contacted by the attackers.

The Arabs, on the other hand, didn't broadcast who had done what.

"What are the numbers for?" Finney asked.

She seemed to take him in for the first time and I introduced Finney to Miss Rom.

She said, "The number of dead."

"British?" he asked, alarmed by the total. I did a quick addition and counted approximately six hundred.

Wolfe said, "No! Only the Jewish terrorists killed our lot. The King David Hotel bombing, the British HQ and the officers' club bombing in Jerusalem."

By my reckoning, there had been over a hundred British deaths at the hands of Jewish terrorists and none by Arabs. Half of those had happened in the early period, before the Jewish Agency and the Haganah had aligned with the terrorist groups.

Finney seemed to relax, but Miss Rom looked daggers at Wolfe, as though he'd said something untoward. I figured she was angry at his reference to Jewish terrorists.

He ignored her stare. There were forty-two rows, starting in December 1947 with the Jerusalem Riots (8 dead) and ending in May 1948 and the Kfar Etzion Massacre (157 dead).

Wolfe removed the last one. He pulled off the card and flicked it across the room.

"Why did you do that?" Rom said. "It's important."

"To you. That happened on the day we left. It was the Arab Legion. I read the papers. We're after the Killing Crew. Kfar Etzion isn't of interest."

I saw her bite at her lip and realized this all mattered to our Jewish secretary. She felt every death, whether it was by the hand of a Briton, Arab or our elusive Killing Crew.

"It's good though," Wolfe said. "A timeline is a good start, so thank you, Miss Rom." Then he surprised me by asking her to go out and get us food for lunch and also another noticeboard.

Once we were alone, Wolfe said we'd leave the rest of the events up and start on the deserters.

We got the boxes from the car and wrote the names and ranks of our soldiers onto cards. Miss Rom returned before we'd finished all eighty-one cards. We propped the board against a wall and, after a brief debate, pinned the names on in alphabetical order.

"What are you going to do now?" Rom said as we tucked into the bread, fruit and cheese she'd brought us.

"We're going to think about these names and events," Wolfe said, "and you, Miss Rom, are going to find a suitable hotel for young Finney here."

"Suitable?"

"The Scopus is full."

She gave him a querulous glance before he continued: "And then you can take the rest of the day off."

Wolfe was staying at the Scopus, which had been an officer's club before we'd left. It may have been full, but I figured Wolfe would rather have young Finney lodged elsewhere.

After Rom left us, we stared at the names and the timeline and I told Finney about the deserters who were responsible for the Ben Yehuda Street bombing. Wolfe removed that event from February 1948 and also the associated three deserters' names from our second board.

"They're not our men," Wolfe said, and went over what I'd discussed with him about the men being set up as a detonation squad and then abandoned by the Arab extremists.

"We're looking for a smarter bunch," I said, which triggered a thought: "We should consider who knew who."

"Most likely they're from the same regiment," Wolfe agreed.

We moved the names around and grouped them. There were seven solo deserters and we moved these to one side.

"Leaves seventy-one," Finney said, and then he pointed out that he'd noticed that none of the deserters had been officers.

With no more insights, we went back to the timeline and talked about the events.

Finney said, "Apart from the attacks you removed, the rest are small: buses fired upon, random people killed on the roads, settlements attacked." He paused. "Except for these ones." He pointed first to the 11th of March when thirteen had been killed by a bomb at the offices of the Jewish Agency. Then he pointed to one, a month later, when a convoy of over forty Jewish doctors, nurses and patients had been slaughtered. Rom had labelled it *the Hadassah Hospital massacre.*

"Mostly small attacks. What do you think it means, Wolfe?"

Wolfe was leaning back in a chair with his hands behind his head.

"I don't know," he said. "I don't have a fuckin' clue."

We stared at the boards until our eyes hurt.

Rom came back and told Finney that he had a room booked in the St Andrews Hotel and showed him on a map where to find it. I'd half expected she would book the kid into Scopus just to rile Wolfe, and I could see from the relief on his face that he'd considered the same possibility.

After Rom left again, I said what had just struck me: "It would help if we knew which of the deserters were pro-Jew."

"To exclude them," Wolfe said.

Finney hadn't considered this and his enthusiasm made me smile.

Wolfe said, "Let's talk over a beer."

We went to a bar and I watched the other men down two bottles of Pioneer as we went around and around with the limited information we had. It got darker outside and the lights came on.

Finney said, "Do we know which ones were pro-Jew?"

I shook my head.

"Most soldiers and police were pro-Arab," Wolfe said, "but some were pro-Jew despite the terrorism."

"Especially men from the Oxfords from 249 Battery," I said. "They'd been some of the first at Bergen-Belsen."

"The concentration camp?" Finney asked.

I nodded. "They saw the horrors first-hand. It had a big impact on attitudes."

"Should we exclude them?"

I looked at Wolfe. "I think it would be better if we knew definitively. We need help."

Wolfe said our fourth man would help tomorrow.

"Will he know pro-Jews?"

"Process of elimination," Wolfe said. He sent Finney for two more beers.

While he was away, I told Wolfe that I thought we should ask Dave Rosen about the pro-Jewish deserters.

"Maybe," Wolfe said. Then: "No, I don't want him involved. We'll do this without their help. We can do that, right, Ash?"

"Right," I said unconvincingly.

Finney returned with the beers and I excused myself. I knew Wolfe was planning a heavy drinking session, so

I retreated to my lodgings just in time for supper and cards with Erika Arnold.

*   *   *

The man with cold eyes was waiting for the teenager in the doorway, like before.

"They have the names," the boy said. "They have eighty-one people they're calling the deserters and they've grouped them by regiment."

"Do they know any of them?"

"The one called Wolfe pulled out three involved in the Ben Yehuda Street bombing."

For a second the boy thought he saw a smile but then decided the man was just moving his lips.

The man said, "They suspect they're the Killing Crew?"

"No, sir. The opposite. They said those men weren't smart enough."

The man nodded. "Anything else?"

The boy told him some detail of the conversations. He'd hoped the man would be impressed by his attention to detail this time, but he showed little interest.

"Anything else?"

"They talked about finding who the pro-Jew deserters were."

The man's face hardened. "Why?"

"To exclude them. Then they left for the evening."

The man handed over some coins. "Pay extra attention to what they learn."

# TWELVE

From the look of him, Finney had the king of hangovers. His eyes looked sunken, his jaw slack and he moved as though on board a boat.

"Can we talk?" he said after I unlocked the office door in the morning. Sylvia Rom arrived so I motioned Finney into the next room.

This one hadn't been tidied after the evacuation and I righted a chair for the lad before perching on the edge of a desk.

"What is it, Bert?"

"It's about the major," he said slowly.

"Wolfe?"

He nodded and looked like he regretted the motion.

"He's a drinker," I said. "Don't feel too bad about it this time, but don't come in the worse for wear in future."

He took a breath. "That's just it, sir. Major Wolfe said there isn't a future."

I wondered what he meant by that and waited for the explanation.

"Wolfe said that I have to go back."

So that was it. Wolfe had decided Finney wasn't any use; perhaps he'd ask for an experienced sergeant instead. There was plenty of our old team in the Canal Zone. He'd request someone he knew.

"He said I was just a courier." Finney looked at me with desperate eyes. "I want to stay, sir."

"It's dangerous. You experienced that at the checkpoint yesterday, and I suspect Wolfe is concerned for you."

Finney said nothing for a moment.

"I'd like…" His eyes brimmed with tears. "Please, sir. I would like to stay."

"All right, Bert, I'll have a word. No promises, mind."

Despite his delicate state, Finney grinned and offered me his hand.

I nodded to the room where Rom would be waiting for us. Maybe Wolfe was also in there by now.

"Come on," I said, "if you want to stay then you'd better make a contribution. Help us find this Killing Crew."

However, rather than Finney make an immediate impression, I was surprised to see Rom at the first noticeboard. Wolfe wasn't there, but she was colour-coding the notes.

She stopped when she heard us re-enter the room.

"I'm using red, blue and black markers," she said.

"I can see that."

She gave a wry smile. "I was thinking about what was said yesterday, about the various Jewish factions taking responsibility. There are very different Arab factions, which may help.

"All right," I said, liking her thought process. "For Finney's benefit, perhaps you'd elucidate?"

"What did the British tend to call the Arab fighters?"

"Irregulars," I said. "We called them that because the Palestinian Arabs didn't have an army like the

Jewish Haganah." What I didn't say was that we tended to view the Jewish combatants as terrorists and the Arabs as fighters.

Whether Rom knew this, I didn't know, because she simply continued: "This past year, the Arabs have become more structured under the guidance of Abd al-Qadir al-Husseini and his Army of the Holy War."

I knew the name. Husseini had been responsible for a revolt against the British in 1939 before fleeing to Iraq.

"OK," I said.

"Then you get the Syrians."

I nodded. "The ALA. The Arab Liberation Army."

"The ALA is less radical than Husseini's militia." Rom pointed to where the note had been removed by Wolfe. "Take the Ben Yehuda Street bombing. Less targeted and potentially more indiscriminate. The ALA wouldn't do those."

I knew Husseini's lot was behind the Jewish market bomb, because of their attitude towards the three deserters who'd helped them.

I directed my next comment at Finney. "Husseini believes in a Muslim state. He not only hates the Jews, but he wanted Britain out as well. His faction was not a good choice for deserters. They'd either be used and discarded or executed."

"Precisely," Rom said.

"What about the Arab Legion?" I asked. The Arab Legion was Transjordan's army commanded by a famous British lieutenant general called John Bagot Glubb. They were the ones responsible for the last entry Rom had put on the timeline. The hospital massacre on 13th April that Wolfe had also removed.

Rom said, "They are the biggest force by far and currently occupying the West Bank."

"But before we left?"

"Unknown—at least, I can't find out."

Finney impressed me by asking Rom the important question we'd discussed last evening.

"There were eighty-one deserters," he said, looking at me for an unnecessary confirmation. "We've excluded three. Do *you* know how many joined the Jewish fighters?"

Rom shook her head then seemed to deliberate.

"Sylvia?" I prompted.

"Seventeen, I believe."

"Which leaves sixty-one," Finney said. "Which pro-Arab faction did they join?"

She shook her head.

"So there were seventeen pro-Jews." I pointed to the board with the deserter names. "Can you tell us which ones?"

"I don't know details. But I understand they all joined the Eighty-Second Battalion."

"The IDF—Israeli Defence Force," I said for Finney's benefit.

I wondered if she'd say more, but nothing was forthcoming, so I switched attention back to the events board.

"Tell us about the colour-coding."

"I was trying to work out which group might be responsible," Rom said. "There seem to be four distinct types of attack. I used red when there may not have been any organization. For example, the attacks by mobs and deaths not involving knives."

"And blue when it's definitely an army?" I asked, noting that she'd put a blue mark against an attack on a cluster of settlements in the West Bank in January. I knew that three hundred soldiers had allegedly been repelled by villagers, resulting in the death of only one

Jew. At the time I'd questioned the veracity of the reporting. It sounded like propaganda, but our starting point was to assume the reports were accurate.

She said, "It may have been the Arab Legion, I don't know."

"Got it," I said. "And the black marks?"

"They're for terrorist-type attacks. Smaller groups attacking buses and convoys."

"You think they're the Holy Army chaps?" Finney asked.

Rom shook her head. "I don't know. I just thought it was a way of looking it at."

"It's good," I said. "Breaking down the bigger picture can help."

"Help with what?"

The question came from behind us. Not Wolfe's voice. I swivelled and was surprised to see David Rosen standing in the doorway.

# THIRTEEN

"Looks like you're making progress," Sub-Inspector Rosen said, walking towards Rom at the noticeboard. Then he stopped and looked at Bert Finney as though only just noticing him. "And who is this?"

"Bert Finney," I said.

"Ah, the third member of your team."

"He brought the army files on the deserters with him."

Rosen switched his attention to the second board with the names on which he scanned it for a beat before looking at me.

"Not all pro-Arab," he said.

Rom said, "I know seventeen were—are—on our side."

"Pro-Jew deserters," I clarified pointedly. The Jewish community might view them as heroes, but they were still deserters. However, it was a moot point because we were after the Killing Crew, not just any bunch of deserters.

Rosen smiled kindly at me. "I might be able to help."

"Can you tell us which of these are your seventeen?" I asked.

He said, "They've all changed their names, you know, all become Jews. Such was their belief in the cause."

Rosen looked at Finney. "Do you know why many did—supported us, I mean?"

"Nazi Germany? The concentration camps?" Finney said weakly, which may have been nerves at being faced by Rosen's strong personality or may have been his hangover.

"Some, but most came over because of the atrocities here. The worst was an attack on doctors, nurses and patients, killing over forty innocent Jews. Many burned alive. I heard a few of your men walked out in protest at Britain's reluctance to condemn the massacre."

Finney paled. "I didn't know."

I said, "Which deserters can we exclude, Dave?"

He turned from the young lad and his eyes were colder than the last time we'd met.

"I need assurances that you aren't going after them."

We'd already given those assurances. Our job wasn't to find just any deserters. I could imagine the repercussions if we deviated from our approved task.

"Your best assurance is to remove the names," I said. "That way, we won't make a mistake."

"Like I said, they've changed their names." He pulled a deserter card off the board. "For example, Martin O'Loughlin here is now known as Avraham Ackermann. You'd have a job tracking them down without access to Israeli identity records." He took a breath, suddenly more serious. "I suspect your pro-Arabs have done the same, so your task isn't going to be an easy one."

If he was right then our task was even harder than I'd imagined. Even removing seventeen names wouldn't help much.

Rosen went back to the noticeboard and started pulling off other names.

When he stopped, Finney said, "That's sixteen."

Rosen looked at me.

"You know about John Spade?"

I'd seen his name on the board and I did know him. He was the man responsible for the dismantling of the Spitfire I'd overseen.

And then I got it. I said, "He's one of yours, isn't he?" I'd suspected as much. When I'd overseen the dismantling of the Spitfire, Spade had been the supervising engineer. I'd already guessed what Rosen was about to tell me.

"John Spade now heads up a team in the IAF." He smiled. "He rebuilt the Spit, Fred."

I didn't like him using his nickname for me in front of the others. However, they didn't appear to notice and I decided to bite my lip.

"He's also working on restoring all twenty Austers scrapped by the RAF."

Spade probably made eight grand for the Spitfire and would be getting even more for the batch of light planes. Plus a good salary.

"A rich man then," I said cynically.

"It's not all about the money, you know. I wouldn't be surprised if he hasn't been paid extra for what he's doing. Not like the other chaps. Not like those who joined the Arabs, paid by the day."

I was sure this wasn't true, but there was no point in arguing. Rosen was looking at the board again.

"I see you've looked for soldiers who were in the same unit."

Finney said, "It seems most likely that the Killing Crew knew and served together."

Rosen nodded thoughtfully. "What do you know about them?"

"Not much," Finney said.

"How many were there?"

We didn't know, and Finney looked at me for support.

I said, "Thanks for your help, Dave. We'll take it from here."

The sub-inspector continued to hold Finney's gaze. "There's nothing concrete in the newspapers, eh?"

"No, sir."

"Not connected to any specific crime. Rumours and conjecture."

"Ghosts," Finney said.

"Invisible… or a myth," Rosen said. Then he looked at me. "Think about it. A myth."

He gave us a curt nod and strolled out. I registered that he hadn't made eye contact with Sylvia Rom the whole time.

After Rosen left, we talked about the names on the board and Finney moved anyone who was a solitary member of a unit to one side. That reduced our list to fifty-four. Still far too many.

We turned our attention to the events, and Finney said, "There were so many in the last two months."

"That was after the UN's Partition Plan," I said, deliberating. "It's muddying the water. We should remove them."

"That's what I was thinking," Rom said.

I smiled at her because she seemed engaged in the process. We'd thought of her as a spy, but ignoring her background, it felt like she was part of the team. Of course, she could have been faking it.

I said, "Let's look at last year's events—and remove the red and blue coded ones." That took out the mob attacks and those with large numbers of soldiers.

Rom pointed to the old map. "I think we can exclude attacks outside of the main areas. I'd focus on here, Jerusalem, Haifa and Acre."

"And anywhere along the Jerusalem–Tel Aviv Road," I said.

Rom nodded agreement and pulled out the events from the original timeline. Without being told, she kept the cards in-line, so that moving them back and forth would be straightforward.

There were eighteen events, and something immediately leapt out at me.

"Snipers," I said. "There are six events involving snipers."

"Invisible," Finney said.

I looked inquiringly at him.

He shrugged. "It's what Detective Rosen said. The Killing Crew was invisible."

"What the fuck?" Bill Wolfe was right behind me. I hadn't heard him come in. His tanned face was creased with anger.

I started to speak.

"Leave the room!" he barked. "You and you," he said, pointing at Finney and Rom. "Get the fuck out of here now!"

The two juniors scampered out, leaving me to face Wolfe alone.

"What's up, Bi—?" I started to speak again as soon as the door closed behind Finney.

"What's Rosen been doing here?"

"He—"

"Did I or did I not say that he wasn't to help?"

"He—"

"I need to be able to trust you, Carter! You going behind my fuckin' back... I may as well do this job on my own!"

I sat down and pointed to another chair. He didn't take it, but he did stop ranting.

When I could see he expected me to speak, I said, "I didn't invite him."

"Then who did?"

"It was probably Sylvia," I said, and told him about how Rosen hadn't looked at her when he was here. She might have been appointed by the Israeli Security Council, but she could have been feeding information to Rosen—maybe others too.

Wolfe growled about getting rid of her, but after discussing it, realized we couldn't.

"And she's doing a good job," I said. "Finney too."

I told him that Rosen had identified the seventeen pro-Jew deserters and that we'd got the list down to sixty-one. Possibly fifty-four if we exclude the solo men. Then I showed him what we'd done to the events.

"Snipers, bus and convoy attacks," he said. "Interesting."

"We're making progress, Bill."

"And we'll make more," he said. "Tonight, you and I are meeting my toad."

# FOURTEEN

A man was sitting in the darkness. Despite the dust up my nose from our journey, I could smell coffee and the strong cigarette he was smoking. His name was Nazeem and we'd driven across rough country to find him.

We'd left the SIB office before the sun set. Wolfe drove us towards Jerusalem in the Bentley and we were stopped three times by soldiers at roadblocks. But our warrants got us through without any problem and some recognized the car. The land became hilly, with the road rising to the holy city about five miles distant when Wolfe turned off the road.

The sun was now splayed out, red on the horizon. We came to an Arab town. From the damage to buildings, I could see that it had been attacked, multiple times probably.

There were thin dogs in the streets and only a few people, looking both dejected and defeated. A woman in black watched us pass, our expensive car appearing out of place amid these ancient, crumbling streets.

"Arabs who've refused to leave," Wolfe said, as a wizened old man stumbled across the road.

"What are we doing here, Bill?"

He'd said very little on the drive. We'd talked about Finney and Rom, and I'd impressed upon him how much they had helped during the morning.

"You should let him stay," I said, referring to the young sergeant.

"He's just an office boy. They only promoted him because of this job."

I could have mentioned that the two of us had recently been promoted. Maybe I deserved to be a captain, but I knew the higher ranks were an attempt to gain respect from our Israeli hosts.

Instead, I said, "Finney's keen. We all started somewhere. And he's useful. He asks good questions."

"I don't want to be responsible for him. I'm no wet nurse."

"Then don't be," I said. "Let me worry about Finney."

"Fine, but you'll regret it," he grumbled. "Your funeral, Ash. It'll be your funeral."

There was much about Bill Wolfe that I admired. He had a reputation as a great investigator; he was tough but fair. However, I'd also learned that he kept his cards close to his chest. He didn't like sharing information, even with me, and he wasn't a team player. It occurred to me that I was only with him because he'd been told to involve me.

I assumed we were meeting Wolfe's informant here, but Wolfe circled the town until we came to a lock-up. Handing me a rusty key that was the weight of a large stone, he told me to open the wooden doors.

Inside I found a Land Rover.

I drove it out and Wolfe put the big black car in its place before swinging up beside me.

"You've got a jeep," I said, stating the obvious. Out in the Middle East, everyone called the topless Land

Rovers jeeps. I think it gave them an air of being American, more cavalier and sexy.

"Needed where we're going," he said before directing me east out of the town and into the hills. But we didn't go to Jerusalem. As soon as we could, we went north, crossed the Jerusalem–Tel Aviv Road and onto another track. Darkness washed in and I left the headlights off for as long as I dared. However the roads were treacherous and I soon needed the lights to avoid rocks and gullies.

Wolfe reached under the backseat and pulled out a Sten gun. He explained that out here we could be mistaken as enemy combatants by either side. People tended to fire first and ask questions later.

We'd been in the old Sector Nine, according to British cartographers. We kept going north and occasionally east, and after an hour I figured we were in Sector Seven.

This was Transjordan occupied territory, and I was relieved when Wolfe told me to drive into the next village.

I approached slowly, and when we saw figures ahead, Wolfe told me to stop and switch my lights off and on repeatedly as a signal. As I did so, he returned the Sten gun to the rear. I prayed he knew what he was doing.

"*Marhabaan*," Wolfe called out. "*Sadiq!*" Hello. Friend.

Two nervous-looking youths approached with rifles held like they had no military training. And they probably hadn't. In the starlight, I could see they weren't in uniform. They were just villagers defending their homes.

"Nazeem," Wolfe said to them calmly. "We're meeting Nazeem."

We were told to drive on. The men held onto our doors and travelled the last hundred yards with us, directing and calling as we went.

My headlights swept over concerned grey faces and pale walls as we were taken to a building with tables outside.

Arabs sat and watched as we stopped the Land Rover and were directed by a different man inside the building.

That was where I met Nazeem.

"Wolfe," he said, with barely a trace of an accent.

Wolfe introduced us and we sat at Nazeem's table. Someone lit a candle and gave us thick coffee and dried dates.

Nazeem held out his hand and I felt calluses in his firm grip.

"Is it safe here?" I asked.

"Nowhere is safe," Nazeem said. "Innocent or militia, nowhere is safe for an Arab today."

"I'm sorry," I said feeling awkward at my words. The Arabs had been our friends for decades and we'd washed our hands of them. Not that I knew how we could have helped resolve the crisis. But then I'm not a politician. I had sympathies with the Jews as well. I understood their desire for a homeland and had seen how they'd transformed areas of this harsh country into farms. The problem was intractable and had been for a thousand years.

The man opposite shook his head as though dismissing my apology.

Wolfe explained to me for the first time. He said that when he'd found Nazeem last week, he'd asked him to help identify the Killing Crew.

"In return for certain assurances," Nazeem said, and held out his hand.

Wolfe reached into his jacket pocket, pulled out a piece of folded paper and handed it over.

Nazeem opened it up, held it into the candlelight, refolded it and stuck it away. "And the other thing."

Wolfe shook his head. "All in good time. You need to deliver the goods first."

The informant lit another cigarette, and after inhaling, turned and blew the foul smoke away from us.

"What do you know?" Nazeem asked me.

So I told him that we had started with eighty-one army deserters and been told which had joined the IDF.

"Eighty-second Battalion," Nazeem said, confirming what Rom had told us, but we weren't interested in the pro-Jew deserters.

I said we'd removed the three we knew were responsible for the Ben Yehuda Street bombing and identified groups of three or more from the same units.

"We're down to a pool of under sixty," I said.

Nazeem took a long drag and blew out smoke before speaking.

"Too many."

"Yes."

"Where did the men go?"

"The pro-Arabs," I said. "I understand there are four groups: Husseini's Holy Army, the Arab League, the Arab Legion and the others—irregulars."

"And every Arab protecting himself and his family," Nazeem said.

"But our deserters were likely to join a specific group." When Nazeem didn't say anything else for a while I added: "And we have the problem that they probably changed their names."

"Those joining Husseini have," he said, nodding. "They will have converted to Islam. They had to if they wanted to survive, but that will be very few of your men."

"That's what we figured," Wolfe said.

"Many of the others are dead," Nazeem said.

"Do you know which ones?" I asked quickly.

"No. Like you say, some changed their names, and one problem we have"—I noted he said *we*, including himself in our hunt—"is the poor records. There is no legal register for us to check."

We talked about what we knew of the various forces and seemed to be making no progress. I thought Wolfe was being very patient, but eventually he snapped.

"I thought you had information for me!"

"All in good time, my friend," Nazeem said, repeating the same phrase Wolfe had used earlier. "More coffee? We have a long night ahead of us."

"Why?"

Nazeem smiled. "Most of the pro-Arab deserters joined the ALA, mainly because they were most active in the north. Your men were in Acre and Haifa and easily contacted. However, the force wasn't as well organized as the Arab Legion."

"The Transjordanian Army commanded by John Bagot Glubb," I said.

"Yes, and having a British commander made it easier to be…" Nazeem struggled with the word.

"Assimilated," Wolfe said.

"Yes. The Legion is structured like the British Army, and your men received promotions as well as guaranteed money. I hear that those joining the ALA weren't paid what they were promised."

Wolfe said, "So you are saying that the men we are looking for joined the Arab Legion?"

"I don't know."

The conversation bounced backwards and forwards like this with the informant acting like a conjurer. He would give us glimpses of information before they vanished in his later words.

I was starting to believe that Nazeem had no real news and that we were being toyed with. However, after an hour, he said something that made us lean forward.

"There's a large group who haven't joined any militia."

"You know who they are?" I said, suddenly excited by the suggestion of real news.

"They call themselves Frank's Band."

I looked at Wolfe and could see this was new for him too.

"There are nine of them," Nazeem continued. "Young men mostly, but led by two sergeant majors. They're working alongside the Legion but are independent."

"Names?" I asked.

"There's also an ex-Nazi in their little band."

"Names?" I repeated.

"I will take you to them. You can ask them their names," he said, and gave an exaggerated yawn. "These are tough men with perhaps something to hide."

The last of the warm air suddenly seemed to suck from the room.

Had Nazeem found the Killing Crew for us?

# FIFTEEN

Nazeem said that we were to meet them at dawn. After checking his watch in the dim light he added: "Which gives us three hours sleep before we must leave."

We each curled up on a wooden bench and had rough blankets to fend off the night chill.

I was uncomfortable but must have dozed because I remember strange dreams then realizing I could hear Wolfe snoring.

Nazeem was sitting by the entrance smoking a cigarette. I checked my watch and saw that we had half an hour before we should leave.

I got up and stretched the ache from my shoulders and back before joining the Arab by the door.

He poured me coffee.

"May I ask why you're helping us?" I asked after a sip of the thick, lukewarm liquid he gave me.

"Perhaps this Killing Crew are criminals," he said.

"Do you really believe that?"

"It doesn't matter what I believe."

"Then that's not an answer to my question."

"Ah," Nazeem said. "What do you know about Islam?"

"Not as much as I should, I suspect."

"There are different sects. Husseini's lot are Shi'ites. They are a minority in Palestine and tend to be more fundamentalist. Husseini argues for a pure Islamic state, for example. There is no place for secularism."

"And the majority?"

"Sunnis," he said.

"Are you a Sunni?"

"No, I am an Alawite, also known as a Twelver. My family originally came from Syria."

I said, "Wolfe gave you a travel warrant."

"He did. You should call me Samuel Macintyre from now on. Scottish, don't you know." This last sentence he delivered with a passable Scottish accent. "No more skulking around. Now I can go through an Israeli checkpoint without fear of execution."

"And if we catch the Killing Crew?" I asked. "If you *deliver the goods*?"

"A passport," he said with a grin. "British citizenship. But you may never catch the Killing Crew. What if they don't exist? There is no proof."

"No there isn't."

"They exist," Wolfe said, approaching. "They fuckin' exist all right."

I saw Nazeem shrug. "But it doesn't matter, because the major will give me a passport for information. Whether or not Frank's Band is the Killing Crew, I get my passport. Right, Major Wolfe?"

Wolfe grumbled his agreement.

"Let's go," he said. "I hate all this hanging around."

Nazeem attached a Transjordanian flag to the front of the Land Rover before we set off in the dark. Its pole was reed-like that bent and wobbled as Wolfe drove. Nazeem sat up front and I took the rear seat with the Sten gun across my lap.

We followed a stream before climbing into the mountains that run north from Jerusalem. This was harsh county and the drop in temperature made me wish I'd brought warmer clothes.

Dawn was a hint on the horizon when we crested the mountains and descended into the valley. Somewhere ahead, I knew the River Jordan cut through the land and the old border. This was all occupied territory now, although I saw no sign of the Arab Legion or any army for that matter.

It was darker again in the valley and Nazeem directed Wolfe south once more. I stopped hugging my body as the air warmed with our descent.

We crossed the river and then vast flatland.

Eventually we stopped.

"Here?" Wolfe asked doubtfully.

We were at a crumbling building beside a cluster of date palms. There was no one about.

Wolfe said, "I thought you were taking us to them."

"They're meeting us here," he said. "We wait."

And we waited.

Nazeem prayed.

The sky lightened and the hills of Transjordan lit up with gold.

We breakfasted on dates and water and continued to wait.

"What's the red card for this?" I asked. The *red card* provided the rules of engagement. If this was the Killing Crew, we were entering the lion's den.

"No guns. We stay relaxed and ask questions."

"Unless they start shooting."

"There is that." He paused. "I want you to do what you do best."

"What's that?"

"Read people, Ash. We'll ask questions. They won't come straight out and admit to being the Killing Crew. So you decide whether they're lying."

It was almost eight in the morning before we saw the dust of vehicles approaching. There were two Land Rovers like ours. They both flew Transjordanian flags. The first jeep had a Bren gun mounted on the back. The second had a passenger standing, one hand on the windscreen, and I wondered if he fancied himself as a charioteer.

As he neared, I noted the white kuffiyah—an Arab headdress—tied around his head.

"Fuckin' Lawrence of fuckin' Arabia," Wolfe muttered, and we raised our hands to show we weren't armed. The jeeps stopped and the man in the kuffiyah jumped down. This was clearly the leader of this band. Frank maybe?

There were six of them, and three showed they were armed by pointing rifles at us. No one was in a military uniform, although their clothes tended to be white or near-white shirts and trousers.

They all wore beards, more unkempt than Wolfe's and, with the exception of the leader, their heads were either shaven or crew-cut. Maybe his hair was the same under the headgear.

The leader said, "Right, let's go. You two in your jeep"—he pointed to me and Wolfe—"and the Arab in that one."

We got into our jeep, me driving, Wolfe in the passenger seat.

"Hey, Creech, there's a Sten back here," one of the militiamen said as he got in behind us.

"Good!" the leader shouted, before making a *wagon's roll* gesture and driving off.

Our vehicle was in the middle. Nazeem's, with the mounted Bren, took up the rear.

I followed the lead jeep, which travelled fast, kicking up dust and stones. We went east and came to an old Ottoman Empire-style town with cramped houses that enveloped the hillside.

After twists and turns, the lead jeep turned into a courtyard. I followed and stopped and wiped the dust from my face.

The walls of the compound were yellow ochre, crumbling in places. I looked over my shoulder. There were gates we'd come through. Nazeem wasn't behind us. Had we lost them among the winding streets?

The man on our rear seat was holding a pistol. He flung our Sten gun to a mate and then gestured for us to get out. Suddenly I felt like a prisoner rather than someone here for a friendly meeting.

Ahead were doors into a cluster of buildings. The leader, Creech, was marching through the one in the middle and we were told to follow.

I relaxed again once through the door because Creech sat at a table with bottles of beer set out, apparently for all of us.

He pointed opposite for us to sit.

"Sergeant Major Creech Towers," I said. "The Sussex Infantry."

His eyes widened.

"One of the most senior men who stayed behind," I said. "Your men called you Creech. Not many Creeches around—I recognized the name."

"Very good," Towers said.

He was a hard-looking man. He was in his thirties, but exposure to the sun had aged his skin considerably.

"And you two?" Towers asked.

"Bill Wolfe and Ash Carter," Wolfe said.

"Help yourself to a beer," Towers said, and took a swig from a bottle. Wolfe and I imitated him, although I didn't drink any.

He watched us then said, "You're military police."

Wolfe inclined his head. "That's true."

"Looking for deserters."

"We're not looking for you."

"You redcaps are hated as much as the enemy. And you're officers to boot! So maybe we should consider you worse than the enemy."

"We're not after you," Wolfe said, and I could hear the strain in his voice as he held back frustration.

"Really? We're deserters. At least, you lot think we are."

"Then what else are you?"

"Heroes. That's what we are, we're bloomin' heroes."

"Really?" Wolfe challenged. "Looks to me like you're mercenaries."

"We're fighting a proper war," he snapped. "We're finishing the job what the British Army failed to do."

I showed my palms. "We're not after you. We're looking for the Killing Crew," I said, hoping to defuse the situation.

Towers smiled.

"What?" I asked.

"You're looking for ghosts."

"You're saying the Killing Crew doesn't exist?"

Towers looked past us as a door opened. I turned to see another man, who beckoned.

Towers said, "Wait a minute."

He headed for the door and then we were alone in the room.

"Nothing but a bunch of thugs," Wolfe said.

"Red card?" I asked. "Time to shoot our way out?"

90

He shook his head. "We're fine. This Towers chap isn't the real leader, it's the other one: Frank."

I said, "From what I remember of the names on the deserters' board, there isn't a Frank or Francis."

"You think Frank's Band isn't their real name?"

Towers came back in and we waited in silence. Two of the juniors came in pointing rifles at us.

"Your lucky day," Towers said. "I was going to shoot you, but we'll trade you instead."

"Let us go," Wolfe said.

I said, "Keep our Land Rover."

Towers laughed, genuinely. "Oh we always planned on keeping the jeep. Really, you redcaps are dunces. Supposed to be the brightest of the bunch." He laughed again, although this time it was forced. "Lock 'em up, boys."

# SIXTEEN

As we were taken out of the room into the courtyard with the jeeps, Wolfe said, "Where's Nazeem?"

One of the two guards said, "Paid off. You shouldn't have trusted a snitch now, should you?"

There was an open door into a sidewall of the compound. We were pushed through and into a room that was probably for storage. It had rough stone walls and a thick wooden door with metal studs. The way it thudded shut made me suspect the metal was for reinforcement. Not a store then, a prison.

A small slit of a window provided a little light to the otherwise dark, airless room. It had a bench and two buckets, one with water and one presumably for our toilet.

Wolfe didn't seem as concerned as I felt. He sat on the bench and closed his eyes.

"We should have drawn our guns," I said from the window. I couldn't see anything except the outside wall and a shape that I figured was a Land Rover's bumper.

Wolfe said, "What do you think? Is it them?"

"The Killing Crew? Hard to know. They didn't say much." I'd hoped they would talk rather than lock us up. We should have had a better plan.

Wolfe said, "I don't think it's them. Which is progress."

I sat on the bench thinking that any progress was bugger all use to us now.

He said, "They'll come to their senses. We'll be fine. I predict they'll let us out before midday."

However, the room got hotter and hotter. Midday came and went. We both sipped at the water in the bucket. It was gritty and tasted of metal.

By late afternoon I could see Wolfe's cool had evaporated. I was irritated, not just with the situation but with my partner. Finally, I said something that had been playing on my mind.

"You, me, Finney and your informant. Nazeem was our fourth man."

"Yes. How did you find out?"

"He said. It should have been you who told me!"

"What difference would it have made?"

"I don't know, but it's what being in a team is all about."

"Nazeem is important. I didn't want to risk the Jewish authorities undermining my relationship with him." He looked at me with accusation in his eyes. I think he was referring to yesterday morning again when Rosen came and told us who the seventeen pro-Jews were.

"I didn't tell Dave Rosen."

He said nothing and closed his eyes.

I said, "So how's it turned out with Nazeem?"

Again he didn't speak. He didn't need to. Nazeem had sold us out.

During the afternoon we occasionally heard voices, but no one came to our prison room. Vehicles came and went and, as the night approached, we heard more activity out there.

Wolfe pulled his gun from the ankle holster.

"Change of plan," he said. He didn't need to elaborate and I unclipped my own gun.

When the door finally opened, our captors were in for a surprise.

But no one came, not then anyway. Darkness descended. We heard the echoes of an Islamic call to prayer. An hour later, we heard vehicles and men leaving. One vehicle had trouble starting, and we heard someone bark: "Leave it. Sort it in the morning."

A few minutes later there was silence.

Maybe nothing would happen until the morning.

I was breathing slowly, more relaxed, and wondered if Wolfe had fallen asleep, when I heard the scrape of a stone outside.

I nudged my partner and we both got up, our guns ready. He went to the left of the door and I went right. It would open outwards, which would afford us no cover.

Wolfe pointed. He'd go high, I'd go low.

Metal sounded against metal; a key was inserted and turned.

The door moved a fraction.

I tensed.

"Wolfe?" a voice whispered.

Wolfe pushed on the door with his foot, and in the pale light we saw the face of Nazeem.

The Arab grinned. "Hurry. I don't know how long they will be."

We followed him into the courtyard and saw our jeep was still there. I thought about the vehicle that hadn't started.

Nazeem was holding a distributor cap and quickly raised the bonnet to reconnect it.

I had a thousand questions but now wasn't the time. We jumped into the jeep, Wolfe driving, Nazeem in the rear, and just as we turned around I saw a man on the floor.

Nazeem confirmed it was a guard and I sprang from my seat.

"What are you doing?" Wolfe asked.

"I want answers."

The guard had been bound and gagged. With Nazeem's help, I manhandled the man onto the back seat and jumped in. Wolfe pressed his foot down and we shot out of the compound at breakneck speed.

Wolfe didn't know his way out of the town, but his logic was to take wider streets and those going downhill. His reasoning was good because we were soon away and on the river plain.

We kept on going long after we had crossed the Jordan. Wolfe took a less obvious route and we were back in the mountains on the western side.

Only when he felt safe did Wolfe stop and take a look at the man we'd abducted. He was awake and agitated, but Nazeem had him subdued with a grip around his neck.

We got out, and after the prisoner was propped against a wall, I held him there with my gun.

Wolfe said, "I knew you wouldn't let me down, Naz."

"I was tempted," the informant replied, but a smile suggested otherwise. "Perhaps if they'd paid me double. Twenty pounds for your jeep didn't seem like enough."

"Where did the gang go?"

"Drinking. I found out that they discovered a brewery and happily help themselves each night. It seems that they were heroes initially but have done nothing for weeks."

Our prisoner looked like he wanted to speak so I removed the gag.

"We are heroes," he spat.

"Really?" I said.

"We cleared Neve Yaakov of mines. We were the first men there after the Jews were driven back." He looked at me and shook his head. "You have no idea. You bloody redcaps! We lost friends fighting the Yishuv, and all you want to do is punish us for doing what we should have done years ago."

I said, "We don't want to punish you."

"That's not what Creech says."

I said, "We're after the Killing Crew."

Despite the poor light, his eyes showed recognition.

I said, "What do you know."

"Nothing."

"You aren't them."

He grunted.

"Who is Frank?" I asked. "You're Frank's Band."

"Franz," he said. "He's the SS chap, not the leader, but they used his name, kind of."

I said again, "You aren't the Killing Crew, but you know something."

"Didn't we all? We all knew about them, just didn't know who they were until that chap came. He wanted to join us, but Creech and Bill weren't having anything to do with him. They said he was bad news."

"Bill?"

"I'm Rich Lynch." He hesitated. "Bill's my brother."

William Lynch was the other sergeant major on our list. That made sense. The two of them together.

I asked, "What was the name of the Killing Crew chap?"

"If I tell you, will you let me go?" our prisoner said.

"Yes," Wolfe said without hesitation.

"How can I trust you?"

"Because we're not after you. We're after the Killing Crew."

The young deserter considered his options then nodded. "All right, I'll trust you."

So we untied him, and before we let him walk away he told us a name.

"Charlie Mason," he said. "You need to look for Charlie Mason."

# SEVENTEEN

We left Nazeem in the same village where we'd picked him up. Wolfe and his informant had a heated conversation, with Nazeem insisting he'd earned the British passport that Wolfe had promised.

Wolfe said that we only had a name and no guarantees. Neither of us could remember Charlie Mason from the deserter files.

Wolfe also wanted Nazeem to stay with us now that he had the travel warrant in the false name, but Nazeem wouldn't agree.

"I'm better working alone," he said. "You look for Mason your way and I'll do my thing. I'll call your office as soon as I know something."

"Call every two days," Wolfe said. They then debated the code they could use since neither of them trusted Sylvia Rom.

Before we parted, Wolfe thanked him for rescuing us and promised that he would get his passport if we proved Mason was one of the Killing Crew. That satisfied the Arab and I suspected he'd always hoped for that outcome.

Wolfe and I took it in turns driving through the night as we retraced our path south towards the Jerusalem–

Tel Aviv Road. We didn't talk much, but when we did it was about Frank's Band.

I believed Rich Lynch had been telling the truth. He hadn't elaborated and padded the story like liars do. We'd had to ask questions and learned that this Charlie Mason had tried to join Frank's Band three weeks ago. His brother, Bill, had said that Mason didn't have the right values. Lynch believed in adventure, they all did. Anyone came asking about how much money they'd earn and the sergeant majors would kick them out.

My interpretation was that Frank's Band was more about having fun than doing a serious job. That's why they weren't part of the Arab Legion. I suspected Charlie Mason had been more about fighting the Jews than drinking their beer.

I wondered why Wolfe had so easily let the man go after obtaining the name. I was driving at the time and I think Wolfe had been trying to get some kip.

"Firstly," he grumbled, "if Frank's Band is the target, then I want them on our terms. Next time, we go back prepared and they don't expect us."

"But we don't think they're the Killing Crew."

"Precisely. I don't want some crazy gang coming after us. They aren't our problem and we should keep it that way. It's a lesson you should learn." I knew he was referring to my altercation with the Slovak debt collectors.

If he was bating me I didn't find out because I stopped talking and focused on the rough terrain. We should have switched again, but I kept on driving all the way to the war-torn village where we'd left the Bentley.

It wasn't quite three in the morning when we put the Land Rover in the lock-up. If we travelled to Tel Aviv now, we were sure to be stopped and challenged. Plus, we were as tired as hell. So Wolfe drove us out of the village to a copse not far from the main road and we waited for dawn.

I awoke with a start. I'd been in a deep sleep and someone was banging urgently on my window. IDF soldiers were all around us, and for a horrible second I forgot where we were and worried about the Sten gun we'd previously had in the rear. But we were not in the Land Rover and Frank's Band had taken our machine gun.

An angry young man questioned what we were doing and didn't like our answer about not wanting to travel at night. Of course he didn't. Why would we have left Jerusalem so late, knowing that we wouldn't make it to Tel Aviv by nightfall?

Wolfe remained calm, and I figured he'd been in similar situations before. He made up a story about being kicked out of a drinking club in the capital and we were so inebriated we'd thought we could make it home.

"But we only managed seven miles."

"Idiots," the young soldier said. He checked our papers and took our home addresses before letting us drive away.

Wolfe dropped me at my lodging house on Gordon Street, where I cleaned up before grabbing breakfast and heading into the office.

Finney and Rom were already there and huddled together over a table, deep in discussion.

"You're back!" Finney said when he realized I was standing there.

"And still alive!" I said.

The other two waited for me to tell them about our trip, but I'd agreed with Wolfe that I'd wait for him. So instead, I asked what they'd been doing.

And it turned out they'd not wasted their time. At Rom's suggestion, they had visited the offices of the *Palestine Post* and interviewed Saul Levi, the reporter who had most frequently mentioned the Killing Crew in his pieces.

"We asked whether he believed they existed and he did," Finney said.

"OK." I wasn't surprised by that news otherwise the guy wouldn't have been writing about them.

"But," Rom said, "he couldn't help us. He didn't know who they were, just that he had informants within the military and they told him."

I pointed to the timeline board with the list of attacks. "Anything specific?"

Rom said, "We got nothing from him. Unfortunately, he was in the middle of something and couldn't give us long."

Finney's head bobbed with enthusiasm as he continued the story. "But a colleague chipped in just as we were about to leave. He didn't know anything specifically either but he had an opinion. He said they all did."

"And?" I prompted.

Rom said, "Sniper attacks. Not all of them, but he said his gut told him that the attacks were targeted rather than random."

I looked at the board. Most of the attacks were in Haifa, which made sense since most of the British Army had been there at some point. But there were also attacks in Jerusalem.

"Two other interesting ones," Finney said. "No evidence but—"

"—But the other reporter highlighted three murders in Tel Aviv: two guards and a nightwatchman," Rom finished.

I noted that none of the pieces mentioned a sniper.

"And," she continued, "an attack in January, here in Jaffa, baffled him."

Finney took up the story, his voice full of excitement: "Sniper, or snipers, again but killing two Arabs as well as a Jew."

"Well done," I said. I particularly liked the way the two of them seemed to work as a team. They'd used initiative and gleaned some information. Maybe it was useful.

When Wolfe arrived, I gave him a quick summary of their findings before we told them what we'd discovered.

We'd found a pro-Arab unit of deserters that wasn't part of an official Arab military. We'd identified the two leaders, Creech Towers and William 'Bill' Lynch. Wolfe separated them on the board of names and I added his brother, Rich—the young man we'd abducted and questioned. From their photographs, we recognized two of the others at the original meeting.

Above their cards, Finney wrote: *Frank's Band*.

"Are they the Killing Crew?" Rom asked.

"Unlikely," Wolfe said. "Not impossible, but unlikely."

"More likely is that they came across one of them," I said. "We got the name Charlie Mason."

Charles 'Charlie' Mason wasn't one of Frank's Band. However, we'd excluded him as one of the seven who weren't in a group.

Finney pulled the file and told us about him.

Mason was twenty-six, good-looking despite a scar across his forehead like a deep frown. He had a square jaw and dark features. Although he was only five foot eight, his photograph suggested a hard-as-nails body beneath his uniform.

In 1940 he'd joined the 3rd Kings Own Hussars, a light armoured unit with a big reputation. He'd fought in Crete and Italy and been part of the 8th Army forced to retreat from El Alamein by the Afrika Korps. He'd been injured in Algiers in '43 and been awarded the Distinguished Conduct Medal in recognition of his outstanding bravery for rescuing three British soldiers alone and under fire.

Despite the serious injury, as soon as he was fit enough, he'd rejoined the fight, this time recruited into the 2nd SAS Regiment, and he'd worked his way up to the rank of sergeant.

However, he'd been posted to Palestine, back in the King's Own but part of a recon unit attached to the 6th Airborne based in Sarafand.

"Does that make sense?" Finney asked.

No, it didn't.

"Buggeration!" Wolfe spluttered, looking at me. I could see he'd guessed the same thing. Finney was right to question whether it made sense. It didn't. Why go back into his old unit? Especially since that old unit wasn't based in Palestine. Mason was here on his own. It would have made more sense to have been transferred to the Paras.

Which meant one thing.

Mason wasn't what he purported to be.

The British authorities didn't admit it, but Field Marshal Montgomery had approved a plan when he took charge. The police had failed to handle the terrorists and so an unofficial police unit was created, one unencumbered by routine police matters—and regulations it seemed.

They were referred to as the Special Squads by both the press and within the rank and file, and yet they were explained as military personnel recruited to bolster an understaffed police force.

"When did he go AWOL?" Wolfe asked.

"March nineteenth," Finney said, still frowning at us.

I nodded. "There was a big hoo-ha. Four of them disappeared with a major to Syria. But then he returned to face the music and all the focus was on him."

Rom realized what we were talking about. "The police Special Squad," she said pointedly.

No one spoke for a minute, each of us lost in our thoughts.

Then Wolfe said, "We need to check the files for the others. And beware, they could be from any unit."

"We're looking for anyone assigned to a group that isn't theirs," I said. "History with the SAS or Commando is a good indicator."

Wolfe said, "Let's list all the main units that were here. We're probably also looking for anyone who's out of place—like a sole man from the King's Own."

Wolfe and I then called out all the British Army units that had been operating in Palestine at the end. Finney and Rom took turns in writing the names on paper and pinning them to the board with names.

Then Wolfe told Finney to split the files four ways. Rom thanked us.

I know Wolfe was dubious about her, but I said, "Of course! You're one of the team, Sylvia."

We added back the seven solo deserters. There were eighty-one, less the seventeen pro-Jew deserters, less the three idiots from the Ben Yehuda Street bombing, less the eight Brits in Frank's Band, less Charlie Mason.

Which left fifty-two. Fifty-two files, thirteen each. Like we were playing a game of cards like bridge.

I got through mine in twenty minutes and had found none. Finney took longer and asked about a couple, but they didn't sound likely candidates. None of us found anyone like Mason.

"Switch," Wolfe said. He took Finney's pile and I swapped mine with Rom and we started again.

No one.

We stood up and stretched.

"What are you thinking?" Finney asked.

"Maybe we're only after one man," Wolfe said.

"There could have been more," I said. "The Killing Crew might have been connected to the Special Squads. Could be one and the same."

"And," Wolfe said with a sigh, "only one of them remained. Only one of them deserted. Charlie Mason is our target. Our priority now is to find him."

# EIGHTEEN

Where was Charlie Mason? We knew he'd been based with the 6th Airborne at Sarafand, which was about six miles south of us. So he hadn't been far from Jaffa and Tel Aviv. The Special Squads went wherever there was trouble, but local made most sense. So I understood the sniper attacks around here. Haifa fit any scenario, but what about Jerusalem?

"You know the 6th Airborne and the 1st Infantry swapped locations," Wolfe said, as though reading my thoughts. "After Sarafand, they were at Jerusalem barracks."

I didn't know that. There had been a lot of units at the end. Most stayed put, but the 6th had a big reputation and it made sense that they were deployed where needed.

Finney said, "So where is he now?"

Rom said, "We know he was in Syria and... the West Bank?" This last word she said as a question since we still hadn't told the others where we'd found Frank's Band.

"Transjordan. Official Transjordan," I said. Before we left him, Nazeem had told us the town was called As-Salt.

"So he's in Transjordan," Finney said.

"Not necessarily."

"Where do you start an investigation like this?" Wolfe asked rhetorically. "You start with *what* you know. We also gather information from *where* we know."

"Sarafand, Jerusalem and Haifa," I added.

Wolfe nodded. "I want us to split up and gather information. You do the smart thing like you two did yesterday. You find people who might know something about Mason—anything. You ask questions and gather information. From that, we build a picture."

"And put it all together," Finney said.

"Right."

And then Wolfe told us what he'd decided. I was to cover the local area including Sarafand. He was going to Jerusalem and he wanted Finney and Rom in Haifa.

Wolfe and I chatted alone afterwards, and he confessed that it was a risk including Rom, but Finney would be lost on his own. I said they worked well together.

"As long as that's all it is," he said.

"She's too serious, and if he tried anything, she'd eat him alive," I said.

He laughed.

I thought about someone else who was too serious: Erika Arnold. That evening after supper, she asked me about where I'd gone the night before. Why I'd not come home.

I gave her some bullshit about visiting a friend but she didn't buy it.

We played cards and I was even worse than usual.

"I'm too tired," I said.

"So you were with a girl last night?"

I shook my head.

After a drink, she said, "It's all right you know, we're allowed to see Englishmen now your army has gone."

"British soldiers dated Jewish girls," I said. They also dated Arab girls too.

"Did you walk out with one?"

"A few. Nothing serious."

She nodded, as though it explained a lot.

"What?" I said.

"Why did Jewish girls have relations with British soldiers?"

"For the obvious."

She smiled, as though my *obvious* probably wasn't the same as hers. Then she said, "For information. And if a girl wasn't doing it for information, she would soon be pressured into it."

"You seem to be well informed," I said, for a second wondering if she'd had relations, but then shook away the thought. Her husband had been killed by us. She'd told me that she could never forgive the British. Surely she couldn't then sleep with the enemy?

"I knew girls who did it," she said. "It was encouraged by the Haganah."

I thought back to the girls I'd kissed. They seemed genuine enough, but maybe I was being hoodwinked along with all the others.

I felt awkward asking, but couldn't stop myself. "What about you, Erika?"

She might have been cross with me, but she wasn't.

"No, I didn't."

"I'm glad," I said.

When I went to bed, I was still thinking about old girlfriends and whether I'd been played, but I soon fell into a deep sleep and woke up refreshed and ready to visit the haunts of Charlie Mason.

\*　\*　\*

"They met a group called Frank's Band," the boy said to the man with the scary eyes.

"And they think they're the Killing Crew?"

"No. They're going to split up."

"What does that mean?"

"They want to find someone called Charlie Mason. He seems to have been a hero or something, but deserted. They said he's the target."

The man shook his head, thinking before he spoke. "Pro-Arab?"

"Yes."

"Where are they looking for him?"

"They thought Transjordan, but Wolfe said they should gather information." The man looked frustrated and so the boy answered more directly. "They're splitting up and going to Sarafand Garrison, Jerusalem and Haifa. They'll meet again in two days."

"All right. Keep watch in case they come back sooner."

# NINETEEN

Wolfe had taken his Bentley, and the others had travelled by bus to Haifa. My mode of transport would be a taxi. There was a Kesher Passenger Car office at the far end of Allenby Street. The employees were all in a casual uniform of tan shirts and matching trousers. The drivers were chatting and drinking coffee outside, with some sitting on the wall, others at tables like it was a café. It must have been a slow day.

Inside, I showed them Mason's photograph, just in case. No one recognized him.

I asked for a taxi to Sarafand Garrison and the clerk produced a formal ticket. Then he looked over my shoulder and said, "Going to Sarafand."

A driver stood at the door and signalled to the clerk and then nodded at me. He was tall, with a disarming grin that showed a snaggletooth.

I sat in the front of his Israeli-made Olds and he drove south through the vast orange groves. Although this was out of season I could see fruit on the ground and trees: splashes of bright orange against the green. The war had impacted the harvest. I wondered how many labourers had fled, how many businesses evacuated.

Snaggletooth talked about the war. He told me that the taxi business was suffering because people were afraid to travel. Plus the Tel Aviv–Jerusalem train hadn't been running for a month. It seemed they normally got a lot of business from train arrivals.

The subject switched to me. He asked about my visit to the old British Army barracks, which I deflected. I claimed my interest was historical curiosity. Whether or not he believed me, he accepted my answer.

We passed three commercial trucks, but I didn't see a private car beyond the city limit. Also, I only saw a couple of people in the fields.

The orange farms ended abruptly and we passed through desert. The land was flat. A boring plain between the mountains and the coast.

A rail line ran parallel before it swept east and west, and we crossed the tracks, continuing south. To the right, I could see the enormous garrison. Date palms scattered around the main gates and officers' sectors. Low brown buildings with dull metal roofs. Fencing around the perimeter.

An old Arab was shuffling along the road and I asked Snaggletooth to stop.

"Anyone at the base?" I asked the Arab.

He didn't break his stride, just looked at me through thousand-year-old watery eyes and said, "No one."

I watched him continue. He was heading towards a town outside the base. I figured this was where most of the civilians had lived. It looked ruined and deserted.

"Sarafand al-Amar," Snaggletooth said to my unasked question.

"What happened there?"

"An Arab militia came here before being driven out by the Haganah."

"And the villagers?" I asked.

He shrugged but knew. They had been Arabs and either been killed, fled or evicted.

After I pointed to the main gates, my driver started the engine and we turned right.

The entrance used to have gates across. No longer. The gates and what would have been a sentry box were gone, ploughed down by a tank I suspected.

I'd visited Sarafand Garrison a year ago, but now I hardly knew the place. Then it had been full of activity, vehicles and men. Now the buildings looked forlorn and the slight breeze carried a creepy silence.

I asked the driver to drive and wait as I explored. Then drive and wait again.

I saw British Army unit signs and abandoned items. Everyday things that wouldn't normally be allowed to litter the place: pans, a kitbag, a single boot.

In the canteen, there were still plates on the tables. This was the army equivalent of the *Marie Celeste*.

I found the Signals and Intelligence blocks, where Mason might have worked, but any insightful paperwork had been taken or destroyed. I could see patches on the ground outside where bonfires had burned.

Sarafand was the ultimate representation of British failure. There was nothing here for me. So I walked back to my taxi one last time and asked him to take me to the offices of the *Palestine Press*.

Snaggletooth looked at me, a fleeting frown on his face.

"What's the matter?" I asked.

"I'm sorry, sir. Just curious of the connection."

I lounged in the seat as he drove back. "Probably none," I said. "Just somewhere else to go."

I suppose he had more questions because I hadn't really answered, but he didn't chat anymore and I was grateful. I closed my eyes and had images of how Mandatory Palestine had been before it all started going wrong. Before we'd become the enemy.

When the taxi pulled up outside the newspaper's offices, my driver volunteered to wait. However, I had no idea how long I'd be and it was only a mile walk back to the SIB office.

Once inside, I asked the receptionist for the same reporter who had spoken to my colleagues: Saul Levi.

He was available, and my initial impression was of a timid man. Every journalist I'd previously met exuded confidence, and I was surprised a major name from the *Palestine Press* didn't fit the mould. He was small with unkempt hair and wore a crumpled suit.

We chatted for a short time over a cup of tea and I decided my initial impression had been wrong. Perhaps it was an unassuming manner. It probably worked well in getting people to talk.

Levi told me everything Finney and Rom had related. But I asked for the names and addresses of the sniper and other murder victims that his colleague had mentioned. Rom hadn't given me a name, but Levi acknowledged the suspicions. He gave it some thought before deciding he could help. Ten minutes after leaving me alone, he returned with the names, but no addresses. A compromise, he said, although I would find public census information at the records office.

"We went through the newspapers and didn't find a mention of the Engineer," I said.

"The Engineer," Levi said. It wasn't a question, but I heard doubt in his voice.

I waited for more and watched his eyes.

"The alleged bomb-maker," he said.

"The man behind the Killing Crew."

"But not one of them?" he asked.

I frowned. Why was he avoiding this?

"Captain Carter," he finally said, "there was no mention of the Engineer in any of my articles because none of my sources ever mentioned him. They mentioned the Killing Crew but not any Engineer. I don't report on myths."

When I asked him about Mason, he said he didn't know the name. However, the town hall on Bialik Street also held copies of travel warrants, so if Mason had documents they'd also be held with the other records.

The town hall was an imposing building at the end of Bialik Street. As I approached I thought it looked like a stunted front section of the American White House.

It wasn't Independence Hall, which celebrated Israel's independence. Even so, the entrance was festooned with the new state's flags. The walls proudly displayed photographs of David Ben-Gurion and other officials.

After showing my identity papers, I had no problem accessing the census records. I found myself in a dark room with cold metal shelves and ledgers. A quick scan suggested there were around forty books. Taking one down, I found exactly what I expected, lists of names against property addresses for the Tel Aviv sector.

These were recorded during the British Mandate and I found I was looking at a census taken in 1938. I pulled another book, then another. There was nothing since the end of 1946.

British Army personnel wouldn't be included— unless they were undercover or establishing themselves. I thought success was unlikely, but checked for the name Mason and found none.

Returning to the reception area, I asked if there were any records since 1946. I was certain the new government would have organized a census as soon as possible. Was it too soon? There would also be the warrants and permissions that were bound to be filed here somewhere. However, I was told that such records were not available to me.

"Where could I find those?"

"Start by asking the police," was the reply I received. I suspect it wasn't serious judging by the tone of the man's voice. But even if it was, Wolfe had impressed upon us all that we weren't to talk to Rosen or anyone from the police or government. He'd directed the comment at Rom, who'd agreed. However, he may as well have been talking to me. I was sure he still believed I'd gone against his wishes and invited Rosen to the office.

I was determined it wouldn't happen again, either deliberately or otherwise.

"More recent records are available," the clerk said, much to my surprise. He directed me into a different room. This wasn't stark and dreadful like the other. It was a small library-style room with a thick pile carpet and smart wooden tables. They were painted white and had glass on top, presumably to protect the furniture.

There was a row of ten burgundy leather ledgers and I took one from its shelf. The format was identical to the British Palestine ones I'd looked at. With one large exception. Everything had been produced by the Jewish Agency and was in Hebrew.

I had no clue what I was looking at. I couldn't read a word past the covers.

Again I thought of Rosen. If I could only rely on him to help, we could review the files together. In fact, I could have used Rom if she'd not been shipped off to Haifa with Finney. I'd have to come back in a couple of days when we were all back together.

Giving up, I strolled towards the coast where all the old army clubs, like Scopus and the Ritz Officer's Club, used to be. I would ask locals and show them Mason's photograph. Perhaps they'd remember him.

But before I reached the first old army haunt, I discovered a solution to my immediate problem.

# TWENTY

My landlady stepped out of a baker's shop. It took a second for me to recognize her because of a scarf over her head, but she smiled when she saw me.

Five minutes later, we were back in the town hall looking at the Jewish Agency books.

"I'm searching for a man called Mason, Charles or Charlie Mason."

"And you think he's in here?" Erika Arnold asked.

"Not really," I said. "I'm just covering all bases."

She opened a book and ran her fingers down the right-hand column. The British documents tended to be left to right. I realized that these were the mirror image.

She turned the page and read on.

It took her forty minutes to go through the first book.

"Not in here," she said with a sigh.

"How many people are there in Tel Aviv?" I asked, looking at the other books and thinking there were about seven hours reading here.

"I don't know exactly. Somewhere near three hundred and fifty thousand perhaps."

I watched her skim through pages for a while longer but I was no help to Erika so decided to go back to the older records.

Within thirty minutes I'd found one of the names Levi had given me—a man killed by a sniper in Jaffa. His religion was noted as Muslim and his job was bank guard rather than *guard*—the job title we'd got from the newspaper. Since we were looking for Jew killers, I decided we would exclude this gentleman.

After an hour I'd found the address of the murdered nightwatchman and noted that he ticked the Jewish box.

Erika came into the room looking exhausted.

"I've been through three," she said. "I'm at the start of book four."

"Any Masons?"

"No," she said, "and I need a break. My eyes hurt."

We went outside for air, and after a stroll in the garden in front of the building, she asked me what I'd been doing here.

"I'm sorry, but I can't tell you why I'm looking for Mason," I said.

"No, not Mason. Not generally. I wondered why you had been walking towards the beach when I spotted you."

"I was going to ask people along the front if they knew him." I wondered about how much I could say but decided it was all right to continue. "You know, the old places British soldiers went. They might remember him."

"Ah, so Mason was a British soldier?"

I said, "I can neither confirm nor deny that."

She flashed a smile, and for a brief moment her attractiveness shone through.

I said, "I have a photograph too. People may remember his face if not the name."

"Let me see."

I fished the photograph of Mason from my pocket and held it out.

She looked. She blinked. She shook her head.

"What?"

"It can't be," she said, drawing the picture closer, examining it. "I think I know this man."

"You know Mason?" I exclaimed.

"No," she said, her face contorting with doubt and confusion. "I think this is Caleb Maaz. No, it can't be."

"Who is Caleb Maaz?"

"A friend. Well, a girlfriend's friend. Looks just like him, but maybe five years younger. He has the scar on his forehead."

I took a long breath. My heart thudded with excitement.

"This Maaz chap—where can I find him?"

"I don't know, but I can take you to my friend."

Erika's friend lived two blocks north. Her name was Ruth Gotting and she gave me an appreciative smile when she opened her front door.

"My, my, Erika! And who is this young man?"

"Ruth! He's just a guest at my house," my landlady admonished her friend. "A paying guest, mind you."

The look on Ruth's face suggested she didn't believe it, but she ushered us inside and offered us tea and cake.

Once in her living room, with the food and drink, I produced the photograph of Mason.

The girl's face changed like a switch had been thrown.

"What's this about?" She looked at Erika with wide eyes.

I said, "I'm looking for this man."

"All right," our host said, turning her hard gaze on me, "tell me who you are exactly."

"My name's Ash Carter," I said.

"You're British," Ruth said accusingly. I could see defensive walls going up.

"It's fine," Erika said, calming her friend. "He's here on approved, official business. I wouldn't let him stay if he wasn't."

"I'm sorry to surprise you like this," I said, hoping to placate the woman. "I'm just looking for him. He may have information that I need."

"What sort of information?"

I couldn't share that. I couldn't tell her about our hunt for the Killing Crew. But I could tell her that it may be of national security.

"For Britain?" she scoffed.

"Yes, but also for Israel," I said. "That's why I have approval." To aid my justification, I produced the travel and authority papers.

She glanced at them, seemed satisfied with the Israeli seal and signature and breathed out. I wondered if she'd been holding it in.

"Tell me about Caleb," I said.

"What do you want to know?"

"When you met. What he does. Where I can find him."

She shook her head. "I haven't seen him for two weeks."

"But do you know where he is?"

"No." She stood up and walked to the window, stared out for a minute and then turned. "I met him a year ago and... I'm sorry, Erika."

Erika sat up. "What for?"

"I knew he was British."

Erika looked confused. "So he really *was* this man, Mason?" she asked, pointing to the photograph.

"Yes. I didn't dare admit it. You know how girls were treated, and I refused to act as a spy." She swallowed and sank back into her chair. "You see, I loved him. And he loved me."

Erika shook her head. "But we talked about—"

"I know! I couldn't see other British soldiers... I couldn't work for the Haganah because I was already seeing one. He never wore a uniform. He wasn't like a regular soldier."

No, he wasn't, I thought. He was more like the secret police.

"And how did that work out?" Erika said, disappointment heavy in her tone.

Ruth was now on the verge of tears. "He'll come back," she said. "These are difficult times. He had a job but got laid off. He went to Jerusalem to find work."

I asked, "So was he working afterwards—after the British left?"

"Yes," Ruth said. "He worked at a security firm over by the brickworks. They have an office there but cover the whole country."

"What's their name?" I asked.

"Shomrim," she said. "He worked for Shomrim Security."

# TWENTY-ONE

The brickworks was north-east of the city and I strode there after a session in the gymnasium followed by a hearty breakfast. As anticipated, I found an industrial area busy with trucks and machinery. Tel Aviv was expanding rapidly and this factory was probably the source of most building materials. The air had a whiff of clay and the dust caught in my throat.

Shomrim Security's building backed onto the brickworks and had a blue and white sign written in both Hebrew and English above a shiny black door. Apart from that, my initial sense was of a small, shabby operation.

A receptionist seemed surprised when I walked in, like she wasn't expecting any customers. Or perhaps she expected me to knock first. Then I noticed a telephone on her desk and supposed most clients telephoned rather than came through the front door unannounced.

"Can I help you?" she asked.

"The boss," I said. "Could I speak to him, please?"

"He's busy."

"Anyone else then? I don't mind who."

The woman got up slowly, like it was all too much effort, and left me alone in the reception room. A minute later she returned to her desk and told me someone would be out shortly.

There was a window in the door she went through and I saw a figure hesitate behind it before coming through and greeting me.

"How can I help you, Mr...?" He glanced at the receptionist as he hesitated, an unsubtle message that she should have asked for my name.

"Carter."

"You're English."

"I am. Is that a problem?"

He smiled. "Not at all. Not at all. In fact, it's a founding principle here at Shomrim." He spread his hands wide. "We accept anyone, irrespective of nationality, heritage or creed."

"Accept them for what?" I asked, acutely aware that we were still standing in the reception. He might have invited me into a meeting room and offered me water at least. I also noted that he hadn't introduced himself.

He scrutinized me. "How can I help you exactly, Mr Carter?"

"I'm looking for a friend. I'm looking for Caleb Maaz."

"Ah. And you think we can help because...?"

"I was informed that he used to work here."

The man nodded thoughtfully.

"Do you know where I can find him?" I prompted.

"Mr Maaz was employed by us for a few weeks," he said. "Then one day, he didn't turn up for work."

"What happened?"

"We don't know. It was three weeks ago and he just vanished."

Three weeks, I thought. That tallied with what the young soldier from Frank's Band had told us. Ruth Gotting, his girlfriend had seen him since.

"Now may I ask why you are looking for him?"

"Like I said, he's my friend and he's missing." Of course, I hadn't said he was missing but hoped that would sound reasonable based on what I'd just been told. "Do you think he might be in trouble?"

The man shook his head and rolled his shoulders with it. "No. Mr Maaz was a lazy so and so, if you want my opinion. I'm sorry to say it because he's your friend, but it's true. To be honest, if he hadn't disappeared, he'd have been dismissed anyway."

I was about to ask another question when he held up a hand. "Now, if you don't mind, I need to get back to work. Sorry I can't be of more assistance."

He opened the door for me and I found myself on the doorstep facing the building.

I waited a few minutes then opened the door and stepped back inside.

The receptionist looked shocked for a second time that day. She started to stand.

"It's all right," I said. "I just wanted one of these." There were glossy brochures on her desk with the company name emblazoned across the front. It looked more impressive than this office suggested.

I took a brochure and thanked her.

"Oh and I didn't catch his name."

"Mr Cohen," she said. "That was Mr Cohen, head of operations."

# TWENTY-TWO

"There's not much in Jerusalem," Wolfe said as I walked into the office. I hadn't expected him until tomorrow, but he was back. He'd pinned a map of the old city on a wall and had marked the locations of the three deaths by sniper on it. Against each one, he'd written their name and the date of the killing.

He said, "And it's dangerous up there. Lots of clashes between the IDF and Arab Legion despite the alleged ceasefire."

I told him I'd discovered nothing at Sarafand Garrison. I'd been to the newspaper's offices, and the reporter, Levi, had given me the names and locations of the three killings in the Tel Aviv sector. However, I hadn't found their addresses.

"Did he say anything about the Engineer?"

The Engineer, the bomb-maker who worked with the Killing Crew. Allegedly.

"Levi said the Killing Crew were real. It was the Engineer who was a myth; a story told by the British soldiers."

"Why?"

"He didn't say, but you know how men make things up—fill in gaps when they don't know. Levi said he only reported true stories—news from his trusted sources. Of course, he was careful what he told me. He wouldn't betray his sources."

Wolfe nodded.

He pointed to the wall and a map of Jerusalem. "I've marked the locations on here. We should do the same for what you found in Tel Aviv and Jaffa."

I'd hesitated, not wanting to blurt out my discovery about Mason and his name change. I'd made significant progress and hoped Wolfe would be impressed.

"I found out something more interesting," I said as I picked up the local map and pinned it up next to the one of Jerusalem.

"Yes?" he prompted as I milked the moment.

"The brickworks are here," I said, pointing to the block north and east of the city. "There's a company called Shomrim Security—"

I stopped abruptly and listened. A noise and then silence. The rats in the room above.

Wolfe looked at me, curious.

I pointed at the ceiling and looked inquiringly at him.

I saw a thought cross his face. The same as mine, no doubt.

He started moving and I followed him out of the room and to the stairs. Our feet clattered on the concrete as we took two at a time to the next floor up.

I realized Wolfe had his gun ready. Mine was still in my ankle holster. He'd pulled it out so quickly and smoothly I hadn't even spotted the move.

Once through the door at the top, we were in a corridor, doors off to the left and right. And a door at the end, thirty yards away, was moving.

We sprinted and burst through into a large room. Overturned desks, chairs and cabinets littered the floor. There were a thousand scattered sheets of paper, and noticeboards hung broken from walls. A strong smell of piss offended my nose.

Our attention switched to the left. An open window.

I reached it before Wolfe, just in time to see a figure dash across the rear yard and scale a wall.

"What the fuck..?" Wolfe growled beside me.

"A boy," I said.

"A teenager or small man," he said.

"Maybe." I looked at the ladder propped against the wall. "Could be innocent."

Wolfe grumbled something I didn't catch because he was marching back the way we'd come. He went through the doors, along the corridor and stopped at the last door on the left. It was open, and we went inside.

The room was directly above our office. It had a camp bed behind the door and a chair by the wall where a water pipe ran from ceiling to floor. It had been modified with a hole in it the size of a fist. There was also an overturned drinking glass on the floor.

A makeshift lavatory, possibly, but I doubted it. The kid had been using the other office as a toilet. The smell in there told us that.

Even before we looked in the hole, I could see a mirror. In the right position, I could see the room below. Two mirrors then, like an inverted periscope.

Wolfe picked up the glass and placed it against the pipe. "Listening," he said. "I bet he was both watching and listening."

It hadn't been rats. I'd heard noises the first time I'd been here. It had been the kid.

"From the start," I said. "He's heard everything."

I expected anger, but Wolfe seemed sanguine as he shook his head.

"At least we now know who told Dave Rosen. I thought it had been you or Rom."

We went downstairs and he looked at the map I'd put up, then he remembered what we'd been talking about.

He said, "He heard you say that security company name."

"Shomrim." I said, thinking. "He reacted to the name."

"The name's important."

"But not the main thing I learned." So I told him about Charlie Mason, told him that our target had been using the name Caleb Maaz. "He was working at the security firm but then disappeared about three weeks ago."

"And found Frank's Band," he said. "Good work, Ash."

I dreaded him asking how I'd found out. I'd have to admit to what I'd told my landlady and her friend. But he didn't.

He was more concerned about the spy and sent me out to buy a hammer and nails. When I returned, he'd removed the mirrors from the pipe and blocked the hole upstairs and in our office. He'd pulled up the ladder, and broken desks into strips of wood. We nailed the wood to bar the windows and then did the same for the door to the office the spy had used.

As we worked, we debated going back to Shomrim Security. Wolfe was in favour. I was not. Mason had moved on and we needed to know where he'd gone after Frank's Band, not before.

However, my words were in vain, and it took us half an hour to walk across the city to the brickworks.

# TWENTY-THREE

"What do you think?" Wolfe asked as we walked. "Was Mason part of the Killing Crew? Was he looking for other members?"

"Or just trying to find a new role for himself?" I said.

"But what I don't understand is why work for Jews after the handover? This security mob are Jewish, right?"

"Of course."

"Puzzling," he said.

We stopped on Hovevei Tsion Street, heavy with trucks, going east and laden with bricks. I pointed out the entrance to the security firm and we sat in the shade while Wolfe deliberated.

Finally, he said, "Let's both go in," and strode to the black door with the signage above.

He entered first. I stepped in behind and closed the door. As before, the receptionist looked surprised.

"Is Mr Cohen available?" Wolfe asked her.

She seemed uncertain then made a decision and jumped up and disappeared through the door with the viewing window.

A minute later, she was back and apologizing that the Head of Operations was occupied.

"We'll wait," Wolfe said.

There were no chairs in the reception area. Wolfe leaned against a wall and flicked through a brochure he'd picked up.

Half an hour passed.

"Please check again," Wolfe said.

The receptionist's face showed relief as she scooted out. This time it was five minutes before she returned. Cohen was right behind her.

He smiled charmingly and held out his hand to Wolfe. He didn't look at me.

"Sorry to keep you waiting. How can I help you, Mr...?"

"My colleague tells me that Maaz used to work here."

"That's correct."

"We are looking for him."

Now Cohen looked at me. "As I told Mr Carter, Caleb Maaz didn't turn up for work three weeks ago, and if he had he would have been fired anyway."

"Where might he have gone?" I asked.

Cohen shook his head with a simultaneous shoulder roll.

Wolfe said, "Where does he live?"

Cohen glanced at the receptionist and back. "I don't know. It's a principle of ours that we don't keep records like that. It protects our staff."

"What about contacts?"

Cohen shook his head.

I heard Wolfe suck in air, and sensed his annoyance. "You must know something," he said.

Cohen pursed his lips as though considering but then did the head shake and shoulder roll thing.

"No. If we knew, we'd have dealt with him."

"Oh?" I said. Not *we would have informed the police.* They would have dealt with him.

Cohen smiled, maybe reading my mind. "He wasn't just lazy, Mr Maaz stole from us. That's why he would have been dismissed. So if you do have luck locating *your friend*'—there was sarcasm in his voice—"then we'd like to know. Now if you'll excuse me?"

"I read your brochure," I said. He'd started to turn away but now he stopped. "When I came before, you said that you provided security to anyone, irrespective of—"

"—nationality, heritage or creed," he finished.

"A founding principle."

"That's right." Cohen's tone sounded suspicious.

"You provide protection services for Arabs then?"

"If they can afford our fees." He raised a finger like he was making a significant point. "And providing they are law-abiding."

I said, "Being a non-Jew is challenging."

Wolfe said, "People still hate the British."

Cohen cocked his head, wondering where we were going with this.

Wolfe said, "We need protection."

"You are asking for protection?"

"Yes."

He looked us up and down, maybe noting our heights and assessing whether we could take care of ourselves.

"You don't look like our typical clients."

"Does that matter?"

He pursed his lips then smiled at Wolfe. "May I ask what you do for a living?"

"We work for the British government," Wolfe said. "With authority from the Israeli authorities of course."

"I see."

"So can you help us?"

"We're overstretched at present," Cohen said. "I'm sure you can appreciate that. But it's a dynamic situation, so we may be able to help at any time."

I said, "If one of your clients is killed?"

Cohen smiled, although the skin around his eyes didn't crease. "We don't claim perfection."

Wolfe said, "That sounds like something that should be in your brochure."

"Good day, gentlemen," Cohen said, turned away then turned back. "And if you do find Mr Maaz, be sure to let me know."

# TWENTY-FOUR

"I didn't like him," Wolfe said as we walked away.

"Do you like anyone?"

"Him less than most."

We went to the coast and turned south. Despite the troubles, people were bathing in the sea. The air was a nice temperature now that the sun was low in the west.

This whole section had once been the purview of the British Army. Not long ago. Signage and names were already changing.

"I used to get English breakfast there," Wolfe said pointing to a café. "Not any more. Stay here too long and we'll forget what pork sausages taste like."

We kept going, into the sectors once allocated to Greek and Polish nationals in the army. And then we were passing through the out-of-bounds sector. When I'd been before, I'd been told about the Arab slums, the ne'er do wells, the brothels and thieves. This was the area my landlady had referred to as Manshiya. Most of the old town was still there, but at the northern end bulldozers were clearing swathes of crumbling houses. Now that I knew what to look for, I could see signs that tenement blocks would be going up in their place. This would be the new social housing. Urgent construction to cope with the rapid rise in population.

Wolfe had said, "Show me where the three killings happened. Maybe we can work out where the snipers were."

We were heading for Jaffa, the mount and the port. But the first place we surveyed was just after the coast rolled west like a carbuncle. We walked past the prison, a bastion of the Ottoman Empire, and followed the narrow road. To our right was the golden sea and Andromeda's Rock. On our left, the buildings climbed, higgledy-piggledy, one on top of another.

I stopped about fifty yards from the prison and said that this was roughly the spot. The nightwatchman had been walking to work at the docks when a single shot killed him.

The reporter had no information about the sniper, just that no one saw the shooter. We looked around. Any number of places on the side of the hill would have worked. He could have been on a roof or shot from a window.

"What about the prison?" Wolfe suggested. "After all, we know that the other two were described as guards. *Prison guards* seems likely."

"I found one in a census. It said he was a bank guard, but he was Muslim, so I suppose we ignore that one."

Wolfe nodded. "There will be a lot of attacks that aren't down to the Killing Crew. We'll just have to be ready to discount those that don't fit."

"And hope we're left with those that do."

"Process of elimination," he said.

I faced the prison, which would have been an excellent shooting spot. The high three-storey walls had plenty of windows and what appeared to be a wall-walk, like you'd expect in a castle. Perfect.

"It's possible," Wolfe said. "Maybe we're looking for soldiers who had access to the prison."

We kept walking along the coastal arc and passed Armenian and Greek churches. I saw a couple of religious men dressed all in black, but no one else.

Then we saw the Jaffa Light, the old lighthouse warning ships of the rocks. Not an ideal spot for a port, I figured. I understood that it didn't have deep water either. What it did have was a thriving orange business—until recently that was.

The second location wasn't in the line of sight of the prison. Which was disappointing.

We walked as far as the warehouses. Here the dock opened up and you could pass either side of a long warehouse that smelled of oranges. After that was Customs and a building for quarantine.

The guard had been found outside a property with the name *Gargour & Fils* above a wide frontage, a three-door, single-storey building. It was made of chalk-white painted bricks and stood out against the four tiers of red-brick buildings that staggered up the hill.

"What did they do here?" Wolfe asked, looking through barred windows into darkness.

Like most properties at the port, it was deserted.

"Unlikely to have anything to do with the prison," I said. "What was the guard doing here?"

We had no answers, but as I looked around, my attention kept being drawn to a St Peter's clock tower—a Christian church in the heart of the old Arab town. It rose above the jumble of buildings, as though surveying the land. Keeping watch.

I pointed. "Another good sniper location."

"Out of interest, could you see the third place—where the bank guard was shot—from there?"

"Undoubtedly. It's just down…" I became distracted by a car at the end of the dock. Not a taxi. I shook my head and continued: "Although we don't know if the bank guard was killed by sniper."

"We don't know if the others were. Not really."

Good point. We started walking. The private car had turned towards us.

"Bill—"

"I've been waiting all afternoon," he interrupted. "Waiting for you to explain."

I switched my attention back to him. "Explain?"

"How you found Charlie Mason's alias."

We reached the end of the Customs building. The car was close now. I could see the driver and another man. Then, as the car turned side-on, I saw the passenger was holding a gun.

# TWENTY-FIVE

I grabbed Wolfe's arm and pulled him back. "Run!"

He didn't question me.

We sprinted back the way we'd come.

The car accelerated behind us. I could hear it gaining, but this wide section narrowed suddenly ahead. We had to get there before the car.

We passed Customs, the long warehouse and reached the end of the dock.

I heard the car braking hard and took a peek over my shoulder. The two men were jumping out of the car, the last rays of the sun glinting off their guns.

"Who the fuck?" Wolfe asked. "Vigilantes?"

"No," I said, having recognized the suits, the look. "Slovak gang."

"Fuck!" he said. "Are they following?"

"Yes."

I thought a gunfight would be risky. We'd attract attention and that would undoubtedly mean the police. I was about to ask but he beat me to it.

"Red card: no guns unless they shoot first."

We rounded the lighthouse, looming and placid, ignorant of our plight.

"We need to split up," I said, and pointed to the passageway between buildings. We went up it and turned sharply, entering the warren that was the old city.

At a T-junction, I went right, Wolfe went left. The lane was rising steeply and cobbles hurt my feet.

I glanced back again and saw one of the gang following.

Another junction. Where to go?

Right then left.

Again I looked back. I wasn't losing him. I needed time to hide or prepare an ambush.

I'm a good runner, but this guy was fast.

Despite his gun, he wasn't shooting at me. Which was good. He was smart enough to know his shots would have gone wild if he'd fired while running so fast.

Which way?

Up and right.

The night was rushing in. The alleyways were dark and getting darker.

I glanced back again, and that's when I slipped on a loose cobble. My holster must have come unclipped, because I watched with horror as my Beretta skittered over the stones. It dropped into a gutter, fifteen feet away.

My mind quickly processed the options. I saw myself grabbing it, rolling and firing. I imagined rolling the whole way, or diving. But each scenario took too long, and I could already see the goon raising his weapon.

Leave it.

I sprang up and continued my sprint, crouching instinctively, expecting a shot. But no shot came.

Suddenly St Peter's Church hove into view and I realized I was nearing the top of the mount. I should have gone left and got lost in the twisting lanes of the old city. Instead, I was running straight down the side of the church.

I got to the end and turned.

A courtyard. Open space. The only cover, a few palm trees.

I could dash across, but now would be a good time for the chaser to stop and shoot.

A dark opening in the wall caught my eye and I darted into it.

And then I realized my mistake.

This was the bell tower. One way in. No way out.

No time to think, I started up the staircase. It wound up clockwise with four square flights to the floor above.

I was on the second set when I heard my pursuer pounding up the steps below.

Up I went. Up and up, floor after floor. At first, there was hardly any light; darker in there than outside. The higher I climbed, the lighter it got. The fifth had a window but it was barred. From there, a wooden ladder took me higher and I found I'd reached the bells. I looked down and saw the church roof was too far. If I jumped, I'd break an ankle. Maybe worse.

I climbed another ladder and went through a wooden hatchway. This section was ten feet square and open to the elements. Above me was the clock section.

My pursuer was on the floor below. He started climbing the ladder. I looked up and considered my options. Climb or stand and fight? My fists versus his gun. I didn't fancy my odds although he might not want to shoot.

If he fired a gun up here, the whole of Jaffa would know about it, maybe most of Tel Aviv.

Metal rods and chains hung down on two sides. Controls for the clocks, I supposed.

I snatched at a rod and it came away in my hands.

His gun came through the hatchway. It turned in an arc, like he was looking for me, but I couldn't even see his head.

And then he bounded up, springing and turning. He'd guessed I was on the opposite side. He hadn't seen me. I hadn't seen him. And he thought I didn't have a weapon, but even as he was landing, I was lunging forward. No time to swing the rod. I jabbed and it took him in the throat.

His eyes flew wide, but the gun was aimed at me.

Another step and I punched with my weaker right hand, catching his cheek. He was already going backwards because of the jab. Now he spun and went over. Through the window.

There was a brief yell before I heard a wet *thunk*. He'd landed on the church roof, his head splitting like a melon. Blood spilled rapidly around him.

And then I heard three shots. But they weren't coming from this guy. No. He was stone dead. The shots were distant and muffled and I wondered whether Wolfe was in a gunfight.

I listened hard but heard nothing more.

Minutes later I stepped out of the bell tower into the courtyard. A priest saw me. He glanced my way but paid me no further attention. Two more men appeared, walking calmly. There had been a fight in the bell tower above them and there was a body on the church roof. It seemed that no one had heard or seen him fall.

I retraced my steps, walking around the church and along its side. Then I turned down the cobbled alley where I'd lost my gun. The Beretta was still there in the gutter. It felt good in my hand and I proceeded with caution. Would I now meet Wolfe or the other goon?

At the T-junction where we'd split up, I went straight on. The dock was down to the left.

As I'd realized, this route wound around the hill through the old town. A maze of passageways and buildings.

An old man saw me—or more likely my gun—and shrank back into the shadows.

I spotted the lighthouse and figured I would have subconsciously headed for it. Had Wolfe? Turning another corner, I bumped into him. He was in shirtsleeves. When we'd parted he'd been wearing a jacket.

"Good!" he said, out of breath. I assumed he was happy that I was still alive.

"Where's your man?" he asked.

"Dead."

"Do we need to move him?"

I shook my head. "He won't be found for a while."

"Good," Wolfe said again.

"I heard shots," I said.

"Yes." He about-turned and led me back the way he'd come. Eventually, we reached a doorway. In it was a crouching man. Only he wasn't crouching naturally because there was blood pouring from his head and chest.

"Three shots?" I said, looking from the dead man to Wolfe.

"You heard them?"

"I was in St Peter's bell tower."

"Blast! I thought my jacket had muffled the sound." He pointed to a lump beside the dead man, and I guessed it was Wolfe's jacket with three new holes burned through.

He said we should move the body and hide it.

We looked around, thought about how the bodies had been found in the tannery so quickly, and decided on the sea.

141

While Wolfe went down the alley to make sure no one was coming, I checked the dead man's pockets. I found no identification but noticed a tattoo on his forearm. Then I checked for a money belt. It had blood on and I took it.

Wolfe beckoned, and I realized that I was doing the heavy lifting. With Wolfe's ruined jacket on my shoulder to protect my clothes, I carried the man down and out of the old town. When I reached the bottom of the alley, Wolfe was waiting and indicated for me to put the body down. He took the man's arms and I took his legs.

After checking the coast was clear, we shuffled across the road to the sea and dumped him in.

We could see the body bob just below the surface. It washed back and forth.

I stepped away. "What happened to the *no guns* rule?"

"I compromised. You know the saying: when the shooting starts, all plans are off."

We started walking along the dock, beside the warehouse that smelled of oranges.

Wolfe said, "You owe me a new jacket."

"I do?"

"The Slovaks. This was because of you. They were looking for you, not me."

# TWENTY-SIX

The secretary snatched up the telephone. "Shomrim Security." Her tone was off. She knew it and silently rebuked herself. The visit by those two Brits had unsettled the boss and, in turn, had unsettled her.

"Put me through to Cohen," a man said abruptly. She recognized his voice. Thank goodness it wasn't those men.

"It's him," she said as she patched the call through to the Head of Operations. No other introduction was necessary.

"Thank you, Irene," Cohen said, and she connected the caller. However, for the first time in her life, she kept the line open with a hand over the mouthpiece. It was coming to an end, she knew that, but her boss didn't share much else.

"Sir," Cohen said.

The caller said nothing for a second, and she could hear Cohen's tense breathing.

"Sir?"

"I shouldn't need to call you."

Cohen breathed. "But you have."

"Because you've made a mess."

"Me? What—?"

"You. Shomrim. Whoever. A bloody mess."

Cohen said nothing.

"You said you'd deal with that man."

"We did."

"Well, it's not been dealt with well enough, Cohen. His body has turned up. He's in the morgue."

Cohen breathed heavily. "Is it a problem?"

"Not yet, but it could be. It could be! We are so close, and incompetence could have ruined it. I shouldn't need to point out what your role is here. It's not that difficult, Cohen. Now is it?"

"No, sir."

"So you need to fix it."

"Get the body out of the morgue?"

Now it was the caller's turn to breathe heavily. Irene could feel the restrained anger through the wires.

"I shouldn't need to tell you how to do your job, Cohen. The last thing we need to do is draw any attention to the body."

"Right. I'll make sure no one talks."

The call ended abruptly and Irene quickly replaced the handset. Her boss came through the door, his jaw tense.

"I'm going out, Irene. Close up for the day."

"Is everything all right?"

He stopped with his hand on the door. "Not a problem. Just a bump in the road." He smiled. "Keep thinking about the destination, Irene. We're almost there."

# TWENTY-SEVEN

Wolfe made me buy him dinner and repeated that I owed him a jacket.

"So now you can tell me how you discovered Mason had changed his name?"

I'd been thinking about how I could spin it. How I could justify telling my landlady. In the end, I told Wolfe the truth. I'd shown Erika Arnold Mason's photograph and she thought her friend had been in a relationship with him. That had led me to Shomrim, where he'd worked.

"I have a theory," Wolfe said after making sure we couldn't be overheard. "These sniper attacks cluster. They start in early December last year and end three months later."

"Right."

"Remember the attacks when British soldiers died?"

Of course I did. We all had them imprinted on our brains. "Which ones?"

"Early January—the fifth and sixth. Shot by snipers. Both attacks had resulted in the death of a British soldier. The first only injured a Jew. The second attack killed one."

"Yes, I remember."

"What were they doing—the soldiers?"

"Protecting the other men."

"And that's my theory. This is about protection."

"Protection?"

"Personal security," he said with eyebrows raised.

"Shomrim Security?"

"Removing the competition?"

"Remember what Cohen said about Mason. *If we knew, we'd have dealt with him.* Not: handed him in to the police. Dealt with. They wouldn't think twice about killing him."

"Possible," I said. "But Mason wasn't working for Shomrim then. If he's Killing Crew then it's not them. And why leave a Jewish company and find Frank's Band."

He nodded and thought while polishing off a bottle of beer.

Then he said, "Mason is killing Jews."

"He was looking for targets? You think he intended to kill someone at Shomrim?"

"Or someone they're protecting."

I pondered this and nodded. "He was looking for support. He tried to enlist the men in Frank's Band."

"I agree."

"So we need to get a list of Shomrim's clients."

He said, "But it doesn't move us forward. Mason went from Shomrim to Frank's Band. Where did he go next? Where is he now?"

We bounced around a few ideas, punctuated by longer and longer silences, but nothing was any good.

I didn't know much about Wolfe's history and I suspect the beer loosened his tongue because for a while the chat became personal. I knew he was from Yorkshire but learned his family had lived in Keighley for generations. His dad owned a garage and Wolfe grew up assuming he'd become a car mechanic.

We talked about why we were in the military police and he said he'd planned to join the mobile division. He'd taken and passed the officer's exam and was encouraged to join the RMP because of his height.

I told him a little about my father without confessing to his name or role in the war and said I'd not expected to be a military policeman either. Wolfe liked that we'd both stumbled into a role that suited us.

The conversation switched to Palestine and events and then back to our new role.

Finally, I said something that had been troubling me.

"I saw his tattoo. The man we threw into the sea."

Wolfe said nothing but he knew what I was talking about. I could see it in his eyes.

I said, "It was a concentration camp tattoo. He survived the Holocaust."

"And your point."

"He suffered so much—"

Wolfe shook his head dismissively. "Don't be soft. Look, there are good and bad people everywhere. Just because someone survives a terrible experience, a horror like that doesn't make him a better man."

I breathed in and out and nodded.

We sat in silence again. People came and went from the café. I checked my watch and thought about my landlady. She'd be expecting me for dinner. I'd eaten a little here, but she'd have prepared enough for me.

"I better go," I said.

He nodded. There was a strange look in his eye. "I'd like you to think about how we find Mason."

"All right. And what are you going to do?"

"Me? I'm going to ponder what we know about the Killing Crew. Pray for divine inspiration. And get blind drunk."

★   ★   ★

The boy found the scary man. He'd delayed meeting the man, wondering whether he should run rather than deliver the bad news. But the money was good. He'd take final payment, but it was over.

"They were told the Killing Crew is real but the Engineer is a myth," the boy said. "Does the name Engineer mean something to you?"

"Who told them?"

"Someone called Levi."

The man with the menacing eyes smiled at the irony.

The boy said, "I can't go back. They found my hiding place." He swallowed. "Can you pay the rest of the money now?"

"I've got the money inside," the man said, and opened the door behind him. Inside was darker than the shadowy doorway.

The boy went in but never came out again.

# TWENTY-EIGHT

My landlady wasn't home. I didn't mind too much, however the other paying residents were furious.

Mrs Epstein, who lived on the top floor with her husband and two kids, was in the kitchen.

"What is Mrs Arnold thinking? How dare she not prepare dinner for us? It's not like we don't pay for it!"

She was opening all the cupboards, checking what food Erika had available. The cupboards weren't as well stocked as I'd imagined. I supposed then that she shopped a day at a time, probably deciding on the evening's meal based on the ingredients she could lay her hands on. These were difficult times and food supplies were limited, staple goods rationed.

Mrs Epstein was still ranting.

I said, "Have you thought for a moment that something might have happened to her?"

"What?" She turned to me and glowered. "What?"

"All I'm saying is it's unlike her. Maybe something is wrong."

"And that's *my* problem now? No, it is not. I have four mouths to feed. It's easy for you to say. And why she lets British dirt stay here, I don't know!"

I shook my head, determined not to become angry at her tone or attitude towards me.

She pulled some things from a cupboard before spinning back and confronting me. "You shouldn't be here. I've a good mind to demand that Mrs Arnold turns you out. It's not good for the rest of us. And the police were just…"

She kept going, but I didn't hear any more. I'd walked away and closed the door on her. I was worried about Erika, wondered where she was, what had happened to her.

I bought falafel and pitta and walked down to the seafront. Sitting on a bench, I watched the waves roll in and breathed the salt air.

Wolfe was in a bar trying to find inspiration in the bottom of a beer bottle. I stared at the blue velvet sea and pale light on the western horizon. Home was once that way, although I felt nothing drawing me back. My father and I didn't get along and my mother was dead. Most of my friends were scattered across the globe rather than in Britain. There was nothing there for me.

I was here in Israel with a job to do. But were we really making progress?

I'd discovered Mason had been living under the name Maaz and pretending to be a Jew. He'd worked for a short time at Shomrim Security before disappearing and visiting the pro-Arab outfit called Frank's Band. Was it as simple as that?

Was Mason part of the Killing Crew? The more I thought about it the more sense it seemed to make. A Jew-killer posing as a Jew.

Perhaps there had been more of them. We hadn't considered the possibility of them dying. What if Mason was the last?

There was another possibility. Mason could be the mythical Engineer. That would also explain his visit to Frank's Band. He was travelling around trying to recruit like-minded killers.

It was fully dark, the sky spangled with a billion stars by the time I returned to my lodgings on Gordon Street. All the lights were off except for a lamp in Erika's living room. I looked in to check on her and immediately heard a low moan.

I rushed in. "Erika, are you all right?"

She was curled up on her favourite chair and looked at me with red-raw eyes.

"Is it Mrs Epstein?" I said, crouching down beside the chair. "Has she upset you?"

Erika swallowed as though trying to speak.

I touched her arm. "It's all right. I'll speak to her in the morning. She had no right upsetting you like this. If you want her to go, I'll—"

"It's not the Epsteins." She reached for a tumbler of brandy and I could smell the alcohol on her breath.

"Are you hurt?"

She swallowed a mouthful and topped up her glass. "I've spent the evening with Ruth."

"Is she all right?"

Tears were running freely down her cheeks now.

"She's convinced Caleb is dead."

Caleb Maaz-Mason, the man I suspected. *She's crying because of a killer.*

"He was a good man," she continued, although I heard a catch in her voice. "He was a good man."

I waited a moment before I spoke. "Erika, Maaz was using a false identity. You know that. His real name was Charles Mason. Doesn't that trouble Ruth?"

151

Erika sucked in air and focused on me, like I didn't understand anything. "She knew him, Ash. She knew him! He was a good man."

I said nothing.

"He loved her, Ash. They were in love."

I still didn't know what to say.

She said, "Do you know what it's like to truly love someone, Ash? Truly be loved?"

I thought for a moment then shook my head. "I can't honestly say that I do. I've thought—"

"We all think," she said, taking another drink.

I touched her arm. "I think you've had enough."

She pulled away. "Not nearly enough!"

I stood, then took the chair opposite her and leaned forward, still close.

She was looking at me through what I suspect was blurred vision. And then she started talking. But it wasn't about Ruth Gotting or her boyfriend Maaz-Mason, it was about Horace, Erika's husband.

"It's the anniversary of his death," she said quietly. "I thought I was fine, but…"

"It's all right."

She shook her head. Then, after another drink, she started talking about him. She must have forgotten because she told me again about them fleeing Nazi Germany before the war, before the concentration camps and settling in Tel Aviv. I'd assumed they'd come directly, but it took them a hard year, travelling, living rough, staying in a town for a while before moving on. Finally reaching Greece and catching a boat from Piraeus to Haifa.

"We didn't have children, because we couldn't," she explained. "I couldn't. Internal problems—my tubes. We suspected, but didn't find out until we saw a doctor in Tel Aviv."

She stopped and looked at me harder. "I wish you would drink, Ash."

"Pour me one," I said. When she handed me the glass I took a sip, and she smiled like I was joining her on the dark side.

"I told you before that we'd been happy. We were in Tel Aviv. The Homestead! We had survived and we were in the Promised Land. What could be better? But Horace became bitter. He never complained about my infertility, but he didn't need to. It changed our plans. Ridiculous." She shook her head. "We planned a hotel! We wanted a family, but the two weren't mutual... mutually..."

"Mutually exclusive?"

"Right! They weren't mutually exclusive. We could have still had that big hotel, not this house that I share with cows like Mrs Epstein!"

"And Englishmen," I added.

She smiled, but there was no humour. "Horace joined the police. I told you that, right? He joined the police and then the Haganah. No, he wasn't a terrorist, but it was as though he wanted to die." She put down her glass heavily. "It was as though he wanted to punish me!"

I reached out, and this time she accepted my hand.

"Erika, I'm sure—"

She took her hand away. "No, you don't know! You can't know. Horace didn't love me. To think of it. I always knew in my heart. He was a waster. He would gamble and drink our money away. That's why we took so long to get here. He said it was his dream but he got so easily distracted."

I mirrored her, picking up my glass and taking a sip. She gulped then cleared her throat.

"He put money in a crazy investment," she said, "He lost our nest egg on a stupid gamble. That's why we could only afford this house and not our dream hotel."

The tears flowed again. Only this time, there was no accompanying sobbing.

As a military policeman, I had informed soldiers' wives that their husbands were dead. We were trained in how to do it. Firstly you stand there and they guess. Then you sadly confirm their worst fears. Then they collapse.

You have to wait, because eventually, fairly quickly, they pull themselves together. It's the shock and acceptance of the truth.

Erika hadn't had that. She'd had four years of denial. Now it was coming out.

The drink was talking, but this grief had been bottled up for many years and turned into anger against the British. Only because her friend thought Mason was dead, only because Ruth had felt real love, did the truth finally come out.

I wondered how she would feel if Mason was our target. If he was the Engineer or one of the Killing Crew murdering Jews. It was an irony that I couldn't bring myself to share.

When she was cried out, her eyes remained full of sadness but she smiled wryly at me.

I said, "You should smile more often, Erika. You're an attractive woman."

"Thank you."

"Let's play cards," I said. "I stand a chance of winning when you're drunk."

She laughed. Not heartily, but enough to tell me she was over the worst.

We moved to the card table and I shuffled and dealt.

154

"I'm a strong woman," she said after she lost another round. "Don't get the wrong idea. I can't forgive the British."

"I don't expect you to. I'm just a lodger."

"Who also expects dinner. I'm sorry about that."

"Don't worry, Erika. It does people good once in a while. Hopefully, the Epsteins will understand. And if they don't…" I raised my fist and she smiled.

"I'm drunk," she said, putting down her cards. "I better go to bed. And tomorrow we'll arrange that meeting."

"Sorry?" I said "What meeting?"

"With Ruth." She shook her head. "Didn't I say? I spent the evening with Ruth—about her Englishman—about him probably being dead. She just feels it."

I nodded, thinking there was nothing to say, not really. But then Erika shocked me with her final words.

"Ruth says she has something for you."

★   ★   ★

The man with the limp opened his front door. His boss was there.

"What's up?"

"The body," the boss said, his tone surly. "They've found the body."

His first thought was, which body? but then he realized. "Is it a problem?"

"It could be."

"What do you want me to do?"

"Nothing. It's been dealt with. I dealt with it."

The man with the limp said nothing, waited.

His boss shook his head, as though disappointed. But he didn't care. This was almost over, and after their final hurrah he wouldn't have to see the boss's ugly mug again. He wasn't even one of them. The man was more of an overseer than one of the team.

"What are you thinking?" the boss asked.

"Like I said, what do you want me to do?" He looked into the dark street. There was no one else around and the boss didn't look armed. "Why come here?"

"To tell you to stop surveillance."

"It's that urgent?"

"Maybe. Wolfe and Carter might be getting too close."

The man with the limp agreed then watched the boss walk away. He'd talk to the lads. The team would decide what they should do, not the boss.

# TWENTY-NINE

My landlady wasn't up by the time I left for the gymnasium. I'd spent the night wondering what Ruth Gotting could possibly have for me. Had it just been Erika's alcohol talking or did Ruth have useful information?

I left Erika a note saying that I hoped she felt better this morning and that I would be available later if Ruth wanted to talk to me.

Despite the early hour, there was a warm wind and I suspected it would be a hot day. Wolfe wasn't in the office when I arrived and I wondered how bad his head would be this morning. Collecting bread rolls and jam, I made myself some coffee and sat at a desk and waited.

But the next person through the door wasn't Wolfe, it was Finney. He was grinning, like the excitable puppy I'd first met.

"How was Haifa?" I asked.

"Hot," he said. "The buses are a nightmare. So damned hot and airless. I never want to travel on an Israeli bus ever again." He paused and looked at me awkwardly. "I mean, please don't make me!"

I offered him some bread and jam and he tucked in. While I finished my coffee I waited for him to speak, but he seemed lost in his own happy thoughts. Eventually, I had to prompt him.

"So, Finney, did you learn anything?"

"Oh sorry, I er… I promised Sylvia that I wouldn't talk about it until she got here."

"Why?" I asked, noting that he'd called her Sylvia rather than Rom.

He continued to look awkward. "I er… well it's what she came up with and it's… well, a bit different."

I understood. Wolfe and I had learned something but it was better shared between all of us rather than one at a time. However, I suspected that the reason Wolfe had sent Rom and Finney to Haifa was to get them out of the way. He'd involved them to appease me but didn't really expect them to find anything.

"How was it generally," I asked. "Get on all right with… Sylvia?"

He didn't pick up on my use of her first name and grinned.

"Oh, yes."

"Finney?" I asked, raising an eyebrow. "Are you suggesting…?"

"Oh… er… well, she's nice. Nothing happened. Not that I wouldn't… you know."

"Wouldn't what?" Rom said, standing in the doorway, hands on her hips, a disapproving expression souring her features.

I covered for Finney's blush. "He was just saying that he likes you. Sounds like you had a useful trip."

She joined us, her attitude relaxing. "We got on well," she said, nodding at the lad. "He's a good boy and an asset."

Finney grinned. "I feel like a rewarded dog."

"Puppy," I said, and Rom chuckled. She felt like part of the team at last. "So you've learned something?" I said.

"Shall we wait for Wolfe?"

I'd been thinking about it. Would he be the worse for wear? Probably. I shook my head. "I'm not sure what time he'll be here, so let's get started."

Rom began by telling me what they'd learned. They'd found a reporter in Haifa who knew where the shootings had taken place and they'd walked around and spoken to people. But that wasn't the interesting part.

"We met a policeman who said something that made me question everything," she said. "We asked him what he knew about the sniper attacks and he remembered one. I asked about who had done it, and he said the police."

"The police?" I said, wondering.

"That's not it!" Finney jumped up, excited. "We started thinking wider."

"Wider?"

"Back to the start," Rom said. "Changing what we'd assumed. But it was actually something a rabbi said to me when I asked him about the Killing Crew."

"And what was that?"

"He said it was Jews."

Finney added, "We assumed it was a pro-Arab group."

I shook my head. "Everything points to that. Like Frank's Band. Like Charlie Mason. You found nothing about him I suppose?"

"You're not listening," Rom said sharply. "We need to start again. We need to look at all of the events. We need to ask ourselves whether the Killing Crew were Jews."

"There's more," Finney said. "Tell Carter the other thing, Sylvia."

# THIRTY

"I have a confession," Sylvia Rom said. "I wasn't Haganah—not in the beginning. I was Irgun."

I stared at her. Our secretary was confessing to being a terrorist. Finney was grinning like it was a sexy confession. He didn't understand. They weren't as bad as the Stern Gang, but the Irgun were responsible for many atrocities. My stomach knotted like a fisherman's rope.

Rom held up her hands. "I know what you're thinking."

"Did you kill any British soldiers?" I asked, trying to stay calm and rational.

She shook her head and had a genuinely sorry look in her eyes. "I was one of the group that helped immigrants. I helped smuggle them ashore."

I breathed out.

"That's not the point," Finney said.

"Well, it is," Rom corrected him. "I was Irgun so I knew most of the actions we took. The point is that sometimes attacks were associated with us, but internally we couldn't explain."

"For example?"

"The Tel Aviv bank robbery in September last year. It was reported as Irgun. Someone called the newspapers and claimed responsibility, but why?"

I remembered the robbery, not a hundred yards from the prison we'd walked around yesterday. The Anglo-Palestine Bank. Four British police officers were killed and the gang were said to have escaped with over a hundred thousand pounds.

Finney said, "Yes, why would anyone claim responsibility for a bank raid? There's a difference between criminal activity—"

"—and terrorism," I said sarcastically. "Remember, British citizens died that day."

"Consider it. Don't just dismiss it, Captain."

It was a reasonable argument. I should at least consider the possibility. I indicated that we should sit in a huddle. Once settled, I said the other thing that was troubling me.

"What would be their motivation? Why would pro-Jews be the Killing Crew?"

None of us spoke for a moment before Rom pursed her lips in thought.

"Why does no one know who they are?"

I said, "They were very careful."

"But why? The Detonation Squad were blatant."

I said, "They were different, and that wasn't their name. They never identified themselves as that. They were just disillusioned, misguided soldiers persuaded to do a terrible thing by the Islamic extremists."

We bounced the question about for a few minutes before Rom said, "So where is Wolfe?"

I checked my watch. It would be midday soon. Where the heck was he? But I didn't want to let the others know about my uncertainty.

"He's busy," I said, and then to distract them further, added: "I haven't told you what we discovered."

And so I told them about Charlie Mason adopting the name Caleb Maaz and working for Shomrim Security before travelling to Transjordan.

"Oh my!" Finney said.

Rom nodded. "You know, that seems to back up my theory. Maybe Mason was pro-Jew all along. You've assumed he was the opposite, but from what you've said, it would be more likely that he wasn't. It backs up the idea that the Killing Crew were either Jews or pro-Jew." She looked at me earnestly. "Don't you think?"

I looked at the timeline on the noticeboard. We'd started with pro-Arab attacks and then whittled them down. We'd found Mason but that had been fortuitous. Our analysis hadn't yielded any insights. Now our Irgun secretary was telling me why.

"All right," I decided. "We have nothing to lose. Let's get another noticeboard and look at all the pro-Jew attacks."

"Or assumed to be pro-Jew," Finney added.

I said, "Let's start with the King David Hotel bombing that killed ninety-one, including twenty-eight Brits and seventeen Jews."

Rom took a long breath. I could see I'd disturbed her with the suggestion. It was the terrorist atrocity that shocked everyone, including the Jewish community. After that, for a period of time, the Irgun were even the enemy of the Jewish Agency. The United Resistance Movement was dissolved and the Haganah worked with the British authorities to stamp out terrorism.

Finney found a board and Rom started paper notes for the events. While they prepared, I went to the shops and bought a working lunch for us.

When I got back, they were ready.

The new noticeboard had a piece of paper with *The King David Hotel bombing* written under the "Where" column. The "When" was *July 1946*. And the "Who" read *Irgun*.

Finney said, "We put that up because you mentioned it, but stopped there. The newspapers we have here in the office start in 1947. The first one in the *Press* is the British HQ bombing in January.

I looked at Rom.

"It was Irgun," she said. I'd expected her to be resistant to declaring her former terrorist group's activities, but she spoke without emotion. Clear and clinical, just like anyone would be reading a shopping list. Maybe that was the problem. She didn't feel the horror of the events.

Finney put up the notes then said, "Were there events in between?"

"Lots," Rom said. "We regularly attacked the railway and fuel lines. In the early days, it was all about disruption rather than terror."

"Except for the hotel," I said cynically.

She looked at me long and hard but didn't say anything. She didn't need to.

I nodded, accepting the unspoken criticism. Like her, I needed to keep my feelings out of this.

I said, "We're ignoring the small attacks. We focus on the major events where people died. Maybe later we can in-fill if necessary."

The other two nodded.

"What's next?"

"In September there was the bank robbery we talked about," Rom said.

"Who?" Finney asked Rom. "You said Irgun before."

She shook her head. "High Command didn't claim responsibility."

"Then who did?"

"I don't know," she said. "I think it was just easy for the papers to assume it was Irgun."

"Let's put a question mark," I said. "But we missed one. There was the officers' club bombing in Jerusalem. Seventeen died."

Finney stared at Rom.

She nodded. "And the day after, your High Commissioner declared martial law."

"Who did it?" Finney asked quietly. I guessed he was thinking of all those soldiers being murdered in a cowardly attack.

"Can we say Irgun?" I asked Rom.

She nodded mutely.

After a moment's silence, I asked if anyone knew of others prior to January and the British HQ bombing. No one spoke.

"All right, let's go through the newspapers like before. We'll split them. Find any event and note it down. Then we'll combine them later."

Rom said, "Note who the paper thinks is responsible, and when we put them on the board, I'll let you know if I question any."

And so we started, allocating the days randomly because we knew that the last few months would be packed, sometimes with multiple attacks in one day. As I worked, I thought we should identify all those we weren't sure about and then approach the journalist, Levi, again.

I was about two-thirds of the way through when a uniformed policeman knocked on the door.

Finney let him in, but the man addressed me.

"Captain Carter, Sub-Inspector Rosen would like to see you."

★   ★   ★

Three men met in a remote spot off the Jerusalem–Tel Aviv Road.

The man with the limp said, "The boss told me to stop surveillance, but the MPs are looking at the pro-Jew deserters now."

The one on the right said, "I thought they'd discounted them."

"They did, but they've changed their minds."

"It could lead to us."

"If they're any good, it *will* lead to us."

The one on the left nodded. "We need to move. Let's plan for three hours from now. You know what to do. Take the old car and make sure they're stopped."

# THIRTY-ONE

The policeman had a car and I expected him to take me to the police HQ, but he didn't. Instead, he went the other way on Allenby and drove the short distance to the hospital on Balfour Street.

"Rosen's here?" I asked as we got out.

"Follow me, sir."

We went up steps and through the entrance. The hospital reception was ahead but we turned left and I saw signs for the morgue.

Dave Rosen was standing outside red double-swing doors. His face was full of tension.

"Ash."

"Dave. What can I—?"

He didn't wait for me to finish, pushed through the doors and started asking questions.

"What were you doing at Jaffa Port yesterday?"

"Checking on some of the recent incidents."

He stopped halfway along the corridor. "Recent incidents?"

"Attacks where Jews were killed… sniper attacks."

His eyes searched mine. "And in Jaffa?"

"Well, not just Jaffa. We're looking at Jerusalem and Haifa killings too."

He started walking again.

"Did anything happen?"

"What do you mean, Dave?" Of course, I knew exactly what he meant. I'd already got a good idea what this was about.

He pushed through more double doors into a pathology lab. There was an uncovered body on a table. Naked and bloated in the cruel blue pathology light. An orderly—at least I assumed he was just an orderly rather than the pathologist since he wasn't introduced—stepped back, looking uncomfortable.

Rosen said, "Recognize this chap?"

"No. Should I?"

"He was found this afternoon in the sea. Shot three times and then tossed into the water. Whoever did it probably expected that he'd wash out, but he washed in. Bobbing by the dock he was."

I said nothing.

Rosen faced me, his eyes hard and calculating. "Tell me what happened, Ash."

"Me? You think I had something to do with this man's death?"

"A coincidence, don't you think?"

I shook my head as though not understanding.

He said, "You were seen a week ago in and around where two dead Slovaks were found. Now you're been seen when another one turns up."

"Another Slovak chap?" I asked, trying to sound surprised. Rosen's face suggested he didn't buy my innocence.

"See that?" he said, pointing to the number tattooed on the man's right forearm. "He was at Auschwitz—he survived Auschwitz. How does that make you feel, Ash?"

"Sorry for him," I said. "Sorry for anyone who went through those horrors. Sorry for anyone who ends up murdered."

"Hmm," he said. "Tell me what happened."

I looked uncertain.

"Ash, you were seen running. You and Wolfe were seen being chased."

I shook my head. "Whoever said that must be mistaken or is lying. Anyway, there's one thing wrong with your accusation—and it is an accusation, Dave. The problem you have is that this chap was shot. I don't have a gun."

"Where is Wolfe?"

"I don't know." When he clenched his jaw showing disbelief, I added: "Honestly, I don't know."

"When was the last time you saw him?"

"Yesterday."

Rosen nodded. "We went to his hotel. Searched his room. He didn't sleep there last night." Pause. "Was he with you in Jaffa Port?"

"Yes."

"Where did he go afterwards?"

"I don't know. He didn't say."

"Really? I find it hard to believe he wouldn't tell you. You're a team after all."

I also found it hard to believe. Wolfe wasn't around and had yet again failed to tell me his movements.

"I'll tell you what I think, Ash. I think you had a run-in with this Slovak chap and were forced to kill him. Maybe you didn't intend to… yes, let's say it was self-defence. I can buy that."

I said nothing. The smell down here was rank. I thought their refrigeration system couldn't be up to scratch. It was an odour that got in the back of my throat and clawed at the soft tissue, embedding its foul self for as long as it could. The stench of decaying bodies in a hot country.

"But your problem is that the Slovaks were part of a gang, and you know how it works with these fellows. Kill one and they see it as a challenge. They can't let it go. They need revenge. It's a matter of respect and revenge. They can't let someone get the upper hand. They have to win. They have to be seen to win. And so they sent out a hunter—someone to track you down and execute the vengeance. Maybe they sent out a number of hunters." He stopped and watched for a reaction.

I said, "Can we go up? This body stinks."

He said, "We'll go up when you admit you did it—or maybe that Wolfe killed this chap."

"Did you find a gun in Wolfe's hotel room?"

His eyes said he didn't. They also said something else.

I guessed. "You searched my place too."

Rosen's eyes said they had, and I hoped the police hadn't upset Erika.

I said, "We don't have guns. I told you."

He said, "I'll continue, shall I? You and Wolfe were wandering around Jaffa yesterday evening. This hunter spotted you and gave chase." He paused as though this added weight and veracity to his next statement. "You fought him, grabbed his gun and shot him. Then you dumped his body in the sea."

I noted that he was only talking about this one body. Which suggested they hadn't found the one on St Peter's roof. A small mercy.

"Didn't happen," I said. "You need to find the real criminal, Dave, rather than—"

"I think you did it, Ash. And you know what, I wouldn't blame you."

Ah, that old trick. Be casual about it and hope the suspect will confess. Not a chance!

I met his stare and waited. He waited too.

"Can we go up now?" I said eventually.

"Just admit it, Ash. One friend to another."

I shook my head. "I didn't do it, Dave. I'm not a cowboy."

"But Bill Wolfe is."

"Was it him or me? Make up your mind, Dave. The problem you have is that Wolfe wasn't around when the first ones died. So it couldn't have been him."

"You, then him," he said, raising his eyebrows.

Still I didn't bite.

"All right," I said, "tell me what our motivation was. Why would I kill this chap?"

"Because of the other two—those in the tannery?"

"All right, then why would I kill them?"

"Just because I don't know your motivation doesn't mean you didn't—"

"No," I said firmly. "We are here on a specific mission. It has nothing to do with Slovak Jews."

"Doesn't it? I don't know that. Just because our government has approved you searching for the Killing Crew doesn't mean you don't have a secret agenda."

"We don't."

He looked at me with disbelief.

This wasn't going to end, so I made a decision. I took out the photograph of Mason.

"Have you seen this man before? He has a distinctive scar." I dragged a finger above my eyes. "A deep one across his forehead."

Rosen was briefly thrown by my switch in subjects. Blinking, he studied the picture. Instinct made me flash it at the other man too.

"No," Rosen said. But it wasn't his reaction that interested me. It was the orderly's. He'd leaned in, and I caught a look of recognition in his eyes.

"Why d'you ask?" Rosen said.

"Because we're making progress. Because we think this man has something to do with the Killing Crew. He may even be the Engineer."

Rosen's eyes bulged. He took the photograph from me and studied it more closely. "What's his name?"

"Sorry, I'm not ready to divulge anything. Wolfe wouldn't be happy with me sharing even this much."

"Will you let me have the details once you have confirmed this chap's involvement?"

"Of course," I said.

"And this dead Slovak has nothing to do with you or Wolfe?"

"No."

"All right then," he said. "You can go, but be sure to tell me as soon as you're able. For friendship's sake."

I wanted to confront the orderly from the pathology lab straight away. He'd reacted when I mentioned the scar. I was sure he knew something but didn't want to talk about this with Rosen there.

I hung around outside hoping to see the inspector leave so that I could return. After twenty minutes I gave up. I'd come back later. In the meantime, I'd visit Ruth Gotting and find out what she had for me.

# THIRTY-TWO

Bert Finney stretched. He'd been hunched over the newspapers for hours and his neck ached. The light was fading. Sylvia glanced up after finishing a note.

"I wish we'd just got everything the first time," he said. "I keep reading articles I've already read."

"I know."

"Should we stop for the day? Wolfe is obviously not coming and Carter's unlikely to be back until morning."

"Wouldn't it be great if we'd finished when he gets here," she said.

Finney guessed she was right. "We should at least take a break, Sylvia."

Her eyes met his, and for a moment he saw the amazing young woman who had spent the night with him in Haifa. She liked it when he said her name.

"All right." She smiled. "We could get dinner."

"Only if you let me pay." He swallowed his awkwardness and forced himself to say what he was thinking. "You're gorgeous."

She stood up and now she stretched too. "Bert, you are incorrigible!"

He didn't understand her at all. He'd assumed that Jewish girls were like Catholics, that anything physical would only happen after a marriage ceremony. But no.

They'd shared a hotel room in Haifa. At first he'd been excited. She'd booked the twin room without consulting him. But she gave no indication of any interest during the day. Or evening. Or when they went to their separate beds. They had spoken a little before he'd turned out the light: just factual stuff about what they'd learned during the day. Like two men would. No sexual interest whatsoever. Which was a shame.

However, after half an hour, she'd said, "Are you awake, Bert?"

"Yes."

"I'm cold."

The window was open. They just had a sheet over them. It wasn't cold. Not in the least.

Emboldened by the darkness he cleared his throat and said, "I could warm you up."

"No," she said, and then surprised him. A second later she was slipping beside him. He was wearing a T-shirt and shorts. She was naked.

Rom was too thin to be curvaceous, but her skin was smooth and he'd already decided that her brown eyes were deep and mysterious. He could lose himself in those. And he soon discovered that he could lose himself in her touch.

He wasn't proud of his love-making, but she didn't complain and let him hold her tight for a long time. Eventually, she said she needed to sleep, got up and went to her own bed. Within a minute her breathing had changed and he guessed she was asleep. He couldn't. He kept thinking about the touch of her body and what tomorrow might bring.

It brought the same efficient hard work that she'd shown the day before. They walked miles and questioned a hundred people about the attacks and snipers and who the Killing Crew might be. She never once mentioned the sex, never once showed him affection.

He'd fallen asleep on the bus ride back to Tel Aviv and she'd accompanied him to the St Andrews Hotel.

"I think it's against the rules," he said at the door, knowing that the hotel strictly forbade unmarried couples.

She smiled sadly. "I'm sorry."

"Sorry?"

"For last night."

"Don't be—"

She cupped his face in her hand. "It wouldn't work, Bert. I'm sorry for misleading you." And then she went.

"Why?" he asked, sitting opposite her in the restaurant.

"Why what?"

"At the hotel in Haifa. You know. You and me."

"I like you, Bert."

"And I like you. So then I should ask, why not? Why just the once... you know."

She sighed. "It's too difficult. You're British. I'm Jewish." Before he could speak, she started to explain. Most Jewish teenagers had worked for either the Irgun or the Stern Gang—although she explained that was the British name for the Lehi, the Fighters for the Freedom of Israel.

"You'll know about the assassination of Lord Moyne?"

He frowned, uncertain.

"The British Minister for the Middle East. Killed by Lehi in November 1944. They were the real extremists. I joined Irgun because the Jewish Agency was too soft, too supportive of the British administration."

"And you worked on immigration?"

175

"Well, at first, as a kid, I put up posters." She blinked her beautiful brown eyes, looking uncomfortable.

"What did they say?"

"Various things." She pulled a tight, awkward smile. "But the message was always basically the same: kill the British!"

"Wow!"

"I know, but we felt oppressed. We felt like the British weren't going to deliver on our Eretz Israel. Remember, Jews have been vilified and marginalized for thousands of years. This was our time. This was our chance to establish our Promised Land."

"Wow!" he said again.

She went on to explain that when she was fifteen she'd been taught how to fight. They typically had one gun between three, but she was an excellent shot.

He said, "You lied! You were just working on illegal immigration."

"Not at first. For a few months during 1946, I was a full Irgun member."

"You killed people."

She breathed and nodded sadly. "I regret it."

He shook his head. *My God, I slept with a murderer!*

"Don't judge me, Bert. It was war. I know you won't see it that way, but before the attack on the King David Hotel, the British escalated things. There were a hundred thousand British troops here, and in June, two years ago, Cunningham—the High Commissioner— ordered Operation Agatha in Jerusalem. They hit us hard with raids and arrests and brutality. They thought by wounding us it would kill our spirit. But it only served to strengthen our resolve."

"So you're justifying the hotel bombing?"

"No, I'm explaining it. I wasn't involved and, quite honestly, it shocked me. Two months later, I left Irgun and joined the Haganah. That's when I stopped fighting and started helping." She paused and looked at her food. She hadn't eaten, and he suspected it had gone cold.

She said, "Please don't tell Carter or Wolfe."

He rubbed his face, breathed in and out.

"Why are you telling me? Why me, Sylvia?"

She held his gaze. She had such soft deep brown eyes that weren't those of a terrorist.

"Because I have feelings for you, Bert. Because I like you... and I want to explain why we couldn't be together. I killed your people. How could you love me?"

He reached forward and gripped her hand. "Because you aren't the same girl."

She had tears in her eyes, and he leaned over and kissed her lips.

"Tomorrow I'll move hotels. I'll find one where we can be together."

She blinked a tear loose and smiled. "I'd like that, Bert. I'd like that very much."

# THIRTY-THREE

"I want you to find him," Ruth Gotting said to me. She'd invited me into her lounge and asked me to sit. However, she was pacing.

"I'm sorry to call so late."

"It's not that," she said, and finally settled. "I have a confession."

I waited for her to explain.

"I knew his real name. I knew he was Charlie Mason. I loved him—still love him."

I nodded. My landlady had already told me. Was Erika all right? A pang of guilt suddenly gripped my chest as I thought about her. I should have checked how she was today, after the tears of last night and the police search of my room this afternoon.

Ruth said, "We couldn't openly have a relationship, you know that, don't you? He was English—the enemy. I felt terrible. I knew it would hurt Erika to know I'd fallen for an Englishman."

"You're only human," I said, trying to lighten her mood, but she ignored my attempted humour. "It's understandable."

When she didn't say more, I added: "It must have been very difficult for you."

"You have no idea! Charlie changing his identity was a stroke of genius. I don't know how he got away with it, but we could finally see each other without fear of reprisal."

I'd seen his file. I knew how he could get away with it. Of course he could. He was probably encouraged to go undercover. After the last failed attempt, I avoided making a joke of that expression.

"I'm worried about him," she said.

I nodded.

"I don't know what's happened to him." She took a shuddering breath, and for a second I thought she would break down, but she held it together. "Please can you find him?"

"I'll do my best."

"Two weeks. I'm so worried."

"Tell me everything you know, Ruth. What happened the last time you saw him?"

She told me the date and time, then: "He just said he'd need to go away for a few days. He was often doing that. Usually to Jerusalem, but this time was different."

"How so?"

"He didn't go by train and I could see he was anxious. He didn't say, but I could tell."

"And this was after he lost his job at Shomrim Security?"

"Yes. Two days after."

Mason had told her he'd been fired, whereas his brief employer said he hadn't shown for work. They said three weeks and I suspected Mason hadn't been totally honest with Ruth.

I knew that he'd been in Transjordan three weeks ago where he'd met the men from Frank's Band. So he'd been back to Tel Aviv since but there had been no news of him for two weeks since heading for Jerusalem.

"And nothing else?" I asked, disappointed that Erika seemed to have exaggerated her friend's news.

"No."

"When he went to Jerusalem, whereabouts exactly? Where did he go?"

Then she said something that made me sit up. "He had a room there."

I swallowed. "Do you have an address, Ruth?"

And she gave me an address in Jerusalem.

Promising that I would check the Jerusalem address as soon as possible, I went back to the hospital on Balfour Street. It was past nine o'clock and the streets were quiet except for the odd IDF truck and occasional police vehicle.

Most of the hospital's lights were off, although I could still see a blue glow coming from the pathology lab.

There weren't any bodies on the tables in the lab this time, and I found the orderly in a side room, drinking tea.

"What are you doing down here?" he said, half accusing, half nervous.

I showed him the photograph. "You recognized him when I mentioned the scar."

The man shook his head.

"Why won't you admit it?"

"I'm not allowed."

I pulled out the bundle of money I'd taken from the dead Slovak guy. "How much."

"I can't," he said without conviction.

I counted out fifty pounds and he licked his lips.

"When did you see him?" I said, holding out the money.

"Three days ago."

"Where?"

"Here."

"He's dead?"

I saw realization flash in his deep-set eyes. Then he nodded towards my bundle.

"Not just for you to tell me whether he's dead or alive," I said. "I want more."

He smiled. "Another hundred and I'll tell you where and when."

I got the money ready.

"Fifty first," he said, and I dealt out the notes.

Then he told me the body had been found in a shack on a farm in the orange groves. He gave me a rough location and said the man had been dead between ten and twelve days.

"How did he die?"

The orderly waited until I counted out the rest of the money.

"Shot twice. One in the chest, one in the head. Execution-style," he said. "Because it also looked like his hands had been tied."

# THIRTY-FOUR

Despite the late hour, Finney and Rom wondered whether they'd find Wolfe or Carter at the office when they returned. They couldn't remember leaving the lights on, but the room was just as they'd left it.

Sylvia had insisted that they keep it business-like except for when they were alone at night. They had a job to do.

"You really want to catch this Killing Crew?" Finney asked.

"Whoever they are," she said. "Pro-Arab or pro-Jew. Partly because they were real criminals and partly because I want to prove I can do this. I'm not a secretary. The Israeli police don't recognize women officers yet, but they will. Once we've stopped being a facsimile of the British Palestine Police Force, there'll be women in the force. There has to be."

They started again, working faster, more efficiently. Finney put up notes and they moved some, corrected others. After two hours, Finney felt a mixture of elation, despair and exhaustion.

The elation was due to completing the task and seeing almost eighty events on the timeline. However, he'd also noted the number of estimated deaths, and it was horrendous. British citizens' deaths were numbered at 122. Jewish deaths during the Mandate were around six hundred. A low estimate of the number of Arabs killed was seven hundred.

The majority of the Jewish militia attacks were claimed. The Stern Gang / Lehi were responsible for only two, Haganah claimed two, Palmach claimed three, and Irgun claimed responsibility for eighteen. There were twelve Jewish militia attacks, including the Rehovot train bombing which killed twenty-eight Brits. It hadn't been claimed by any group.

"You mentioned Palmach. Who are they?"

"An elite unit of the Haganah."

"OK, so what are we looking for?" Finney asked, nodding. "There are no sniper attacks."

"I don't know," Sylvia said, seeming distracted. "I just want to look at that car."

Finney looked out of the window where the office lights picked out a vehicle parked on the street. For a second Finney thought it might be Wolfe, but it wasn't a big car. Not Wolfe's Bentley.

Maybe somebody wealthy had gone to the cinema opposite. They'd just parked on this side of the road rather than by the cinema.

Sylvia went outside being nosey. She looked in the window and he smiled and waved, then turned his attention back to the board. Wouldn't it be fabulous if they could come up with something before the others arrived in the morning.

"Where are you?" he asked out loud, addressing the noticeboard. "Where…"

*Could that be it?*

Sylvia banged on the window. He beckoned her in. "Sylvia come and look at this!"

She burst in through the door screaming at him. Her face distorted with desperation.

*What the heck?*

"Bomb!" she yelled, grabbing his arm. "Get out. We need to get out the back. Fast!"

Then she was rushing out of the office again and he started to move.

The first thing that registered was a bright orange light. He stopped and looked and time slowed down. Where the car had once been there was just a blooming ball of light. Then the windows were shattering into a million pieces. Finally, he heard the roar, and it expanded, enveloping him. For a second he felt pain in his face and guessed it was glass splinters. Then he was flying through the air.

And then there was nothing.

# THIRTY-FIVE

The explosion was less than a hundred yards south of me. I was walking on Balfour away from the hospital and saw the flash before I heard the blast.

The SIB office. *Someone has bombed our office!*

I don't know how I knew, I just did.

Praying that my instinct was wrong, I started running. It was a shame that I couldn't go direct. I needed to get to Allenby, turn left and then left again before reaching our street.

There was no panic, just annoyance. I wasn't worried because it was late. Rom and Finney would have left the office long ago.

But I was wrong.

There were people on the street, onlookers, starting to congregate in a wide semicircle around our building. I was thirty yards away and could see the windows and front wall had gone, demolished by the explosion. Papers fluttered in the air and scattered across the road. At first, I thought I could see them because of the street lamps, but it soon became clear that the building was on fire.

I was twenty yards away, and beyond the first people in the crowd, I saw a twisted mass of metal out front. It had been a car bomb.

185

And then my heart stopped. There was a cluster of people around something on the floor. Someone was hurt.

"Out of my way!"

I pushed through. Two people on the ground. Two other people were administering first aid.

I heard sirens. I heard someone shouting that the crowd should get back. The fire crackled and whooshed inside. Sparks flew across my vision, moving slowly like a flurry of snowflakes.

And I saw them. Rom and Finney. They were the ones on the floor, the ones injured.

Sounds deadened. My world shrunk to a few feet. I could only see them.

Rom was hunched. Finney was lying. She had his head in her lap and looked up at me, her face blackened and streaked with tears. Finney's hair was burnt, his face grey and lifeless. His dead eyes were open and seemed to be staring at Rom.

She tried to speak. Her mouth moved, but nothing came out. I was crouching, reaching for her, when a hand grabbed me. I fought against them as I was pulled back, but people were suddenly lifting Finney and dragging Rom. Firemen and then medics, I realized, and I stopped resisting.

Fifteen minutes after leaving the hospital, I was back. Only this time, I was following Rom as she was stretchered in.

I was forced to wait as she was rushed into a ward. A screen was pulled around her bed, but I could see medics around her, testing and checking. Rom seemed responsive. I'd travelled in the ambulance with her. She hadn't spoken, she'd been in shock, but physically she seemed all right.

The screen was moved aside and the doctors stepped away, letting nurses take over. Then the screen was redrawn and I couldn't see anything else.

A sick feeling rose in me as I thought about Finney. He would be downstairs now. I should go and see his body, but I didn't want to leave. I wanted to check on Rom as soon as the nurses let me in.

"What happened?" a voice said.

I turned to see Dave Rosen a step behind me. He was looking into the ward.

"How is she?" he asked before I responded to his first question. Maybe he could see I was struggling to speak.

He took my arm and eased me into a chair in the corridor. I realized my hands were shaking.

"It was a car bomb," he said. "They bloody car-bombed you."

"She's alive," I finally managed to say. "Sylvia's alive. Finney's dead."

"Yes."

"They must have been working late." I looked at him through blurred vision and shook my head. "They shouldn't have been working late."

He said nothing for a few seconds and looked up and into the ward.

"They're still with her."

I said, "Who would do that? Who would bomb us, Dave?"

Rosen considered it, scratching his right eyebrow with his left hand. "Is this anything to do with the dead Slovak?"

I said nothing.

Someone gave me a cup of tea. I didn't ask for one or see where it came from. One moment I didn't have anything in my hand, the next I was sipping sweet tea.

He said, "We'll find out who did this. We'll get them, Ash."

# THIRTY-SIX

I was eventually sent away.

"She's sleeping," a nurse told me. Rosen had left me outside the ward and I'd been there for two hours.

"I'll keep waiting," I said.

"No. You can come back in the morning." She wagged a finger at me. "Not until seven. There are no visitors before that."

I walked the streets down to the coast and breathed the sea air. Finally, I went to my lodgings.

No one was up, not even Erika, so I went to bed and stared at the ceiling until the daylight crept through the curtains.

I was back outside the hospital ward at six thirty. A different nurse from the night before took pity on me and let me see Rom.

She'd been cleaned up, but her face was pale and scratched. There was a deep cut on her right cheek but she said it didn't hurt.

"I know he's dead, isn't he?" she said quietly.

I nodded.

She gulped. "I hoped... you know how you hope for the best, but really you know?"

"Yes."

189

"He was a good boy," she said. I saw her hands shaking and guessed the shock hadn't passed. A nurse handed her a painkiller and some water. Rom knocked it back and took deep breaths. "Such a shame. Stupid! He—" she started to say before emotion took her voice.

I felt my own eyes prickle. Holding her hand, I felt the tremble of her nerves through my fingers.

I said, "We need to stop. You need to recover. You've done a—"

She glowered at me and gripped my hand hard.

"We can't stop! I'm not stopping."

I nodded but knew she needed time to recover.

"For Bert's sake, we can't stop," she said.

I was tired. My mind was a mess so I couldn't think, but Rom was right. Then she said something that was like an injection of adrenaline in my arm.

"He wondered whether the bank raid was more important than the sniper attacks."

"What?"

"While I was holding him. He kept saying 'the bank raid, the bank raid'."

"Why?"

"He didn't say. I could hardly hear him." She shook her head, tried to say more, but then began to cry. However, she quickly put the emotion in check and took a calming breath. "He was dying. I couldn't understand."

"It's all right," I said, squeezing her hand. "It's all right."

"He figured something out," she said, her eyes bright with conviction. "If he hadn't been so distracted he'd have gotten out. I was banging on the window but he hardly noticed."

I let her rest a little, which helped me as well. When she was ready, I asked her what had happened, what she could remember.

She told me about them wanting to finish, wanting to impress us. They'd taken a break, eaten dinner and then got back to the timeline.

"We'd finished and were trying to understand what we were looking at. That's when I got distracted by the car parked outside." She took a shuddering breath and I could see she was still in shock, despite sounding almost normal. "I should have told him. I should have voiced my suspicion, but I didn't really expect a bomb. After all, who would want to bomb you? I'm used to worrying about Arab car bombs. So I went to look and thought it was innocent enough. But then I wondered what was under the covers on the back seat." She paused again and breathed. "There was just something about it. I'd seen a car bomb before but this one didn't have any wires showing or anything. Just this lumpy thing on the back seat."

"Go on," I said when she looked at me with sad eyes.

"A minute sooner and… Well, I decided to shake the car. I rocked it hoping the covers would reveal what was underneath. Why didn't I just assume the worst?"

"Because you didn't expect—"

She wasn't listening to me. "An object fell off the seat, onto the floor. An alarm clock with wires! That's when I realized this was a bomb and I was looking at the timer. Bert didn't hear me through the window. I ran in and made him leave his pile of papers. He was excited because he thought he'd seen something—a connection. I don't think he understood the urgency, because he was still in the office when I reached the stairs." She gulped. "He was walking towards me. He was smiling. That's the thing I'll always remember. He was walking towards me, smiling. And then he wasn't standing there anymore. The explosion just blew him away." She shook her head and tears rolled down her cheeks.

"But you got him out," I said with a comforting hand on her arm.

She blinked the tears away. "I was dizzy. I couldn't hear. I think I was shouting. There was thick smoke. The lights had gone out but I saw him in the flames. Crumpled against the end wall."

"You got him out," I said again.

"I don't know how. I just remember being on the pavement. I remember sounds coming back. People shouting. Bert was still alive and trying to tell me about the prison, the safecracker." She shook her head, as though trying to process the memories. "He also said something about Wolfe."

# THIRTY-SEVEN

"Is it you? Are you the Engineer, Wolfe?" I snapped. We were in the burnt-out office. I don't know why I'd gone over there. I was in a daze. Finney was dead. Sylvia Rom was injured.

And where the hell had Wolfe been?

I couldn't believe it when I saw him crouching between the broken and burnt furniture. What was he up to?

He jolted up and I repeated, "Is it you? Are you the Engineer?"

"What?" he snarled. "What the fuck are you talking about?"

"Is it you?" I squared up to him, tense and angry. "Are you the Engineer?"

"You're losing your mind!"

I gritted my teeth. "Bert's dead and Sylvia's in hospital. You're here, Wolfe. Why haven't you—?"

"It's your fuckin' fault," he growled at me. "Finney would be alive if we'd sent him home like I wanted."

My chest constricted. How dare he?

"What were you doing before I came to Israel? What were you doing for those days after I arrived? Where were you, Wolfe?"

"Looking for Nazeem."

193

I shook my head. "All that time?"

He glared at me. His teeth clenched.

"You could have telephoned me."

"I was busy."

I shook my head. "You never wanted me here."

His left eye twitched and he may as well have agreed.

"You never tell me what you're doing," I said. "Why would that be?"

"Because you're weak. I can do this alone."

"You and Nazeem?"

"Yeah, me and the toad."

"Tell me about Frank's Band, Wolfe. That was misdirection, wasn't it?"

"You're talking rubbish!"

"And all this focus on the pro-Arabs and snipers and sending Rom away. That was to get her out of the way."

"Yes, she was in the way. We can't trust her."

"She's an asset, Wolfe. She's good. And now she's in hospital. She could have died."

"Get out of my way, Ash!"

He pushed me.

"That's it, isn't it? I'm in your way. We were all in your way."

"I said, get out of my way!" He pushed me harder and I raised my fists. Instinct. I wasn't thinking.

I threw a punch, a left jab that jolted his head back.

And then he was flying at me. There was no room to move or dodge. I knew he had a reputation as a brawler, and a boxer can always beat a brawler. Providing the boxer can move. Paper slipped under my feet and I tripped over a chair.

Before I was prepared, Wolfe had hit me twice. Two powerful roundhouses that stunned me and sent me tumbling again. But as I fell, he was close, so I managed to get off another punch. Then he was on top of me. Blows rained down. I blocked and rolled and for a moment had the upper hand and was hitting him.

We rolled again and it became more of a wrestling match. I hit my head and shoulder on something harder than rock. I caught him with an elbow and then he was on top again. His forearm jammed into my throat.

I choked. Tried to stay calm. Ignored the pain and lack of breath. Thought about getting out, dodging and punching.

"Enough!" he bellowed.

I focused on him and felt the pressure on my throat ease. *Now's my chance...*

But he was standing, backing up, palms open.

I sucked in air and spluttered.

"You damn fool!" He reached out. I took his hand and he pulled me to my feet.

I said, "Was it you, Bill?"

"Don't be an ass! What possible motive—?"

"To get rid of some evidence. We were getting close, weren't we?"

"One, I have no idea what you were working on today, and two, why would I hurt... why would I kill one of ours?"

"You told me yourself. You thought you'd be a car mechanic when you grew up."

"Right?"

"An engineer. It makes sense. Are you him? Have we been looking for you? Are you the Engineer?"

# THIRTY-EIGHT

My landlady threw her arms around me when I got back to her house. We sat in her kitchen and she plied me with tea and offered toast.

I couldn't eat. My stomach was in a tight knot. I stared into space, saying nothing, and Erika didn't force me. She waited.

Finally, I said. "Bert—the boy died."

"I heard. It's terrible. You must feel awful."

I met her eyes and saw real concern for me.

She said, "Do you know who did it?"

Bill Wolfe, I felt like saying. It was my colleague! But it wasn't. He wouldn't have done that. Granted, Wolfe was difficult. He did things his own way, but he wasn't the Engineer. He wasn't part of the Killing Crew.

He'd stormed out after I'd accused him, and my rage had subsided. Now I talked a little with Erika, and gradually I started to feel more human and the stomach knot eased.

She said, "You saw Ruth last night. Did she give it to you?"

I nodded. "The address."

Erika frowned and shook her head. "No, I don't think it was an address. It sounded like something... something more tangible."

She took my hand. "Come on. If you're up to it, the distraction will do you good. Let's go and see Ruth."

On the way, I remembered my conversation with the orderly at the morgue.

"I'm not sure this is a good time, Erika."

"Why?"

So I told her what I'd discovered. Charlie Mason was dead.

"Are you sure?"

I nodded.

"She knows," Erika said. And when her friend met us at the door, she said the same thing.

"I guessed," she said. "Call it a woman's intuition, but I knew."

We sat in her lounge and for the second time that day I was given sweet tea, only this time I accepted the toast since it gave Ruth and Erika time to talk in the kitchen without me.

When they came back, Ruth asked for the details and I told her everything I'd learned about Mason. She frowned when I mentioned Mason walking out of his job at Shomrim Security three weeks ago. It didn't tally with what he'd told her, but she didn't comment.

After some silence, she said, "You'll still go to Jerusalem and check the address?"

"I will."

"Then you'll need this," she said, handing me a key.

"His door key?"

"I don't know. Before he left two weeks ago, he gave it to me. He said if someone… no… when someone came looking for him, someone I could trust, then I should give them this key."

I found Bill Wolfe at his hotel.

"I'm sorry," I said.

He accepted my proffered hand and said, "We're both upset."

I nodded.

"It wasn't your fault," he said. "Finney's death, I mean."

I nodded.

He said, "And you say…?"

I nodded reluctantly. "You didn't bomb our office."

"Of course I bloody didn't, you idiot!" He pursed his mouth disapprovingly. "Let's get over to the office, there's something I want to show you."

On the way, I said, "You still haven't told me what you've been doing. Where've you been since I left you in that bar?"

"Sorting out your fuckin' mess."

"My mess?"

"The Slovak gang. Me and Nazeem… we dealt with it." And then he told me that he'd left the bar, driven east, found Nazeem, found out where the gang headquarters were—in the slum area on the Jaffa–Tel Aviv border—and then, last night, had made sure none of them would be bothering us again.

"Extreme force," he said. "You don't beat those chaps one at a time. You go in and blow them away."

I thought it was a bad choice of phrase and said, "Could it have been the Slovaks who car-bombed us?"

He didn't answer directly. We'd arrived at the office. Our building was a mess, but others were too. Workmen were outside the cinema opposite, pulling out broken window frames ready for new ones. Wolfe walked quickly inside the office and pointed around. Everything was burned and damaged. But it was recognizable: the newspapers, the bits of noticeboard. The files.

"But there's a box missing. Not burned or damaged. Missing."

I looked around, but couldn't tell what he meant.

"The pro-Jews," he said. "The box with the files of the seventeen pro-Jews is not here. Not even a scrap of it."

I stood with my hands on my hips, thinking.

"There's a positive to take from this, Ash," he said.

"There is?"

"Whoever did this to us is scared. We're getting close and they didn't want us to have those files."

# THIRTY-NINE

I found Sub-Inspector Rosen at the police HQ. His pale face suggested sickness.

When I asked about his health, he exhaled noisily and sighed. "Stress."

"Work?"

"Well, let's just say that I know you weren't involved in the death of those three Slovaks. We seem to have a gang turf war on our hands." He shook away thoughts that seemed to crowd his mind. "Are you here about your office?"

"In a way," I said. "We lost the seventeen files."

"Seventeen files?"

"The pro-Jew deserters."

He regarded me with curiosity. "But you aren't looking for pro-Jews, Ash."

"That's what we thought. But the files have gone."

He smirked as though I was telling a joke. "It was an explosion. Of course stuff's gone."

"There's no sign. No sign at all, Dave. We think someone made sure we didn't have them."

His smirk half remained but his face showed doubt.

"Doesn't sound likely. Why would they?"

"Why indeed." I nodded. "I need to know the names of the men in those files."

"Whoa!" he said, suddenly becoming deadly serious. "I can't do that. I can't support any investigation into anyone on our side. Ash, you know that, don't you? You understand?"

"I need their names. We think it was them who attacked us. We think they're still active."

He shook his head. His normally bright eyes looked dark and cold with sadness. "It's nonsense. Jews aren't the Killing Crew. It's nonsense. Look, every one of them joined the eighty-second"—it was an IDF battalion—"I can tell you that. They didn't attack you."

I tried again but he waved me away.

"I can't help, Ash. I'd get fired for even considering such nonsense. You're here with the Security Council's approval to round up pro-Arab deserters. I can't help you and I've got more pressing and real issues on my plate."

I thought that my friendship with Dave Rosen would have crossed political barriers, but it didn't. He wouldn't help and Wolfe wasn't at all surprised. My colleague was waiting for me in the Bentley as I came out of the police station.

Nazeem was in the back, looking grumpy. He nodded a greeting to me but then shut his eyes and leaned back.

Wolfe drove us east out of Tel Aviv and within minutes I was asleep.

I must have slept through the first checkpoint, but we were stopped by the IDF near Lydda Airport and the car thoroughly searched.

I took over the driving, and Wolfe was soon snoring beside me. Nazeem's eyes caught my attention in the mirror.

"What happened last night?" I asked, referring to the Slovak gang.

"We dealt with them," he said tersely.

"How?"

"A bulldozer." He flashed a smile. "We found where they were based and I drove a bulldozer into the building. Old stone crumbles easily. They won't be troubling you again."

I wondered if that was what Rosen had been referring to. Wolfe and Nazeem had literally destroyed the Slovak gang and their headquarters.

Soldiers ahead blocked the road with a makeshift barricade of barbed wire pulled across the road. We had reached the plateau. Jerusalem sparkled, gold and white, like a mirage ahead.

We were flagged to a halt, searched as usual and handed over our papers. The soldiers scrutinized and debated Nazeem's documents while he stood impassive. He also stayed calm when he was body-searched. If he'd been wearing an ankle gun, they'd have found it. My heart pounded as they turned to me. I could feel the sweat prickling my forehead.

"Strip!" the soldier barked at me.

Wolfe shouted at the most senior soldier—a mere sergeant—and waved our papers.

"How dare you! We are British citizens, here at the invitation of your government. It's an outrage!"

His tone created confusion, and he continued, emboldened, providing the name of the Security Council official we'd met, and claiming a diplomatic incident.

Suddenly there was a burst of fire to our left. Arabs had closed in on the position while the IDF soldiers had been distracted. Now they dived for cover and returned fire.

More evidence if we needed it that the truce was falling apart.

We didn't wait for permission. Wolfe jumped into the driver's seat while Nazeem and I scrambled into the back.

Wolfe blasted through the barrier and raced away. I expected a bullet through the rear window at any moment, but none came. An armoured jeep pounded past us, heading for the checkpoint, and then we were out of the trouble and driving into Jerusalem.

I'd been here a dozen times, but only once ventured inside the old city walls. Even from a distance, I couldn't help marvel at the castle battlements that loomed before us. Immediately behind them, I could see the Tower of David beside Jaffa Gate. And beyond, partly hidden by walls and churches, was the dazzling, golden dome. Beneath that lay the foundation stone of the world, allegedly.

Wolfe must have seen me staring in awe because he spoke. "No tourist trip today, I'm afraid. The city is occupied and barricaded."

We passed the modern heart of the city, the Russian Compound which included the old British barracks. The IDF was occupying them now. Israeli flags flew all around and a Sherman tank stood outside.

So much for the decommissioning exercise we oversaw, I thought.

Wolfe turned off Jaffa Road onto Paul's Road and then right and left. We were outside a modern block with Barclays Bank on the ground floor.

This was the address that Erika's friend Ruth Gotting had given me.

Wolfe and I got out, Nazeem stayed with the car. There was a side door to the building that didn't require a key. On the second floor, there were doors to apartments. We went to the fourth and uppermost floor before we found the door we wanted.

Again, no key was required. The door had been broken open.

There were two rooms, each about twelve feet square: a bedroom and an office. Both had been turned over. The mattress had been shredded. Horse hair spilled across the floor amid tossed clothing. The wardrobe, pulled away from the wall, had its base and back smashed.

The office was in a similar state. It looked like our Tel Aviv place without the burning. However, the things that caught our attention were a field telephone and a calendar with writing on. The field telephone had a cable that ran through a rear window and over a telephone line. Smart. Mason had been piggybacking off Barclay's telephone line.

The calendar had a date circled in red: Friday, July 9th—two days' time. And beside it were the scribbled letters 'SIR'.

# FORTY

There was a chest of drawers, open and rifled through. But inside we found newspaper articles, scraps of paper, restaurant receipts, train tickets, a taxi receipt, a Shomrim Security brochure, and more pieces of newspaper.

The newspaper clippings were about the Killing Crew.

Wolfe picked up the field telephone, checked it worked and called SIB Command. It took almost ten minutes of being connected and put through and transferred before he spoke to the right person.

"I need to know…" He looked at me and then pulled an apologetic face. " *We* need to know about Charles 'Charlie' Mason. He was on our list of deserters."

I heard a tinny voice say something like: "But you have all the files."

"Did have—but that's not important right now. Was there anything excluded? Was anything missing?"

Pause. "No. Why should we exclude something from a file?" Pause. "Are you saying something's missing?"

"No, just asking."

"Is he one of them? Is he one of the Crew?"

Wolfe glanced at me and I shook my head. He said, "We don't know. There's a lot of odd stuff, that's all."

He ended the call and shook his head in frustration.

SIB Command, and by inference the army, didn't know.

I took the handset from him, causing a frown. He frowned even more when I asked the operator to place a call to London. Specifically the Energy Department at Whitehall.

Once connected, I asked for my father's office and the phone was answered by his secretary, Samantha Duffield.

"Sam, it's Ash."

"Ash? Is everything all right? Where are you?"

"Israel at the moment," I said, immediately conscious that she was showing more interest in my career and safety than my father ever did. "Is he available?"

"Meetings all day, I'm afraid. Can I help?"

"I wondered whether I could make use of his contacts," I said. "I'm hoping to speak to someone on the security side."

She said nothing for a moment.

"Sam?"

"What specifically?"

"I need to know if someone is working with or for MI5."

Again a pause. Longer this time. I listened to random electronic noises on the line and I got the impression she was speaking to my father. Checking.

When she came back on the line, she said, "Call back in ten minutes."

I put the phone down and saw Wolfe looking at me with curiosity.

"How do you know him?" he asked.

I shook my head. "My father. Yes, I know he's got a different surname. I changed mine." I didn't want to explain the problems between me and my famous father, but Wolfe kept pressing until he'd got enough detail. I told Wolfe that I blamed my father for my mother's suicide; what I didn't say was that he was also an authoritarian and made my childhood hell. I despised him. He thought little of me.

However, when I called back, Sam answered and asked me to hold while she transferred me.

After thirty seconds, another voice came on the line.

"Hello?" He didn't say his name and I didn't expect him to. "You have a question."

"We're looking into someone," I said.

"And who is *we*?"

Wolfe had his ear pressed to the other side of the receiver, listening in.

"We're a special unit, SIB operating in the Levant, out of the seventy-fifth Provost Company."

"All right. What's the chap's name?"

"Mason. Charles Mason. Have you heard of him?"

"That's a fairly common name."

"Operating in Palestine as was?"

"Yes."

*Bingo!* This MI5 officer knew the name.

I said, "Was he part of the Special Squads?"

"The government always denied their existence."

Of course they did, despite everyone knowing to the contrary.

"All right," I said, trying a different angle. "Were army operatives transferred from the SAS and Commando units into the Palestine Police Force?"

"That's a matter of public record."

Yes, it was, but it led to my next question: "Did these men report through the normal police channels?"

"No."

207

Now for the big question: "Was Mason one of them?"

"Yes."

"Have you heard of the Killing Crew?"

"Yes."

"And the Engineer?"

"Yes."

"Is Mason connected in some way?"

"I couldn't possibly comment."

*Bingo again!* I paused, choosing my next question carefully.

"Are you concerned about Mason's desertion from the army?"

Without hesitation, the man said, "No."

My eyes flared wide as I looked at Wolfe. Mason wasn't a bad guy. MI5 was confirming he was one of them. Typically, the government and army hadn't communicated. The army thought Mason was a deserter. Maybe it was part of his cover.

I nodded to Wolfe, who was mouthing at me.

"Just to confirm, sir, Mason was working for you?"

"I couldn't possibly comment."

"When was the last time you heard anything?"

"He's been off the radar for ten days."

We'd gotten it wrong. Mason wasn't the Engineer. He wasn't part of the Killing Crew. Like us, he'd been investigating them. Until about ten days ago when he'd been killed and dumped in an orange grove shack.

"Now that we know he was one of the good guys, let's go through all this paper again."

I agreed. This time we were looking for clues as to what he found out rather than evidence of guilt. However, it didn't change anything. The solutions didn't jump out at us. Receipts, scraps of paper and

208

pieces of old newspapers didn't miraculously change their information.

Wolfe fetched lunch and we ate it in Mason's office.

"I keep thinking," I said between mouthfuls, "that the bomb at our office was to stop us."

Wolfe nodded. "Or destroy information—the deserters' files."

"And something similar here?"

"No," Wolfe shook his head firmly, "I don't think so. If they wanted to stop Mason they would have blown this up like they blew up ours. No, this place was turned over after he'd died. They were looking for something."

"Evidence."

"They killed Mason but didn't know how much evidence he'd gained."

I nodded. "You think he'd worked out who they were?"

"It's a possibility."

"Or at least, whoever killed him suspected he knew."

I fished the key out of my pocket. Were they looking for this?

Wolfe took the key from me and puzzled over it.

"Too small. We should never have assumed it was for this place. Or any other kind of door."

"It's for wherever he hid. And that's what they were looking for," I said thinking aloud.

Wolfe played with the key, thinking. "Yes... From the state of this place, they didn't find whatever it is. Otherwise, they'd have stopped when they found it. They kept going until the whole place was wrecked." He continued to look at the key.

"What does this key fit?"

We bounced around a few ideas, which were mainly variations of some kind of safety box: not a bank's deposit box because it didn't look substantial enough.

What do people use keys for?

Locking a diary, a drawer, a cupboard. Maybe it was just symbolic. Present the key to someone—the right person—and they would release the information, perhaps.

What did we know about Mason? He had a jeep or similar transport. He'd been to Transjordan visiting Frank's Band. It wasn't a car key, that was for sure.

Mason lived in Tel Aviv with Ruth Gotting, but he had this office-type place in Jerusalem. He didn't use a jeep for going back and forth. Too many checkpoints. Too many questions. Ruth had told me he went by train.

"Let's go to the station," I said.

# FORTY-ONE

The old Jerusalem railway station was identical to the one in Jaffa. However, we had a problem. We were in Israeli territory and the station was in Arab-occupied land.

Nazeem was waiting outside Mason's apartment block and the three of us drove south past the King David Hotel where GHQ and the Palestine government secretariat had been based. There was no sign of the bomb damage any more. We continued along Julian's Way, between olive groves and palms, before coming to an abrupt halt.

There was a tank and about forty soldiers ahead. But they weren't facing us, they were aiming at the Arabs further down the road—where we wanted to be.

Wolfe parked a good distance from the front line and we walked the rest of the way, watched with curiosity and caution as we approached.

We took out our papers and showed them to the IDF guards blocking the road.

Wolfe did all the talking, showed our papers and insisted we be allowed to cross. Eventually, the commander relented, said something about it being our funeral, and let us pass.

We walked fifty or so yards across no man's land with our hands up. I didn't bother counting the number of rifles aimed at me. I figured twenty was no worse than two. And only one shot needed to be deadly.

But we made it all the way to the fencing on the far side and it was Nazeem's turn to do the talking. He had an earnest conversation with the commander and within seconds we were in occupied territory. However, we were accompanied by two soldiers, who made sure that we didn't deviate from our path.

There was also a soldier standing guard outside the entrance to the station, although I didn't know why. There was no one else around. Trains weren't running. The station staff had presumably fled. The concourse was deserted.

After going through heavy oak double doors, our feet echoed on the concrete floor. Five sets of feet: us and our two guards.

I turned and nodded to them as though it was perfectly normal for us to be here and being followed by armed men.

"What are we looking for?" Nazeem asked.

"A locker of some kind," I suggested.

There were rows of wooden benches but nothing resembling a locker.

Through the far side, we came out onto the platforms. There was a train at the buffers with a gaggle of soldiers around it. Now I could see why there was the security and sensitivity. The three wagons appeared to be laden with armaments. This was either an improvised store or they were preparing for an assault.

Despite this interesting observation, the far side of the station held no obvious solution for us. I saw no lockers of any kind.

It was Wolfe who spotted it first.

"Luggage," he said, pointing to a porter's office.

We went inside and were immediately rewarded by a pile of cases. Most of which required a key.

Under the watchful gaze of the soldiers, I went through case after case until the key clicked in a lock. Success! Such a satisfying little sound.

It was a briefcase, and rather than open it there, I tucked it under my arm. We retraced our steps, through the station, to the Arab border, across no man's land, and back to the Israeli soldiers.

"Open it!" the IDF commander said, and watched closely as I turned the key and revealed the contents. He breathed a sigh of relief. Just papers.

He shook his head. "A lot of trouble for a briefcase full of paper," he said. "You must be crazy."

We probably were crazy, but at that moment, I was as excited as a child on Christmas morning.

Wolfe drove fast back to Mason's building. We all got out, and as we stepped towards the door to the apartments, Nazeem barred our way.

"I'm done," he said.

Wolfe shook his head. "It's not over. Let's go upstairs."

"You promised."

Wolfe cleared his throat, uncomfortable.

Nazeem's eyes hardened. "You promised the passport."

"Yes, but—"

"Hand it over. I've done everything you asked." Nazeem had his hand out and Wolfe dug into his jacket. He pulled out a British passport and passed it over.

"Thank you for your help," Wolfe said after a breath.

Nazeem smiled then looked at me. "You should be very grateful. Wolfe burned his last favour on those Slovaks."

So that was it. Wolfe had been holding out, using Nazeem for as long as possible, but the final job had been the elimination of the problem I'd created.

I nodded my appreciation. Something crossed my line of vision behind Nazeem, but only my back brain registered it.

Wolfe said, "Is there something—?"

"You owe me for getting you into the station," Nazeem said. "We're done, my friend and I wish you good luck and God's blessing."

We shook hands and our Arab helper walked away.

I was about to speak when I saw the thing again, and this time my conscious brain registered it.

"Don't look," I said casually, "but there's a man in a doorway opposite. He's wearing a brown suit and grey cap, and I've seen him before."

# FORTY-TWO

"Where?" Wolfe said, deliberately looking the opposite way. "Where have you seen him?"

"When I went to Sarafand. He was my taxi driver. I'm sure it's him and he's watching us."

Wolfe said nothing.

I was still thinking. "You know, now I'm wondering whether I've seen him here, in his taxi. He's been trailing us."

Wolfe said, "Let's grab him. Put the case on the floor in the back of the car. Act like nothing's up."

I dropped it onto the back seat and Wolfe relocked the doors.

"You go right, I'll go left," I said. "Go!"

We darted around each side of the car and across the road. But the man in the brown suit had gone. A quick scan up and down and I saw him, running towards the old town, towards New Gate.

Running hard, Wolfe said, "He can't get that way unless he's bulletproof. Is he an Arab?"

"Jew," I said, considering that he worked for a Jewish taxi firm. "I think a Jew."

The man had gone down a side road still looking like he was heading for the front line. When we got there, we stopped running in case a soldier got nervous and

215

trigger-happy. We strode fast and then saw our man running down a side road. As soon as we'd turned the corner we were running too.

He reached the wall and then walked smartly up to the barricade at Jaffa Gate. With five others, he showed papers, was frisked and soldiers let him enter.

Wolfe shook his head as we approached the same soldiers. He pointed to the sign leaning against the barbed wire. It said: No Jews!

There were three soldiers, young and anxious. But they smiled when we presented our British warrant cards, and let us pass.

Beyond the gate was a cobbled market square. Despite the war, there was a market just like there had probably been for two thousand years. Except for an armoured car with a mounted gun. People milled around, and for a few seconds, we thought we'd lost the brown-suited man in the crowd.

We separated, Wolfe went right and I went left, looking down each of the alleyways. And at the second one, I saw him. He made the mistake of looking back.

Yes, I'd been right. It was Snaggletooth the taxi driver. He'd been walking fast up the narrow passage and, when he saw me, immediately started running again.

I yelled for Wolfe and sprinted up steps and along the cramped alley. Stone buttresses arched overhead; the walls closed in. People got in my way, but I kept my eyes on my quarry.

I vaguely registered that this was the Christian sector, and I was soon on a wider route crammed with pilgrims. But I saw Snaggletooth dart into the church ahead.

Zigzagging through the throng I entered the holy place. Mystical light spilled from the domed ceiling.

Twenty or so men were prostrate on the stone floor. And I spotted a brown-suited man walking fast at the far end.

He disappeared through a side door and I found myself in another narrow passage. I'd lost him. I ran east, hoping to get lucky. At a crossroads, I could see old barricades to the Muslim sector directly ahead. The left appeared to offer little opportunity to hide so I went right. Then I saw Wolfe burst out of a side road.

I shouted and he pointed across the main thoroughfare to the Jewish sector and more of a maze than where I'd just been. I followed but soon caught up with Wolfe. He was breathless and wide-eyed.

"Keep going," he said. "I'll try and cut him off."

I saw the man and sprinted harder. He switched left and right, jigging through the labyrinthine streets. I'd lose him and then spot him again. He'd slowed right down and I figured he was tired and hoped to lose me rather than outrun me.

And then he simply disappeared.

I sprinted to where he'd gone and found stone steps descending deep underground. When I reached the bottom I was in a subterranean passageway just wide enough for a man to pass through. On one side the passage was rough-hewn, the other looked like a wall with massive stones, many about four feet square. The man could only have gone left so I went that way. Light faded fast and then came back from vents high above. I heard distant praying and the scuffle of feet.

After about a third of a mile, I was at steps again. With nowhere else to go except up, I started climbing.

I emerged in the dazing sunshine at the end of the Western Wall plaza. There were a hundred people here including soldiers. Most of the people were standing still. I saw Wolfe fifty yards off. He pointed and I saw the brown-suited man.

He was walking and I sprinted, closing the gap quickly. I heard shouts, presumably because I was running. Then Snaggletooth looked at me and pointed. He yelled something in Arabic, and the way everyone turned and looked at me, I guessed he'd told them I was chasing him.

People closed in like they were forming a huddle with me in the middle. They kept their hands down, but their shoulders bumped me. Dour, angry faces glared and I was blocked by a press of bodies.

Suddenly there was a soldier in my face.

"What are you doing? Hands up!"

I stayed calm. "That man. The man in the brown suit. He stole my wallet!"

The soldier blinked doubt.

"Look!" I turned out my jacket pockets, showing that they were empty—although my wallet was in my back pocket. "He's a thief!"

The soldier stepped back.

The crowd parted, slinking back, awkward and apologetic.

With no sign of Snaggletooth, I hurried to the end of the plaza where I'd last seen him. There was an alleyway and I took it, jogging but no longer expecting to catch the man. He'd be long gone.

I rounded a corner and there was Wolfe. He grinned at me. His left arm was around a man's neck, his right jamming the man's arm behind his back.

"Got him!" he said. "Guessed his route and circled around."

He pulled the man, spinning him to face me, and I confirmed he was indeed Snaggletooth, the taxi driver who had taken me to the Sarafand Garrison.

"Who are you working for?" I snapped.

"I drive a taxi."

"Who?" Wolfe growled in the man's ear.

"I work for Kesher." His voice broke. "Taxi driver!"

I frisked him for a weapon and found nothing.

While I'd chased him, I'd imagined he was a gangster. I'd imagined he was linked to the people who had bombed our office and killed Bert Finney.

Now I saw a frightened middle-aged man. He was just a taxi driver after all.

"Why were you following us?" I said less aggressively than before.

"Because I was paid to."

Wolfe gripped him harder but I calmed him. "It's all right, Bill. Let him talk." Then to the man, I said, "Who paid you?"

"The Palestine Press. I work for them!"

"Bugger!" Wolfe said. "Saul Levi?"

"Yes, sir."

I said, "How long have you been following us?"

"You," he said, "since I was told to pick you up."

Levi told him to pick me up? Snaggletooth had been selected to take me to Sarafand.

"All right. What does Levi want?"

"Information. He said you are investigating a crime. He wants to know what you are doing."

"And you tell him?" Wolfe said.

"Yes, he pays me. I've worked for them before."

Wolfe let him go. "Piss off!" he said. "And don't let me ever see you again!"

"Yes, sir," Snaggletooth said, gave us a timid, grateful nod and hurried away.

"Good to see you've recovered," I said as we walked back to David Street.

His eyes narrowed. "You're referring to me being out of breath after the chase."

I smiled. "I thought you said you were naturally fit."

"I may have been misguided. Perhaps I will join you at that gymnasium you mentioned."

"Yes, so apart from you coming with me to a gymnasium, what do we do next?"

"We get back to Mason's and see what's in that briefcase."

# FORTY-THREE

We cleared the only table in Mason's office and opened the briefcase onto it. The papers could have been put together by us. This was an investigation.

He had the details of the bank raid that Bert Finney had been interested in before he'd died in the explosion. But Mason had added his own notes: *What did they find? This wasn't just a hundred thousand.*

There was a document with Shomrim Security's logo on top. It listed seventeen names. Cohen, the Head of Operations was there. Three names were crossed off. All the names were Jewish-sounding, but Mason had circled three and written a Western name against one of them.

"I recognize it," Wolfe said, jabbing his finger at the name. "Jack Howells. He was one of the deserters. Highland Light Infantry, if I remember correctly."

"Seventeen names," I said. "You don't think…?"

"The pro-Jew deserters?"

"All of them connected to Shomrim Security?" Could they be? It didn't seem likely that everyone would think they were in the IDF when they were in fact private contractors.

We went through the notes hoping for clarity. We found a bunch of photographs, some better than others.

221

All taken surreptitiously. Some had *Shomrim* written on the reverse and all of these matched the names on the Shomrim letter-headed paper. We noted that not all of them looked like ex-soldiers. They were too old or too fat, we thought.

I went through more papers and found a newspaper cutting that covered the sniper attack that killed the guards we'd looked into in Jaffa. One was an Arab the other a Jew. I'd discounted the one I'd discovered was a bank guard because he was Arabic. Now I saw the truth.

"My God, both guards worked for the Anglo-Palestine Bank!"

I pulled out an article with a photograph from before the bank raid. It had the bank's governor flanked by three men who looked like guards. Their names weren't mentioned but I wondered if they included those who'd been killed.

Wolfe had been reading something else. "There are notes here about a safecracker being broken out of Acre Prison. Mason thought the bank robbers needed him."

I wondered if that's why Mason had written *What did they find?* It looked like they had taken a safe, although this wasn't mentioned in the newspaper reports. They needed a safecracker to crack open a safe. What had been in there?

We kept going and found that other deaths we'd been suspicious about were linked to the bank. Of the three British soldiers killed in and around Haifa in January, two had been posted to the bank at the time of the robbery.

The more we delved into Mason's work, the more it appeared that the men who had raided the bank had subsequently killed some of the bank staff, guards and soldiers who had been there.

Removing witnesses perhaps? What did they know?

I pulled out a newspaper cutting about the investiture of the new governor of the bank. On Friday, July 9th. The day after tomorrow.

The same date as circled on the calendar.

The new bank governor was also on the list of names we'd found.

We read some more and Wolfe eventually sat back, his eyes wide.

"So, we conclude that Shomrim is the Killing Crew?"

"Not all of them."

"Some of them."

"And maybe they're going to attack the bank again."

"Mason thought the new governor is a member. He's in on it."

"And it all comes to a head in two days."

"During his investiture? A distraction while they rob the bank?"

We kept looking and Wolfe picked up a piece of paper that I'd missed. It had arrows from and to events we'd been discussing: the raid, the sniper attacks, the governor's investiture. They all had one thing in common. All arrows pointed to a single circle. It had "Engineer?" written inside.

We dug some more and Wolfe pulled out a newspaper. It had another name on it that was on the list of seventeen. This man was an old Jewish property investor involved with the demolition of Manshiya in Tel Aviv.

Could he be one of the Killing Crew?

Unlikely, we thought.

Wolfe said what we were both thinking: "Some of the names on the list could be clients."

"The bank governor could be a client."

We bounced around a few ideas before we came back to the diagram with the arrows.

Wolfe said, "Maybe we've got this wrong. Maybe this isn't about the new governor and a raid on the bank."

I wasn't sure. "But the date?"

"Mason wasn't just looking for the Killing Crew, he was after the Engineer."

"All right," I said.

"Someone with the initials S-I-R." He pointed to the calendar. "A coincidence. Something happening on the same day."

"Could be."

He looked at me hard. "You're being polite."

I shrugged. "Too much of a coincidence. This is connected to the bank or bank governor. The Killing Crew and Engineer are involved but it all links back to the bank."

# FORTY-FOUR

When I got back to Wolfe's hotel, the dying sun cast the long shadow of a woman waiting on the street outside. Sylvia Rom nodded a greeting to me as I got out of the Bentley.

"Where's Wolfe?" she asked.

"How are you?" I said. "How's the face?" I touched my cheek, mirroring where she now had a protective wad.

"Stings a little. But I'm fine." She nodded towards the hotel. "I've been waiting hours. There's no sign of Wolfe."

Just then, a Land Rover came down the road and pulled up behind the Bentley. Wolfe swung out. On the way back, we'd debated the risk of getting the jeep and decided that two vehicles were better than one. We couldn't risk any more taxis based on my experience with the taxi driver we'd chased in Jerusalem. From now on we assumed everyone was on the other side. Now that we were sure they weren't just killing Jews, anyone could be working for the Killing Crew.

We had the briefcase, the calendar from the wall and the field telephone. One principle we both believed in was keeping things that might come in useful in the future.

225

"Let's go in," Wolfe said, and we filed into the hotel.

As soon as the door was shut, Wolfe grabbed Rom by the throat and walked her backwards until she was pinned against the wall.

"Who the fuck are you?" he growled in her face.

"Bill—!" I started to complain, but he held up a hand to silence me.

"Are you working for them?" Wolfe asked.

"No!"

"What's your connection with the Anglo-Palestine Bank."

"What? None!"

"Did you know Charlie Mason?"

Rom looked at me with desperation. "No. Wolfe, honestly I—"

Wolfe didn't let her finish. "Did you know him as Caleb Maaz?"

"No!"

"Are you S-I-R?"

Now I got it. Wolfe thought Rom was the person referred to in Mason's notes. Sylvia Rom. SR."

"What? What are you talking about?"

"What's your middle name, Sylvia?"

She shook her head. "I don't have one!"

I finally reacted. With a hand on Wolfe's arm that held Rom, I said, "Let her go, Bill. She's on our side."

He eased the grip slightly but didn't let her go.

"She was blown up for Christ's sake, Bill!" I said. "Will you let her go?"

Wolfe took a deep breath, dropped his hand and stepped back.

Rom's hand flew to her neck as she sagged and coughed. I gave her a glass of water and helped her into a chair.

"Sorry," Wolfe said unconvincingly.

"She's on our side, Bill," I said. He'd not been there. He'd not seen her after the car bomb. The way she'd cradled Finney's head.

In the hospital, she'd said, "For Bert's sake, we can't stop." She was on our side.

When she'd composed herself, she said, "You need to know about me. I told Carter and Bert, but not you." Then she explained about being in the Irgun, but she also told me she'd lied about her role and that she didn't help the refugee smuggling operation until later.

She said, "When Sub-Inspector Rosen told me I would be working for you, at first I was happy. I thought I could be his spy and support my country again."

Wolfe gave me a knowing nod.

She said, "But I didn't. I soon realized you were investigating for the right reasons. I want to be a police officer, not a secretary. And that means doing the right thing irrespective of whether the crooks are Jews or Arabs."

She stopped, and I could see she was struggling with her explanation. After a pause, she said, "I have never given the sub-inspector any information."

She hesitated again and before letting out a shuddering breath. "And I fell for Bert."

Wolfe looked surprised, but I nodded.

"She's on our side, Bill."

She said, "And I want to help. Let me be involved, for Bert's sake. Let me avenge his death."

Then she shocked us. She reached behind her back and pulled out a revolver, held loosely and down.

"I have a gun and I can shoot."

That final act must have convinced Wolfe. She had a gun and could have pulled it when he'd attacked her. But she hadn't.

He looked at her long and hard then looked at me.
I nodded.
"Three are better than two."
"All right," he said. "Let's start planning."

# FORTY-FIVE

The first thing we did was bring Rom up to speed. She sat on the bed, I perched against the window ledge and Wolfe leaned against a wall. He let me do most of the talking and I explained about the notes in Mason's briefcase. I said that he'd been investigating Shomrim Security.

"So Mason didn't work for them?" she said.

"He did, but only to get information on them. We recognized one of the employee names as being from our pro-Jew deserters list."

"Jack Howells," Wolfe added.

She said, "But Sub-Inspector Rosen said that all seventeen had joined the eighty-second."

"That's right," Wolfe said, frowning.

"Well, it looks like at least three of them joined Shomrim—although we lost the files."

"Why three?" Rom asked.

"Mason had a list of seventeen names. One was Jack Howells and there were two others with 'Brit' against their names."

Wolfe showed her the list.

"Know any of these men?"

She shook her head. "If these are all the deserters, did Mason think they all joined Shomrim Security?"

"We don't think they can all be deserters," I said, and explained about the photographs and the new bank governor.

"They could all be involved though," Rom said.

"They could," I said.

"They might all be the Killing Crew or connected," Wolfe said, "or work with Shomrim or be clients."

We talked briefly about calling SIB Command and going through the names—a process of elimination—to find the seventeen again. But it would take too long and we couldn't rely on having all of the pro-Arab names since many were destroyed by the car bomb.

Plus we needed Jewish rather than British names since they'd changed them.

"Mason took photographs," I said, and Wolfe pulled them from the briefcase for Rom to see.

"So we match people to the faces?"

"Let's come back to that," Wolfe said. "We need to decide the plan first."

I went on to tell Rom about the bank raid and the connection with other attacks. "It looks like the gang—the Killing Crew—were removing witnesses."

"Building a protection business," Rom said.

I think my mouth may have dropped open. "Could be," I said. "They may have got wealthy Jews by attacking some groups and by doing that had made their targets fearful. Anyone could get killed, and so if you could afford private protection, why not take advantage of it?"

"Sounds reasonable," Wolfe said, "but it's more speculation. We need answers."

We didn't have any. All we had were various scenarios and the date—two days' time.

I decided to tell Rom the other thing.

"We've been followed... for some time."

"By whom?" Rom asked, surprised.

"The reporter, Saul Levi. Well not him, but his man. He was my taxi driver when I went to the Sarafand base. I recognized him watching us in Jerusalem."

"And you're sure he was working for Levi?"

"He admitted it," Wolfe said.

"Why?" Rom asked.

"Investigation. Reporters like information." I shrugged. "We could be big news."

Wolfe said, "We should ask him about SIR."

"SIR?" Rom said.

"It's why Wolfe was suspicious of you," I said. "SIR was written on Mason's calendar by the circled date." Again Wolfe fished out the appropriate item from the case, we'd brought the calendar with us.

Rom flicked through the other months. There was nothing else circled or written.

As she handed it back, Wolfe showed her the piece of paper with the names and arrows.

I said, "As you can see from this, Mason thought the Engineer was linked to the bank job and the attacks."

"But Mason didn't know who it was."

"SIR could be the clue."

She nodded uncertainly. "You're connecting the calendar with the bank governor's investiture with the arrows pointing to the Engineer."

I shrugged. Her tone was right. It was the same point Wolfe had made. We were making connections that might be misguided.

"It might mean something else, like a place," Wolfe said, "but SIR is most likely a person."

"The one you call *the Engineer*?"

Wolfe and I both nodded.

"And you thought it was me!" she said with an edge of derision in her voice.

231

"Sylvia Rom," Wolfe said, explaining. "SR. We don't know your middle name."

"I don't have a middle name."

"I believe you." Wolfe apologized.

"The Anglo-Palestine Bank," she said after a beat and changing the subject. "That's still the state bank. It was run by the British, and Israel has taken it over. All currency is managed by the bank."

"What are you thinking?" I asked.

"I don't know, but it can't last, can it? We're still using the Palestinian Pound, which must annoy a lot of folk. Surely there are plans for our own currency."

Wolfe said, "We think there are two possibilities, and the new bank governor is either in on it or not."

I smiled. He wasn't in on the second possibility we'd previously discussed. Unless he had a suicidal wish.

Wolfe continued: "Option one is that there will be another raid on the bank, bigger this time, maybe involving many more people."

"And option two?" Rom asked.

"An attempt on the governor's life. Another sniper attack by the Killing Crew, or a bomb by the Engineer."

"Why?"

"We don't know," I said. "I don't think Mason did either."

"There's lots we don't fu—" Wolfe started to say but stopped abruptly when there was a knock on the bedroom door.

We all whipped out our guns, moved apart, and I stepped to the door. Before taking hold of the handle, I checked the others were ready.

I jerked open the door.

Outside in the hall was the reporter, Saul Levi.

# FORTY-SIX

"You promised to keep me apprised," Levi said through gritted teeth.

He'd stepped confidently into the room. Rom and I put our weapons away but Wolfe kept hold of his.

Wolfe said, "Talk. How did you know we were here?"

Levi shook his head. His mouth tightened in an ironic smile. "Really, Major? All I needed to do was ask the receptionist to call me when you returned."

"You've a nerve showing up," I said.

Levi switched his attention to me. "Me a nerve? You failed to keep your end of the bargain."

"We hadn't found anything to report," Wolfe growled.

"Put the gun away, Major," Levi said.

Wolfe considered it then complied. Then he repeated: "We had nothing to tell you."

"I don't believe you."

"You were spying on us!" I said. "How can we trust you, Levi?"

"Listen, you buffoons," he said, sitting on the only chair in the room, "it's how the *Press* operates. We have investigators, sources and informants—oh wait, you use informants too! You're just like us, so don't act like the aggrieved party here. We have ordinary men on the street with their eyes and ears open and we pay them for the information. If you want to call that spying, then do so. I call it investigative journalism."

Levi paused and folded his arms before he continued. "I'm disappointed in you."

We said nothing. I noticed Rom clenching her teeth.

Levi said, "Right, let's start with why you were in Jerusalem today."

We said nothing.

"The place above Barclays Bank... What was there? What did you find?"

"Nothing of interest," Wolfe said.

Levi pointed to the open briefcase. "Doesn't look like nothing, although I know you got that from the railway station. Hell of a risk you took, crossing into enemy territory to get"—he raised his eyebrows—"nothing of interest."

I said, "Look, Levi, it's too early to share with you. I promise that we'll reveal everything once we've made sense of it."

Levi shook his head. "Not good enough."

"Gonna have to be, pal," Wolfe growled.

"Really?" Levi looked unperturbed. He looked like a man expecting to be told everything.

Wolfe took a pace towards the reporter, close enough to grab, and I thought he was going to pull Levi to his feet.

"Time for you to leave," Wolfe said.

"Tell me what you've learned."

The two men locked eyes. Wolfe was the bigger man, taller and broader, but Levi wasn't intimidated.

I said, "Do the initials SIR mean anything to you?"

Levi's eyes narrowed, then he smiled and switched his gaze to me.

"No. Why?"

"It's someone or something linked to who we presume is the Killing Crew," I said. Wolfe looked at me, and I could tell he didn't agree with me talking, but this wasn't giving anything away and Levi might know something. After all, he'd given me details about the sniper attacks and that had led us to discover a connection with the bank.

"Is that in the briefcase?" Levi asked.

"Yes, and more," Wolfe said.

"Then I'd like to see."

"Not a chance. Not until after."

"After what?"

Wolfe breathed in noisily through his nose and I guessed he regretted what he'd just said.

I said, "You can have it in a couple of days."

Levi's eyes flared wide with interest. "Something is going down tomorrow or the day after?"

I hesitated then said, "Yes."

"What?"

Wolfe shook his head. "We'll tell you in a couple of days."

"When it's too late." Now Levi shook his head with his lips pursed. "No, Major, you'll tell me now."

Wolfe said, "All right, time for you to leave!"

Levi didn't move. "So far I've been nice and friendly, but it needn't stay that way."

Wolfe bristled.

Levi said, "I know about the Slovaks."

"The Slovaks?"

And then the reporter told Wolfe that he knew who was responsible for the attack on the Slovak gang last night. His spies had seen Wolfe and Nazeem go inside the property before Nazeem had driven the bulldozer into the building, killing the boss and his cronies.

"The police would be very interested," Levi finished.

Wolfe said nothing, his face impassive.

I said, "What do your sources tell you about the bombing of our office?"

"It wasn't the Slovaks."

"So who was it?"

Levi waited a beat then stood. "All right, if that's how it's going to be."

"What do you want?"

"I want answers, not questions. I want to know what you know."

Wolfe said, "No."

Levi said, "Tell me something."

Wolfe looked at me and I inclined my head.

He said, "We think we know who they are—the Killing Crew."

"Who? And before you say you'll tell me in a couple of days, that'll be too late. I don't want to know when this is over. I want to be involved."

"Shomrim Security," Wolfe said after deliberation.

"The protection firm? Really?"

"Really," I said, and nodded to the briefcase. "Someone else was investigating. That's who they came up with."

"Was? They're dead?"

"Yes."

"Who?"

"Doesn't matter."

"Killed by Shomrim?"

Wolfe said, "We don't know, but it seems likely. They found out and killed him."

Levi said, "And you think something is going to happen tomorrow?"

"Friday," I said.

"How do you know?"

"The governor of the Anglo-Palestine Bank's investiture. It's relevant. The governor's name was also on Shomrim's list."

Rom spoke to Levi: "Do you know where the seventeen pro-Jew deserters went?"

"The IDF."

"Eighty-second," she said.

"That's right. We all know."

I picked up on Rom's thinking. "How do you know?"

Levi paused for thought. "Ah," he said.

Wolfe leaned towards him. "What's that supposed to mean?"

"Propaganda," Levi said with a smile. "I don't know for certain that they all went there, or stayed there. Why do you ask?"

I said, "Because we know at least one works for Shomrim."

"Maybe all of them do," Wolfe said.

"Interesting," Levi said. He looked at my face and then Wolfe's, probably gauging whether we'd told him the truth about the other stuff.

"What are you going to do?" he asked.

"We were just going to decide," Wolfe said. "We need to find out whether this happens at the bank or if there's something else linked in some way."

I said, "We haven't worked it out yet, honestly."

The reporter nodded and seemed to relax. "Here's the deal," he said, standing. "When you've worked it out and start to move, then you inform me. Day or night. Understand? I want exclusive photographs and to be an eyewitness."

We said nothing.

Levi pointed skywards with both index fingers as he continued: "And if I'm not... if you tell me too late... then I go to the police about the Slovaks."

# FORTY-SEVEN

Captain Janes stretched his neck. He'd spent too long going over and over the details. Seven men had died in the building that collapsed in Manshiya. Slovak thugs to a man, but that wasn't what bothered him. Sub-Inspector Rosen was convinced it was a turf war.

"Another gang. Find the other gang, Janes," he'd said. But the captain hadn't found any evidence. At first, he'd suspected an Irgun faction. They were known to act independently, dealing out their own kind of justice, but they weren't subtle. They had a history of warning first, and no one they'd questioned had seen anyone or heard any threats. And then there was the bulldozer. It had been on the building site. The Irgun would plan ahead. They'd use a mortar, not an opportunistic vehicle. No, this was someone else.

And the clues before had led to the British military policemen, Carter and Wolfe.

The bombing of their office was another sign of terrorism. Was this tit for tat between the Slovaks and Brits? And why was Rosen so against believing the Brits were guilty.

Of course, Janes knew why. Rosen had been one of them. Maybe he was still one of them.

Captain Janes got up and stretched his legs. He walked to the kitchen to get coffee, partly to keep his brain going and partly because the walk took him past Rosen's office.

The office was empty and neat, like Rosen had left for the day.

"Where's the sub-inspector?" Janes asked Rosen's clerk.

"Gone."

"Coming back? I have something to show him," Janes lied, hoping to get the clerk to open up. Rosen had been slipping out a lot lately.

The clerk smiled with feigned innocence. "He'll be back in the morning, that's all I know."

# FORTY-EIGHT

After the reporter had gone, Wolfe paced the room. "I don't like him. I don't fuckin' like the man."

"You don't like *anyone* controlling you, Bill," I said. "We go along with it and use him."

"He better not get in the way."

I smiled. I wouldn't put it past Wolfe to accidentally-on-purpose shoot the man if he got in our way.

Wolfe said, "We've been wasting time. Here's what we're going to do. We're going to pay a visit to Shomrim Security."

But the office beside the brickworks was closed. The place was in darkness and the front door was locked.

"Break in?" Rom asked as we sat in the Bentley, thirty yards down the street.

"No," Wolfe said. "We wait to see if anything happens."

Thirty minutes later, with no sign of anything happening, Rom said, "We break in and find their employee and client records. Then we can work out who on the list is possibly Killing Crew."

"No," Wolfe said.

Rom's eyes told me she was conflicted. I could see she wanted to argue, but Wolfe was the boss.

I said, "If we go in, we might find nothing. And we risk alerting them. It's better that they don't know we're onto them."

"Right," Wolfe grumbled.

I said, "There are two things I want to do."

Wolfe looked at me.

"I want to revisit the morgue and question the orderly. Someone told him to say nothing. I want to find out who it was."

"What's the other thing?"

"I'm bothered that we think there might be an attack on the bank or the new governor. If it's big, we can't stop it on our own."

"You're suggesting we involve the security forces or police? We can't do that," Wolfe said.

"We don't tell them anything else," I said. "We don't mention Shomrim or the Killing Crew. I just feel we should tell Dave Rosen to increase security during the investiture."

Wolfe bit his lip, looked at the dark office and then back at me. "So long as that's all, Ash."

"Of course."

"Right, then we have a new plan. By all means do that, but we get a good night's sleep. Tomorrow we meet at my hotel at six and we resume the surveillance."

At the hospital, Wolfe and Rom waited outside and I went down into the morgue. It didn't take long to spot the orderly. He was wheeling a body into cold storage. After taking one look at me, he abandoned the trolley and ran.

I could have chased him, but all of the morgues I'd ever been in, bar none, had only one entrance, one staircase. And that was behind me.

The orderly was going nowhere.

I found him after five minutes, cowering in a broom cupboard.

"I can't talk," he said as I pulled him out.

"You don't know what I'm going to ask you yet."

He looked left and right. There was no one else around, no one to help him.

I said, "You were told not to tell anyone about the man with the scar on his forehead."

The orderly didn't reply, but his eyes agreed.

"Who was that? Who told you to keep quiet?"

"I can't say."

I took out my wallet.

He shook his head and I saw tears brimming in his eyes. "No money!"

"Who?" I pressed him.

"They will kill me." His voice quaked and a tear broke loose.

"Who?" I said, my voice more threatening.

"They will kill my family."

I felt bad about my next words, but I was desperate for the truth and so said, "I will kill your family."

His body shook, and above the rotten smell down in the morgue, I caught the stench of urine. He glanced down at his wet pants.

"Was it Shomrim Security?" I said.

"Yes." He nodded. "A man from Shomrim."

I walked to the police HQ from the Scopus Hotel. Wolfe dropped Rom at her home before stopping at the hotel. He said he didn't want to visit the police station. So I went alone.

I could have taken the Land Rover but I wanted the walk.

It was a clear night with no moon. The air blew fresh from the west and I hoped it cleansed me of the stench of death as well as my guilt for the way I'd treated the poor orderly. He hadn't known the Shomrim man's name but the description sounded like Cohen, the Head of Operations.

Rosen wasn't at the police station and they couldn't tell me when he'd be back. "Sometime in the morning," was all I got. I said I'd return.

A wasted journey. I should have driven after all.

Erika was up and in her living room and she kindly made me some supper while I took a bath. She gave me some rose oil and insisted I use it because of the smell.

It had been a long eventful day and my night-time stroll hadn't significantly improved my body odour.

Afterwards, we sat and played cards and she wanted to know about the car bomb. She'd been worried about me and gone to see for herself in case I was injured. I thought she'd been in bed when I'd returned home after visiting Rom in hospital, but she'd still been out.

Then I told her we'd been to Jerusalem today and found Mason's place there.

"He was a good man," I said. "You must tell your friend Ruth that."

Erika wasn't surprised but was grateful for the confirmation. I couldn't bring myself to tell her of my original doubts—that I'd assumed he was part of the Killing Crew.

"How did he die?" Erika asked as we played cards. "You know, don't you?"

I checked her eyes and saw she wanted the truth. No platitudes. "Executed," I said.

"Who by?"

"We're working on it."

"Where was he found?"

I told her. Gave her the approximate location south of us. About halfway to Sarafand.

244

She said, "At least it's a nice location. All those orange trees. It somehow seems better to die in the countryside. Closer to God."

She drank her brandy and we continued our game and she beat me. Which made me happy. She was more herself than two nights ago. *I'm a strong woman*, she'd said, and I could see that.

"What's tomorrow got in store, Ash?" she asked as we packed away.

"Progress," I said. "Tomorrow we'll make some progress."

However, I was thinking, tomorrow we go on the offensive.

# FORTY-NINE

The man with the cold eyes removed the barrier. There was a deserted farmhouse at the end of the track. He'd been using it for the last two years, making his bombs in isolation and moving explosives a small amount at a time. And he had the perfect disguise. No one ever questioned what he was doing.

He was the expert.

The Shomrim idiots had taken matters into their own hands with the car bomb. For a fleeting moment he'd been impressed by what they'd achieved, but only a moment. He was the bomb-maker, not them. And he didn't like them making decisions for themselves. Stupid decisions at that. If you want to kill hornets, you don't poke their nest. It's even worse to accidentally kill one of them. All or nothing. You want to stop someone or something then you hit them hard. No survivors. The Shomrim men didn't understand that.

He made his final checks and fed wires up to the loft.

This hadn't been the original plan, but what was the point of intelligence without the ability to adapt? Mason could have spoiled things and needed to be dealt with. But a Special Investigations team couldn't be stopped so easily. Kill them and many more would arrive. Admittedly, it would be over by then, but they wouldn't let up. The British Army wouldn't be fooled. They would hunt him and he would be forever looking over his shoulder.

Since the SIB men had gotten close, the man with the cold eyes had sensed the formation of a new plan. Not a radical change. There would still be the finale he'd intended, but now he would add a new twist.

# FIFTY

I was up early, energized and keen to speak to my friend Dave Rosen before meeting Wolfe and Rom.

I'd told Wolfe that I would mention the potential threat to the bank's governor, but as I walked down Allenby and past the road that led to our bombed office, I thought about Mason's notes. The Special Squad man had known so much, but there was SIR on the calendar with no explanation. It wasn't on his diagram with the arrows.

Either Mason hadn't figured it out, or it was just that. Not a person, just initials. Could there be a military unit called SIR? Like the IDF, military units were often referred to as an acronym or abbreviation. I wondered if the S might stand for Syrian. The ALA was funded by Syrians. Could SIR be similar?

Last night, we'd asked Levi if he knew what SIR stood for. Could it hurt if I asked my police friend this morning? I didn't think so. It would tell him nothing about Shomrim or the link to the Killing Crew.

I asked the desk sergeant for Sub-Inspector Rosen and was told to wait.

A few minutes later, the man beckoned to me and said, "SI Rosen will see you in about thirty minutes. He's just finishing a meeting."

I stood, transfixed for a beat.

"Sir?" the desk sergeant said.

I felt a cold hand around my heart and ice down my spine.

How had I not seen that? How had I not guessed?

"Sir?" the sergeant said again, and I snapped out of my paralysis.

"I'll come back," I said. "I'll come back later."

We saw the Shomrim secretary arrive at their office. She had a green car—a small Morris. Which was impressive for a secretary. She unlocked the office, went inside and shut the door behind her. The blinds at the window didn't open.

We wondered which of the men would be first to arrive. But after an hour no one else had gone in or out.

There was no wind that morning and I had been watching a thin line of smoke. It reached into the clear sky like a fine finger holding up the heavens. But I wasn't thinking about that. I was thinking about Dave Rosen. My old buddy. The Ginger to my Fred Astaire.

Eventually, I said what was playing on my mind.

"S-I-R," I said quietly. "It could stand for Sub-Inspector Rosen."

Wolfe stared at me. "Good God, man, how long have you thought that?"

"Not long."

I could see him thinking and hoped he wasn't considering any duplicity on my part. However, when he spoke he was resigned rather than suspicious.

"It makes a lot of sense. We should have seen it."

I said nothing.

He said, "He's pestered us the whole time. And you know what?"

I thought I did.

"He probably planned this ages ago," Wolfe said, nodding as though he could read my mind. "He probably orchestrated your friendship."

"A man on the inside," I said quietly.

Rom hadn't said anything up to this point and I'd almost forgotten she was there until she spoke.

"Was the inspector a deserter then?" she asked.

"No," I said.

"But—"

Wolfe said, "He didn't need to be. He was in the right job."

"A puppet master," I said. "I feel like a puppet."

Wolfe said nothing for a moment. Then he cleared his throat. "What did you tell him?"

"Nothing."

"But you went to see him about the attack on the governor."

I nodded.

"And?"

"He wasn't there last night, so I went first thing. And he wasn't free. That's when I suddenly realized he was S-I-R."

"So he doesn't know we suspect Shomrim?"

Of course, I wasn't supposed to mention anything other than the bank governor. Wolfe had suspected I'd say more to my friend.

I shook my head. "He knows nothing about this, about what we learned." I thought for a second. "Although, after the office bomb and missing files, I asked Rosen for the pro-Jew deserter names."

"He's no fool. He'll know," Wolfe said.

"What's that smoke?" Rom asked after a pause. "The brickwork's chimneys are on the other side."

My attention snapped back to the line of smoke I'd noticed earlier. It was darker now. Charcoal-grey.

"She's burning something!" Wolfe said, and I was already moving.

We were out of the car and running to the Shomrim office door.

It was locked, and after a quick check, Wolfe used his shoulder and smashed into the reception area.

The secretary wasn't there.

We charged straight on, through the door with the viewing window, into a corridor from which there were two small offices and a rear exit. That door was ajar and Wolfe was first through it into a narrow yard.

A woman screamed.

The secretary was standing four feet away from a burning barrel, panic on her face as she stared at us.

She had a rod in her hand and immediately raised it, threatening.

"Get back!" Her voice was off. There was wild desperation in her eyes.

I realized there was a box behind her. A glance at the barrel told me she'd been stuffing papers inside and burning them.

Wolfe and I raised our hands, palms out. "It's all right," I said.

Wolfe said, "Step away from the barrel."

She didn't. In fact, she did the opposite. Pushing the last box closer, she grabbed a handle on the barrel's side and yanked it over. A huge effort with limited control that made her cry out. Or maybe it was pain caused by a hot metal handle.

The barrel toppled. The fire poured onto the final box, but it also sent a cloud of burning ash and paper into the air.

And then she screamed again. Only this time it wasn't the shock of us charging into the yard. Her dress had caught fire. The flames spread quickly, and I guessed there was some sort of accelerant on the paper.

I dived, caught her midriff and rolled away from the burning pile. As I tried to smother the flames, my jacket caught on fire.

The woman was screaming, fighting me, squirming, trying to escape the fire, trying to pull away from me.

And then Wolfe punched her.

She stopped struggling and Wolfe rolled her on the dirt, patting out the blaze with his jacket.

I tore my own jacket off and stamped out the flames.

Wolfe stepped back from the now unconscious secretary. Rom was trying to pull paper from the fire, leaning in against the heat, trying to drag unburnt sheets out. But it was hopeless. It had gone from a barrel fire to a bonfire in seconds. All we could do was step back and watch the ashes and sparks rise in the column of smoke.

All of the Shomrim Security records had been destroyed.

# FIFTY-ONE

The secretary wasn't grateful that we'd saved her life. We were in the reception area, with her on the chair and us around the table, facing her.

A quick check of the offices had told us there was nothing left. Even the Shomrim brochures from her desk had gone.

Despite the black smears on her face, she had an implacable seen-it-all-before expression. She eyed us with suspicion as Rom handed her a cup of water.

"I'm saying nothing," she said after a sip.

I leaned forward on the desk. "What's your name?"

She looked at me, considered the question then presumably decided it didn't matter. "Irene."

"All right, Irene, we just want to know what's going on."

Her eyes narrowed slightly as her lips tightened.

Wolfe said, "Where are the others? Where's Mr Cohen?"

"I'm not talking."

I said, "You're cleaning up, aren't you? Shomrim Security is finished."

Her eyes were defiant, but they confirmed my assertion. The men weren't coming back and her job had been to destroy any evidence.

"They've left you," I said. "You're out of a job."

Her jaw twitched. "I've been well paid."

"They gave you the car," Rom said, referring to the green one we'd seen her pull up in. It was a big thing to have a private car.

"Yes." She smiled. "Mr Cohen valued my contribution."

"Where are they?" Wolfe asked.

She shook her head, defiant. "I just answer the phone."

I said, "Irene, it's important. They are killers."

A slight movement of her head suggested she didn't believe me.

I said, "They plan to raid the Anglo-Palestine Bank."

She looked at me. Cold eyes. I couldn't read them. Did she know? Was I wrong?

Wolfe lunged and clutched her dress at the throat.

"Fuck this!" he growled into her face. "You won't talk if we're nice. Maybe you respond better to pain."

With his other hand, he grabbed hers—the one she'd burnt on the barrel.

She cried out.

"Talk!" he said.

Rom pulled her gun from the waistband behind her back. For a second I wondered what the hell she was doing. Was she going to defend the secretary?

No. Rom leaned across the desk and jammed the barrel between the other woman's eyes.

A flicker of approval played in the corner of Wolfe's mouth.

Rom calmly said, "You talk or I shoot."

The secretary's eyes bulged with terror.

Rom clicked off the safety. "Doesn't matter how much they paid you. You can't spend it dead."

Wolfe retained his grip and I saw the secretary tremble, the defiance melting from her eyes.

"I just answer the phone," she said.

"You've told us that!" Wolfe growled. "Tell us something that won't get you shot."

"I'm not one of them!" There was desperation in her voice. She wasn't one of them. She was just a secretary. However, secretaries know stuff.

"You answer the phone," I said, repeating her words. "What then, Irene?" As I spoke I pulled on Wolfe's arm and he dropped his grip.

The secretary locked eyes with Rom, licked dry lips.

I said, "Lower the gun, Sylvia."

Rom hesitated then took a step back from the desk, but the gun was still raised. Which was fine.

The secretary took a sip of water. I could see she was calculating, wondering if she could get out of this somehow, but there was no escape.

She said, "How do I know you won't shoot me anyway?"

"Because we don't do that," I said, hoping I sounded sincere. "We want them not you. You're just a secretary."

She nodded, took another sip. "All right," she said. "I'll tell you what I know."

# FIFTY-TWO

The secretary told us that she knew the operation was over. She'd been there for five months. The business had been operating for six.

"But this goes back about a year," she said. "They'd been working on it."

I said, "Did you know about the ex-army men?"

"Yes. Three of them. They were the main ones."

"Mr Cohen wasn't one?"

"No. He was head of operations. He coordinated everything. I think he was... I think he was smarter."

Wolfe had the photographs we'd got from Mason's briefcase. He spread them on the secretary's desk.

"Point out the employees," he said.

The secretary split the photographs into two groups: employees and clients.

"The clients were all wealthy," I said.

"Of course! Protection wasn't cheap. Two of our men died. And one client."

I thought about Charlie Mason but decided to wait with my questions on him.

Wolfe asked which were the ex-army men and she pointed to three.

"Who's this one?"

She gave us his Jewish name.

"British name?" Wolfe asked.

"Jack Howells."

Excellent, she was confirming what Mason had noted, which suggested she was telling the truth.

We asked about the other two and she gave us names.

"Jack, John and Zach." I repeated what she'd told us. "Which one is going to shoot the new governor."

"I don't know anything about that."

"I don't believe you!" Wolfe said, but I thought she'd been telling the truth.

I said, "So this isn't about the bank, Irene?"

She shook her head. "It was never mentioned."

"What was mentioned?"

"The finale."

Wolfe said, "What finale? The shooting of the governor?"

She breathed out. "He's one of the clients."

"What's the finale, Irene?" I asked.

"I don't know, honestly I don't know. They never discussed it with me." She looked at me pleadingly, before adding: "My last job was handling the calls. The men all had to confirm they were on their way. I took the calls and let Mr Cohen know."

"And they all confirmed?"

"Yes," she said, blinking, trying to convince me. "That's all I know."

"Tell us about Caleb Maaz," I said.

"You know that. He was an employee briefly. He took the place of one of the others who got himself killed."

"You told us you didn't have addresses, but you did, didn't you?"

She deliberated, then decided to admit it. "Yes."

"You had an address in Jerusalem for Maaz?"

"Yes." She gave us the address we'd visited.

I asked if she knew whether anyone from Shomrim had been there after Maaz disappeared, but she didn't know. But it was likely. Shomrim had his address and had turned it over, maybe looking for the briefcase we'd found.

"Who killed him?" I asked.

She hesitated. "I don't know."

"But you know he was executed?"

"I suspected they had him killed."

"Why?"

She thought for a second. "It was odd. Mr Cohen employed him. He was happy that we had a replacement, but then after the phone call, he was worried. Very worried. He started making calls, talking to the other men."

I said, "Who did he have the call with? Who worried him?"

"The boss. He wasn't happy that Mr Cohen had employed Maaz."

"Who's the boss?" Wolfe asked, leaning in.

She said nothing.

I eased Wolfe back. "Who's the boss, Irene?"

"I don't know. I never met him and he didn't call very often."

"What do you know?"

She breathed out but didn't answer.

I lined up the photographs. "You know who killed Maaz. Which one was it?"

She looked in the direction of the first three—the three deserters. "I can't be certain."

"Which one?"

She tapped the photograph of the one called Zach. "But I can't be certain. I just know Mr Cohen called him after the call with the boss." She paused. "And

Zach was the... the one most likely to do that sort of thing."

I felt my chest tighten and didn't speak for a second.

Wolfe filled the silence. "Who is S-I-R?"

She shook her head. Genuine puzzlement.

"Is he a policeman?"

"Who?" Again the puzzlement in her face.

"The boss."

She breathed out. "I never heard the boss's name. He used to... wait"—she smiled—"S-I-R. You mean *sir*, right? Yes, I heard Cohen call him, sir. I used to say 'sir' out of politeness. Not a name."

I exchanged looks with Wolfe. He shook his head. She didn't know. It didn't mean it wasn't Dave Rosen.

Wolfe said, "Are Shomrim the Killing Crew?"

"I don't know what you mean."

"You know the name?"

"Of course. Anyone who reads the papers has heard of the British soldiers who called themselves the Killing Crew. Mr Cohen wouldn't have employed them!"

"What about the Engineer?"

She shook her head. "Which engineer?"

"Have you heard anyone referred to as the Engineer?"

"No."

I believed her. After finding out Charlie Mason's likely executioner, Wolfe asking questions had given me the break I needed to think properly again.

Forget the bank governor's investiture, she knew nothing about that, but did she know something was happening?

I said, "Your job was to destroy all evidence."

She cleared her throat. "I'm not sure about *evidence*. I was just getting rid of everything."

"Right. You just handle the telephone calls."

She nodded.

"What was the evidence of?"

"I don't know. You called it evidence, not me."

"But you know there will be a finale. You said the word yourself."

She nodded, and her eye movement said she was wondering whether she shouldn't have said it or where I was going with the questions.

"You heard them talking."

Tentatively she said, "Yes."

"What's happening tomorrow?"

She breathed deeply, maybe considering her options. "You're not going to kill me?"

"No," I said, thinking about the private car she drove. "You just answer the telephone."

"I want you to promise."

"We're not going to kill you," I said. "I promise. Just tell us what you know, Irene."

"As you say, I heard them talking—heard Mr Cohen tell them. They all needed to know. It's not tomorrow, it's today. It was brought forward."

My heart thudded. "When today?"

"Before sundown. Seven o'clock."

Wolfe said, "And what happens then?"

"The finale—that's all I heard. That's all they said."

I believed her and asked, "Where's this happening?"

"I don't know."

"All of them together. All the employees?"

"Yes."

I said nothing, thinking. Then I saw Wolfe tense and wondered if he was going to grab the woman again.

Quickly, I said, "Think, Irene. Where might they go?"

I saw a thought cross her mind, but she said, "I don't know."

"Where?" I persisted. "Where might they go?"

"They used a place for practice. They talked about dummy runs. You know, training, practising in case of attack. You know, after one employee was killed…"

"Think, Irene. What was the name of this place?"

"I don't know. It's north of here. Ruins of a farm in Krum er Raml."

I looked at Rom, who nodded. She knew the area.

As I turned my attention back to the secretary, I saw it in her eyes. There was something she wasn't telling us.

"There's another place," I said.

"I don't know. Maybe. It was south. An old British barracks perhaps." She carried on, saying something about a deserted town, but she didn't need to.

"Sarafand!" I said.

She blinked confirmation, but said, "Could be."

I looked at Wolfe. Sarafand was the place all right!

He said, "Is there anywhere else?"

She shook her head. "I don't think so. I don't know anywhere else. This was the office and the rest worked out in the field."

I had no more questions. In the lengthening silence, the secretary looked from me to Rom to Wolfe.

"I've told you everything I know," she said.

I nodded.

She said, "So you'll let me go?"

Rom said, "Which of them planted the car bomb two nights ago?"

The secretary looked at me, but I wasn't asking the question.

"I don't know," she said. "They didn't tell me that. Now, can I go?"

Before I could answer, I heard a click and turned.

Rom was pointing her gun at the secretary, jaw tense.

She fired, and the secretary's head crashed back against the wall. A hole between her eyes.

# FIFTY-THREE

"What the fuckin' hell?" Wolfe exploded as Rom put away her weapon.

"Someone had to do it," she said.

Wolfe held out his hand. "Give me your gun. Now!"

Rom hesitated, gave a slight shrug and then pulled out the gun. Wolfe snatched it from her.

"Never, ever—!" he started, but was so apoplectic with rage he could hardly speak. He took a deep breath. "You never do that again! I decide whether we shoot someone."

I think I was in shock. I'd promised we wouldn't kill Irene and had meant it. I hadn't seen this coming. I was staring at the dead woman. Blood had splattered on the wall from the back of her head. It was running down to the floor.

Finally, I came to my senses.

"We need to go. Someone might have heard."

Wolfe said, "Someone might have seen us come in. This is a fuckin' nightmare."

I grabbed his arm. "Let's go!"

Outside, there were the usual street noises and brickworks' trucks. We drove back to Wolfe's hotel room in tense silence and I noticed two things: the army was out in force, and on every street corner, newspaper sellers announced the resumption of the war. The truce with the Arab nations was officially over.

Less than ten minutes later, inside the hotel bedroom, I could see Wolfe was still angry. Rom could too, but she had calmed down.

"The receptionist was complicit," Rom said, her voice firm, her face set.

"What?" Wolfe growled.

"The secretary knew about the car bomb." Rom nodded to reinforce the statement. "She said they didn't tell her which of them did it. So she knew one of them did."

"She knew what they were up to," I said. "She knew more than she was saying. And we know she knew who killed Mason."

Wolfe was pacing.

Rom said, "So what were you going to do, just let her go? She'd have called her boss or gone to the police."

Wolfe said nothing.

She continued: "Or were you going to tie her up and hope she wouldn't escape? That would have been a big risk."

I'd thought the same, and it seemed that Rom had got there faster than both of us.

Rom continued: "Taking her out of the equation was the only option."

"But not *your* fuckin' decision!" Wolfe snapped.

She shook her head as if telling him he didn't understand. "I did you a favour. Someone had to do it."

The argument went back and forth a few times before I interjected.

"What's done is done. We need to move on."

"Right." Wolfe took a deep breath then told Rom to wait outside.

She shrugged and left the room.

Fifteen minutes later I opened the door and called her back in.

"You're lucky, Carter defended you," Wolfe said. "You're still part of the team."

After she thanked me, I said, "The starting point is to accept that this so-called finale is happening tonight at seven."

"What do you think it is?" she asked.

"Does it matter?" Wolfe said, his tone suggesting he was still annoyed.

"Perhaps. It could just mean the end or something more theatrical."

I said, "It's probably just the end of their operation. Maybe it's when they'll split the proceeds and leave."

Wolfe seemed to be pondering. "Yes, but why a specific time?"

"A deadline to meet?" I suggested.

Wolfe shook his head. "It'll be more, but we won't second guess it sitting here. The plan is this, Rom. You go to the ruin in the north. Carter and I are going to check out Sarafand."

"Are you just getting me out of the way?" she said accusingly.

"No," I said. "The plan is we investigate both locations. We recon the places for Shomrim activity, assess and then meet back here for five pm."

"Why the two of you to Sarafand?"

Wolfe was about to say that he didn't need to justify the plan to her. I knew this because he'd told me, just minutes before. However, I responded before he could speak.

"The Sarafand Garrison is a much bigger area. Plus, being a military base, Wolfe and I will have a better idea about layout and purpose."

She pursed her lips but then accepted my argument.

"Fine," she said, holding out her hand, "but I want my gun back. You saw the notices. The war is back on and I might need to defend myself."

Their eyes were locked in defiance as Wolfe slapped the gun into her palm.

"Don't use it," he said. "Not unless you have to."

She said, "What did you decide about Sub-Inspector Rosen? How do we handle him?"

We didn't answer immediately. Wolfe and I had argued about him too. I wanted to confront him sooner rather than later, Wolfe said we should wait. I'd said that Rosen was the root problem and Shomrim might be a symptom or a distraction.

"We don't know that," he had said to me. "You're just letting emotion get in the way. Like Rom did at the Shomrim office."

But she had controlled her emotion. I liked that about her. Yes, she'd killed the secretary without approval, but it hadn't been out of rage.

So, Wolfe explained that we'd deal with Rosen after we'd dealt with Shomrim. He was the boss and I accepted his decision, however frustrating.

"And the reporter?" she asked.

"We tell Levi when we're ready," I said.

# FIFTY-FOUR

We took the Land Rover and left Rom with the big Bentley.

As we drove through Jaffa, I said, "You don't think it's at the ruins in the north."

"Do you?"

"Not a chance. We might have guessed at Sarafand since Mason's body was found in the orange groves about halfway between their office and the garrison."

He nodded.

I said, "Sending Rom north was getting her out of the way."

"She's a liability, Ash."

We went through the orange groves and passed where Mason had died. I pointed it out to Wolfe and he just nodded. I couldn't help looking and imagining I was in his situation, held captive, probably aware that they intended to execute me. Something similar had happened in Cyprus. That had been a warning.

Had Mason thought it would be a warning? Would there have been an opportunity for him to escape? I doubted it.

We drove on and into the desert. The road was straight, the land flat, except for a slight rise to the west and the mountains to the east. It was a dusty plain good for very little, ideal as an army base.

And then about a mile further we saw the grey, corrugated roofs of Sarafand Garrison. The sun was low and Wolfe drove as fast as he could without creating a plume of dust. In such an open space, a dust cloud would give away our approach.

I spent the last ten minutes of our journey describing the layout.

"They'll have a sentry," he said. "If they're there."

"Probably."

We crossed the rail line where I'd seen the old Arab on my previous visit. I pointed right to where the base's entrance lay beyond the palm trees.

Wolfe continued past.

At the end, the perimeter fence curved west and Wolfe stopped at the cluster of houses. It took us a few minutes going from house to house before we found the old Arab. He wasn't alone as I'd previously assumed. A large family was eating at a long table.

They eyed us nervously as we entered and I wondered if it was because of the situation or the fact that the table and chairs looked army. A quick glance told me there was a lot of ex-army stuff here. A cooking stove in the room beyond looked like a typical barracks hut stove.

"Excuse us," I said, bowing.

The man said something to the others before walking over to us.

"We are a simple people," he said. "No trouble, please."

Wolfe said, "Have you seen anyone at the army base?"

The Arab looked at me. "Yes. The army," like it explained everything.

Wolfe grunted. "Anyone else?"

Still looking at me, the old man said, "They are back."

I guessed what he meant. "The soldiers you saw before. The ones practising. They're back?"

"Yes. Five cars came."

"Where are they?" Wolfe asked. "Where are these men?"

"The OC."

Wolfe looked at me. I wasn't sure where the officers' club was, but before I said anything, the Arab called out and a young boy no older than ten ran to his side.

He spoke urgently to the boy and then said, "Ahmed will show you."

"Secret," I said.

The Arab grinned. "But of course."

The boy scooted away and we followed.

He led us to a broken section of the perimeter fence. I figured this was how they got in and out. Easy access for their scavenging trips.

Wolfe grabbed the kid as he clambered through the gap and raised a finger to his lips. The universal sign for 'quiet'.

The boy grinned and nodded.

There was fifty yards of barren land and then the first huts. We kept low and ran.

One good thing about this cantonment was the height of the buildings. Nothing was two-storey. There was no watchtower. The guard post at the main gate was no longer standing. Even the headquarters, infirmary and church were on one level.

Which meant that, so long as we kept low and away from open spaces, we would be fine.

Providing we didn't run into or past the Shomrim men.

269

We moved slowly and cautiously, checking as we went. The first huts we came to were regimented lines of barrack sheds. On the far side was the parade ground. To the right were playing fields, to the left was the road leading to the main entrance and headquarters.

Ahmed pointed across the playing fields. Far right, I could see officers' housing, and I figured he was telling us where the OC was.

I pointed the other way with a circling motion and the kid nodded his understanding.

We went around and picked up a road that went up to the main gate. We passed a garage and workshops before the road split. Ahead was the main gate and guard huts. There was no one in sight and still no evidence of the men we were looking for. Left went to where I'd found the Signals office and right went past the HQ. We went behind the HQ, keeping close to the wall. I noticed again that the place looked wrecked. Now I wondered whether some of these buildings had been used for military exercises.

Ahmed kept going and trees along the road gave us additional shelter.

We passed more buildings, including the magazine, which was nothing but a shell now. Then came the single officers' quarters, and after the fourth block, Ahmed stopped. Ahead, we could see faint light spilling from what I now recognized as an officers' club.

I nodded 'thanks' to the boy and Wolfe pulled a coin from his pocket and placed it in Ahmed's palm. He grinned and scurried back the way we'd come.

Keeping a distance of over forty paces, we circled the building. On the far side, we found five Shomrim vehicles. Five cars, five men?

Wolfe signalled that we should go into an adjacent building. It was the comms office and one of the few with a flat roof.

We went through and up onto the roof.

From there we had a good view of the OC. Lying on our fronts, Wolfe took out his binoculars and trained them on the building opposite.

I kept a lookout, watching the road and other buildings in case one or more of them were elsewhere.

Wolfe whispered that he could see men drinking. There appeared to be a celebration. Then he told me the names of the men he saw: the three deserters and Cohen, the head of operations. But there were others too. Five cars but not five men.

"There's more of them," Wolfe said. "There's fuckin' loads of them."

# FIFTY-FIVE

Rom took the main road north and then jinked right and left onto the next main road through the farmlands of Krum er Raml. It ended at sand dunes and she realized she'd not taken the easiest route. She had to loop back around to the east before picking up a track that ran along the urban boundary.

The odds of the Shomrim men being out here were as remote as the ruins she was looking for. Wolfe wanted her out of the way, she was sure. She had seen it in their faces. Wolfe and Carter thought Sarafand was where they were preparing for the finale.

However, she wanted to prove her worth. She could follow orders and so she wouldn't complain. Although they damn well better include her later. If they didn't show at 5 pm, she'd jolly well go to Sarafand anyway.

She found the track to the ruins and only went a hundred yards before she stopped and gave up. The Bentley wouldn't make it much further, and even if it did, she ran the risk of irreparable damage.

So she started walking the remaining two hundred yards to the farm at the end of the track.

There were lots of tyre tracks, but no sign of another vehicle or person. This was not the place.

★

Rom drove back into town and purchased cleaning materials, an Israeli flag and a bottle of lemonade. Then she drove to a garage and got a canister of fuel. She tipped out the soft drink and decanted petrol into the empty bottle before heading to Shomrim's office.

The street was busier than before, with more trucks coming from the brickworks. The chimneys poured out smoke and she could hear the clatter of machinery beyond the brickworks' walls.

The office looked the same as they'd left it. No sign of disturbance. No police. However, she drove past and parked out of sight on the next street, just in case.

When the coast was clear, Rom dashed from the Bentley around the corner and into the office.

The secretary was slumped forward, her bloodied head resting on the table like she was asleep. Wasting no time, Rom pushed the secretary back, tilted the chair and dragged it out of the reception area. She went through the door, down the hall and out into the yard.

Without ceremony, she tipped the body into the pile of smouldering paper. Returning the chair, she then set about washing and scrubbing the blood from the wall and desk. It wasn't perfect, not by any stretch of the imagination, but at a glance, no one would immediately suspect what had happened.

However, when she pinned up the Israeli flag, all sign of the discolouration was hidden.

Once she was satisfied, Rom returned to the yard. She added the cleaning cloths to the pile and poured the petrol over the secretary's head. She set light to it, waited to make sure it was burning well, and then left the building quickly.

From the smoke, it was clear to her that a fatty object was burning in the yard, but she hoped it might look like an accident. If the police first thought there had been an accident, it would buy them time. If they needed it.

Hopefully, Wolfe would see that she could use her initiative and help their cause. Providing he came back to collect her.

She reached the Scopus Hotel with twenty minutes to spare and wasn't surprised that there was no sign of Wolfe's jeep.

With the intention of cleaning up before Wolfe and Carter came back, she opened the bedroom door.

And stopped dead.

A man was sitting cross-legged on the chair.

# FIFTY-SIX

I was sent to get Rom, and Wolfe stayed on the roof watching the officers' club.

I suspected he had planned to do this without her, but we'd counted at least eight of them, and two against eight didn't sound too good. Plus we had no idea how heavily armed they were.

Apart from telling me to fetch Rom, Wolfe also told me about his weapons stash. He said he had Stens and boxes of ammunition hidden in a goat herder's shack outside Tel Aviv.

If I could have driven straight out, I would have saved twenty minutes, but I had to retrace my steps around the base to the hole in the fence and the cluster of Arab houses. Despite seeing the men inside the OC, I was still cautious. We'd expected five men and seen eight. Could there be more out patrolling?

I saw no one but still drove carefully alongside the fence, over the rail track and a straight line through the plains towards Jaffa. Just like Wolfe had on the approach, I kept my speed down and the dust cloud to a minimum.

Wolfe's description of where I'd find the goat herder's hut wasn't great. "Between two olive trees," he'd said. There were hundreds of olive trees! I drove around for fifteen minutes before locating the place he'd described. The two trees provided the only shade for half a square mile. I'd been in the wrong area.

The hut looked like a portable toilet and smelt almost as bad. There was a false floor. Wolfe had dug a hole, boarded over it and then stamped earth down on top.

I scraped away dirt and got my nails under a board, still unsure whether I had the right place. There was a space underneath. I pulled up another hoping to reveal the stash.

Empty. The space was empty. The weapons had gone.

As I drove into Tel Aviv my head was spinning. Where were the guns? Who had found them? Was there a chance that Rom had collected them?

No. Wolfe hadn't planned to involve her. He hadn't told me before, so he wouldn't have told someone he barely trusted.

They'd been found by someone else and we now only had three handguns between us to defeat eight men who could be heavily armed.

I'd need to improvise.

Molotov cocktails were the homemade bomb used widely by terrorists here against the British. The first thing we'd do, when I picked up Rom, was to buy bottles, petrol and rags. We would make the bombs when we got back to Sarafand.

The streets were even busier than earlier. In addition to the taxis, buses and military vehicles, I passed a small dark blue car and saw an old beat-up, pale Soviet car in my rear-view mirror. I took a few random turns in case I was being followed. I wasn't. By the time I reached the Scopus Hotel, I'd forgotten about the old car.

Rom wasn't outside. Nor was she waiting in the room.

I checked my watch. Hunting for the missing weapons had made me late by ten minutes. Surely she'd have waited.

Or perhaps she wasn't back yet. Could she have found something at the property to the north? I thought it unlikely.

Then I noticed a map on the little vanity table. No not a complete map. A section had been torn out. It showed the coast south of Jaffa for about twenty miles. There was an X beside a place called Palmachim. Handwritten was the word 'Shuldik'.

I was just considering whether this was a message from Rom—telling us she'd gone somewhere else—when there was a knock on the door.

"Nazeem!" I said as I swung the door open.

Wolfe's Arab informant grinned at me from the hallway.

"What…?"

"I thought you might need help," he said. "I don't like unfinished business."

I shook his hand with relief, but rather than welcome him into the room, I pointed outside.

"We need to hurry," I said. "Something is going down at Sarafand Garrison at seven."

"What's happening?"

"I'll explain as I drive."

I stopped on the street. There, behind the Land Rover, was an old beaten-up Soviet car. A Kim-10. The car I'd spotted earlier.

I pointed to it. "Shall we take both?"

"No, it's rubbish. Drives like a bag of nails," he said as he swung into the passenger seat of the Land Rover. As I got in I noticed a scruffy brown holdall in the rear.

It was lying next to the field telephone we'd picked up from Mason's apartment in Jerusalem.

"A little extra." He grinned at my expression and reached for the bag. "In case we need it."

He opened it up and I saw Stens and boxes of ammunition.

"Wolfe's stash," he said, still chuckling. "We got them off a bunch of Slovaks."

This took the pressure off the timing. We didn't need Molotov cocktails after all.

I could have told him about my relief that it'd been him who'd recovered them, but I'd save that for later. Instead, I told him about us going to the Shomrim office and confronting the secretary. She'd been destroying evidence because the business was over.

"But the deadline isn't tomorrow as Mason thought. It's seven tonight. We found the Shomrim men at Sarafand. No idea what they're doing, but this is clearly coming to a head."

"How many of them?"

"At least eight."

"And Wolfe's there?"

"Waiting for us."

"What about the girl—Rom?"

"Gone off on some wild goose chase it seems," I said. I might have worried, but I was in a good mood.

I may not have Rom with me, but I had Nazeem and we had guns.

However, on the far side of Jaffa town, I spotted a checkpoint. No way could we explain a bag of weapons, so we'd have to find another way.

The detour would add another half an hour to our journey.

# FIFTY-SEVEN

Wolfe had been watching for an hour, wondering what the Shomrim guys were up to, when one of them came outside carrying a bag over one shoulder.

He was one of the deserters, John, and Wolfe noted a slight limp as he favoured his right leg.

John turned left, walked around the side of the building and stopped at a post in the ground. Wolfe hadn't noticed it until now. It looked like a stumpy flagpole.

Seconds later, Cohen appeared with another, fatter man. And Wolfe realized this changed everything. He'd got it wrong. They weren't all Shomrim men. From his limited view through the OC windows he'd sensed the interactions weren't normal.

At first, he'd thought it was just a gathering, a celebration. He decided the finale was a kind of party. However, some of the men were subdued and, on one occasion, argumentative.

Wolfe hadn't seen clearly, but five minutes ago he there had been a scuffle.

Now he could see the man with Cohen was a prisoner.

The man sat on the dirt and they lashed him to the pole. The low sun created weird elongated shadows: two stretched men, a pole and a lump at its base.

John, the deserter, pulled something from his bag and held it to his face: a cine camera!

Cohen talked and John filmed Fatty tied to the pole. Was this some kind of interrogation?

Because they'd gone to the side of the building, Wolfe strained to hear and only caught the odd word.

He decided to get closer. On the ground floor, he wouldn't get such a good view of the proceedings, but he would hear more.

Wolfe slipped from the roof and into an adjacent building. A broken window meant he could listen within thirty yards.

He immediately knew this was not a straightforward interrogation. Cohen was trying to get Fatty to confess to a crime, it seemed. The fat prisoner said nothing at first and then Wolfe heard him talking as though trying to explain. His voice came across as calmer than Wolfe would have predicted.

"You don't understand!" Fatty repeated.

John moved, trying different angles with the cine camera, as though he thought he was a real film cameraman. Or maybe the shadows were a problem.

Cohen's voice got louder.

"I want a confession!"

Fatty shook his head.

Cohen lashed out, slapping the prisoner's face, and the cameraman moved in for a close-up.

"Now, talk!" Cohen barked. "Tell the camera what you did."

Fatty shook his head, even more defiant than before Cohen had struck him.

Cohen growled into Fatty's ear. "Last chance."

From his waistband, he whipped out a gun and jammed it between the prisoner's eyes. He glanced at the officers' club as though checking that the others were at the windows, watching. They were.

"One last chance. Start talking by the time I get to zero or never talk again. Three."

"No."

"Two."

Fatty turned his head away. "You won't get away with this."

"Neither will you. One."

John stopped filming.

Cohen took half a step back, the gun still aimed at the prisoner's head.

Fatty started to struggle, twisting against the pole.

Whether or not Cohen actually said "Zero" Wolfe didn't hear, because the gunshot rang out a split second later.

It wasn't a small calibre pistol, because Wolfe saw a big hole blasted in the back of Fatty's head.

Cohen looked over at the others, again making sure they'd been watching. Then he had a quick word with John, who then cut Fatty free of the pole. Between them, they lifted it and threw the body aside.

Cohen waved to the men inside, and a minute later a second prisoner was brought out by a different employee. Wolfe didn't recognize this man. Not Zach or Jack, so not one of the deserters, just a later addition to the team if the secretary had been telling the truth.

Five cars, five Shomrim employees and four prisoners, Wolfe realized, as he counted heads and the second man was tied to the pole.

The new captive kept staring at the body on the ground.

Fatty had been stoic and unyielding. This second man was quaking before he was even bound up. However, Fatty might have thought they were bluffing. This second prisoner had no illusions of that.

He started speaking too soon. John wasn't ready with the camera and limped into position.

Cohen made the prisoner start again and the man spoke fast but quietly. Wolfe could tell they were getting the confession they wanted but couldn't hear any detail.

It looked like this prisoner still wondered whether he'd be executed, but that would be foolish. The Shomrim men needed their prisoners to talk, and that meant giving them hope.

So Wolfe wasn't surprised when the second prisoner was untied and returned to the officers' club building.

The third man needed more persuasion, with a slap and a threat of the gun, but he eventually talked too.

Wolfe was watching the fourth man being tied up when he heard a noise over the random night sounds. A scuffle, like footsteps.

Carter finally back?

He turned to signal where he was standing but he never completed the move. As if from nowhere, a heavy object slammed into his head and darkness rushed in.

# FIFTY-EIGHT

As before, I approached Sarafand slowly so that any dust was limited. The jeep bumped over the rail and we were at the junction. Straight on to the Arab village and the way through the fence. Right to the main gate.

I went right.

Nazeem put a Sten gun on his lap, ready, as I went through the gates.

On the way, I'd told him the layout, so he knew the officers' club was beyond the headquarters to our left. We'd also discussed a plan.

I rolled forward and parked at the garage, out of sight.

My watch said it was forty minutes to go before the 7 pm deadline. The finale. Whatever that was.

Nazeem handed me a Sten and we each took two spare magazines. Almost one hundred rounds each. Overkill? I hoped so.

We split up. The plan was to enter the building at the same time, Nazeem from the west—the near side— me from the east.

I had further to go, so jogged off, back towards the main gate and then cut right. I used the palm trees that lined the road as shelter, then there were buildings beyond that I slunk behind.

When I was in position, I blew into my hands, making the hoot of an owl. I couldn't imitate an Israeli owl but hoped it was close enough.

After a pause, I heard one hoot back. Wolfe knew the signal. Was that Wolfe or Nazeem? Maybe Nazeem had been delayed.

One short hoot followed by a longer one meant *go*. I gave the single owl hoot again instead, in case one of them hadn't heard me.

At the same moment that I heard a single reply again, I spotted a hump on the ground beyond the target building.

There was a body and what looked like half a flagpole with ropes on the floor.

Had they tied up and executed a prisoner?

My God, was it Wolfe?

The area around the body was exposed. I didn't dare approach from my side, so I retraced my steps and went to the west side. Nazeem must have seen me through the trees because he gave a low whistle.

"What's up?" he asked, as I found him behind a building.

"There's a body in the open."

"Wolfe?"

I pointed to the comms office where Wolfe and I had been on the roof. Was he still there?

We slipped in and went up. No sign of Wolfe downstairs or on the roof. However, up there, I could see the body on the ground better.

It was wearing a bloodied white shirt. Wolfe, like me, had been wearing black.

I said, "It's not Wolfe."

Nazeem breathed out. Then: "So where is he?"

"Worst case, they've got him." I couldn't imagine another scenario, but thankfully Nazeem didn't question me.

As we descended he said, "The new plan?"

"We assume they've got him. Maybe they've got other prisoners. We go in hard and fast, but we're careful."

"Of course."

"I'll hoot again as soon as I'm in position. This time we just go."

He nodded and I left him outside the comms office.

I ran faster this time and maybe that was my mistake. Because someone saw me.

"Hey, you!" It was an uncertain challenge, as though he might know who it was and yet not.

I froze behind a tree about three-quarters of the way.

"Show yourself!" he said, sounding more confident.

I peered around the tree and he was looking right at me. The British Army deserter called Zach. The one who had killed Charlie Mason—probably, according to the Shomrim secretary.

He had a gun pointing at me.

"Who are you?"

"Captain Carter, SIB."

"Ah! The military police scum sent to get us."

"Don't shoot," I said, "I'm here to talk."

"What do you want to talk about?"

"We're really after a spy called Charles Mason. You may have known him as Caleb Maaz."

Zach grinned. A genuine smile. "I knew him."

"I heard someone killed him in the Jaffa orange groves. Was that you?"

He grinned again. "Yeah, that was me."

"Good," I said, stepping out from the tree. For a second he looked surprised by my response. He should have pulled his trigger, but his mind was trying to process what I'd said rather than what I was doing. And he didn't register my gun until much too late.

A short burst from the Sten spun him around and down.

Probably not my smartest move ever, but Nazeem knew how to react. No need for an owl hoot now. When the shooting starts, all plans are off.

He started firing at the building.

I heard shouts from inside and saw shadows flit across windows, towards Nazeem's shots. But I wasn't waiting to see what happened next. I sprinted to the far wall and pressed against the wooden planks so close that I could smell old creosote.

I was between a door and window. A quick glance—out and back—through the window told me no one was near. No one I could see anyway.

One kick smashed open the door and I was inside and diving for one of the upturned tables.

Nazeem was still drawing fire on the other side, but at the end of the room, I saw movement. A man darted across the doorway, finding shelter behind a pillar.

We both waited, both assessing where the other man was.

I moved, scrambling to the next table, working my way around. His pillar would only be an effective shield if I was by the door I'd come through.

I moved again and he must have guessed my intention because three rapid shots pinged off wood close by. However, I kept going. One more table, then I sprawled and strafed the space on the other side of the pillar.

But he wasn't there.

I hadn't recognized the first one but I did know the next man who came into the room. Another deserter.

Jack. And he had a machine gun. He was also smarter because he found a barricade of tables like I had.

He fired a burst and moved. A burst and moved.

I grabbed tables as I went, pulling them over, pushing them together, trying to create a better defence.

He fired, I fired. He fired, I fired. Wood splintered around me and I flattened as a string of holes appeared in the table beside me.

I moved position, firing all the time until my magazine emptied.

As I inserted a new one, Jack used the pause to find a better position. I heard an order barked out and saw movement by the far door.

I thought it might be a ploy to draw fire, but it appeared to be a switch of men. Maybe the first man had been hit. Whatever, he scurried out and then there were two of them again. Jack with a Sten and someone else firing single shots.

I couldn't hear Nazeem's Sten anymore. I had two men here. Had he been fighting five or six? Was he down? Just as I began to fear the worst, the distant firefight started again.

"Who are you?" the new man in the room called to me, and I recognized his voice: Cohen, the head of operations. Probably the one in charge here.

"Where's my colleague?" I shouted back.

"Who's he?"

"Bill Wolfe."

"Never heard of him!" Of course, we'd met in the Shomrim office but hadn't given any genuine names. Maybe Cohen didn't know Wolfe's name, although I thought it unlikely.

They fired again and I realized they'd worked together, moving either side of my position.

I crawled and saw Jack now on my left, exposed.

My gunfire blasted into him and he sprawled away. I saw his Sten slide across the floor into the open.

After my burst, I realized Nazeem's firefight had also paused again.

"Give up," I shouted to Cohen.

He countered: "You're outnumbered."

"You're outgunned, Cohen."

I saw a hand in a gap between the tables and realized he'd somehow thrown his voice. He was crawling towards the available machine gun. Aiming at the fallen weapon, I sent it spinning far out of his reach.

A bullet clattered close to my head. I scrambled away and aimed at where I expected him, but nothing came.

I fired again and the Sten jammed.

"Doesn't sound good!" Cohen said.

"Can we talk?"

"Who are you?"

"Captain Carter, SIB."

"Ah!"

I said, "Who is SIR? Who is the Engineer?"

He laughed. "You'll find out soon enough."

The 7 pm deadline.

"What's the finale?"

"We're going to tell the world."

"Tell them what?"

"Throw your Sten out. Let me see it."

I tossed the machine gun aside.

"Stand up."

"Don't shoot!" I said. "Lower your gun. Talk. Tell me what's going on."

I could just see him through a crack between overturned tables. His gun hand dropped.

I raised my right hand, kept my left low, and started to rise.

I could see his face and read his intention. But it was like slow motion.

His gun hand started to come up.

"Stop!" I barked, and he hesitated, the foot soldier instinct in him perhaps. "Before you shoot me. Tell me about the original bank raid. Tell me what you found."

It was a wild punt on my part. His gun had been rising again but he hesitated. And I shot him in the head with the Beretta in my left hand.

# FIFTY-NINE

I heard running and shooting. It had been going on while I talked to Cohen, but I'd tuned it out. There was a long burst of gunfire followed by the eerie silence there always is after a loud gunfight.

Nazeem shouted, "Carter?"

"Here," I called. "I've got three."

"I got two. I think there were only five." He paused. "And I checked. The body outside isn't Wolfe."

"Search the building," I shouted back. "But watch out, the others may be hiding."

I opened four doors before I found a small room. Inside, men lay shackled on the floor. Three terrified chained prisoners.

"Found three more," I shouted. "Wolfe's not here!"

I could have tried to set them free but my priority was to find Wolfe.

Nazeem was coming towards me.

"He's not here. Any luck?"

"There's a cellar. I'll check down there."

I watched him run back the way he'd come. I followed, went through a kitchen and saw an open hatch in the room beyond.

A ladder went down to a cellar. The space looked huge, maybe as big as the ground floor.

I could hear Nazeem down there making scuffing sounds, moving objects. Then running feet.

"Nazeem?"

"Bomb!" Nazeem shouted. "There's a bloody big bomb down here."

I was descending the ladder.

"And the timer's running out!" he screamed at me. "Get out!"

I was up through the hatch and running for the exit. After twenty paces outside, I stopped and turned.

"Keep going!" Nazeem shouted.

He was in the doorway. One second he was there and the next he was flying, his arms and legs flailing in the air.

Behind him, the building blasted into fragments. I remember shards of flying wood and flames—bright orange and white and then black.

My whole body shook. I was trembling, lying flat in the dirt. I could smell burning, a choking stench, a chemical mixture of rubber and fertilizer.

I opened my eyes and forced myself onto my hands and knees. My ears rang and my body felt pummelled, but I had no injuries.

Nazeem, on the other hand, lay in the dirt fifty feet away, a torn and bloody mess. I crawled to him and knew he was dead. His body was wrecked, chunks missing, blood still leaking out turning the ground rust-brown.

Behind him, the officers' club was a pile of burning rubble. It looked like an ugly imitation of the setting sun. One was soft gold with streaks of orange. The other had jagged edges and black acrid smoke.

No way anyone inside had survived that blast.

Seven pm. The deadline had been a bomb.

Had they intended to blow themselves up?

I got to my feet.

I saw movement in the corner of my eye to my right. A man lit by the glow stood in a doorway.

# SIXTY

I was swinging my weapon up and towards the man in the doorway when I realized who it was.

Bill Wolfe.

His hands were tied and he shook his head groggily.

"Did you do that?" he asked, nodding towards the remains of the officers' club.

I cut his bindings. "Are you all right, Bill?"

"Fine. Fuckin' headache, but apart from that I'm fine." He flexed aching wrists then felt the back of his head. "So did you blow this place up?"

"Not me."

"Are they all dead?"

We were now walking towards the burning building. I had my gun ready, but no one could have survived that blast and I'd seen no one escape.

Then I wondered.

"You were knocked out? Who hit you?"

We stopped thirty yards out and stared at the flames. He told me that he'd watched a 'display' and then heard something in the room. That was the last thing he remembered.

"Before any shooting started? Before we arrived?"

"Shooting? There was an execution. I saw that."

What he'd called a display had been the Shomrim men

filming the others. He told me that they'd brought out the first one, tied him to a pole and interrogated him with a cine camera.

"Then they fuckin' executed him!" Wolfe said.

So that was the body at the back by the pole.

"What happened to the others?"

"I think they were trying to get confessions. The first execution was a message to the rest. They all cooperated. At least, I was watching the fourth one when I was whacked."

Was it one of the Shomrim guys who had found Wolfe? If not, then who was it? Why leave him tied up in the comms office rather than take him to the other prisoners?

I was still trying to make sense of it when Wolfe asked where Rom was.

"I don't know."

"But you said *before we arrived*." He looked around. "Who else is here?"

I took a breath. "Nazeem."

"Nazeem?" Wolfe grinned. "I knew the bugger wouldn't let me down!"

I was looking at him and he started frowning.

"He's dead, Bill."

"Oh! Bugger."

So I told him how I hadn't found Rom in Tel Aviv, but that Nazeem had joined me. We'd assumed Shomrim had captured Wolfe and we attacked.

"He's over there somewhere," I said, pointing to the far side.

"Definitely dead?"

I pursed my lips as I remembered the mess of Nazeem's head. "I'm afraid so."

"Fuck." He started walking. "Show me."

After we found him, Wolfe said, "Call Levi."

"Right." We'd promised to involve the reporter, and although he'd missed the action, the story was here.

"I don't suppose the comms telephone works?"

He shook his head. "There are telegraph poles running along the train line. Still got the field telephone?" It was in the back of the Land Rover. When I nodded, he continued: "You make the call and I'll look after my friend."

"What about the police?" I said, not really thinking it through. We still thought Dave Rosen was involved, possibly as the Engineer. "No," I said before Wolfe responded.

"We can't trust anyone, especially not Rosen," he said nodding. "I would have expected the Engineer to be here, but no one else arrived."

Except for maybe the unknown assailant, I thought as I jogged away. Could that have been the Engineer rather than one of the Shomrim men?

I jumped in the Land Rover and tore out through the garrison's main gate. As I turned right towards the rail crossing, I saw another car to my left. Small and black, I thought. Hard to tell because of the dust cloud behind its racing tyres.

It took three attempts, throwing the cable over the telegraph line, but I managed and got through to an operator. From there I was put through to the *Palestine Post*.

"Saul Levi," I said.

"Who is this?" the newspaper operator asked.

When I told her she said, "Ah, he said someone might call. Let me put you through."

Seconds later a man came on the line. "I'm afraid Paul's gone."

"Sorry, who's Paul?" I asked.

"Sir. Paul Sir."

My heart stopped. "You're saying his name is Sir?"

"Yes."

"I thought his name was Levi."

"That was his pen name. You know, after that terrible incident... the murder of Thomas Flynn..."

My God! Levi was Sir. Levi was the man identified by Mason as being involved. Which probably meant that Levi was the Engineer.

"Hello?" the voice on the line said. "Are you still there, Captain Carter?"

"Yes," I said quietly.

"He said you might telephone. He said to tell you he was going to that little place in the south... where was that note?"

"Palmachim?"

"Yes, that's the one!"

"He said he was going there with a secretary... a girl called Rom."

I dropped the handset and leapt into the jeep. My wheels spun as I U-turned at pace then accelerated south, parallel with the rail track.

Palmachim had been marked on the map left at Wolfe's hotel. Levi had Rom. Thank goodness she'd had the chance to leave it for me.

Now I pictured the map in my mind. The location was about halfway between Tel Aviv and Ashkelon, the next large town on the coast. I didn't know the place but it gave me a rough idea of where I'd find Palmachim: approximately two miles south and then at least a mile west.

I thundered back down the road, past the main gate, past the rail terminus and then left skirting the garrison. Because of the flat landscape, I could see something in the distance ahead. A black lump on the road. Only it wasn't a black lump, it was a dark blue car. A small car.

There was a man at the wheel, just sitting, staring ahead. I braked hard when I saw who it was.

Snaggletooth.

"You!" I said. "What's going on?"

Still sitting, he looked at me nervously, as though expecting me to hit him.

"What the hell's going on?" I asked again.

"He told me to…"

"Levi?"

"Yes. He told me to make sure you went to Palmachim… to a farm called Shuldik. He wanted me to take you." He gave a juddering breath and shook his head. "I'm afraid. I can't do it."

"No need," I said, jumping back into the Land Rover. "I'm going."

My wheels spun on loose stones and I left the taxi driver cum reporter's investigator in my dust.

I'd wasted time talking to Snaggletooth, and when I hit the coast road going south, I knew I was driving like a madman. If there was a checkpoint out here, any IDF units, they'd probably shoot first and ask questions later.

But by the time I came to a track, I'd seen no one. The land had changed. Sarafand had been in the desert. Now I was surrounded by vegetation. However, the road to the coast was a rutted track. No, the map in my head told me it was too soon for Palmachim.

Another half mile and there was a signpost. The correct road.

I bounced and swerved and prayed that this would take me to Shuldik. I prayed that I wasn't too late to save Sylvia.

# SIXTY-ONE

Two hours earlier, Sylvia Rom had been in the Bentley with Levi driving.

There was something off about him. Twitchy. When they'd met him earlier he'd been confident and a little cocky. Now he was uncomfortable.

"What's wrong?" she asked.

He breathed out. "Time pressure."

"Where are we going?"

"I told you—to meet up with Wolfe and Carter."

She nodded. It was what he'd said in the hotel room and it made sense. They hadn't turned up and Levi had come instead.

"So it's over?" she said. "They've found Shomrim?"

"Yes," he said, but she still sensed something was off.

"You have information you aren't saying," she said firmly. "Tell me."

"All right." He passed her a flask of water and she took a sip. "What do you know?"

"That it looks like three of the Shomrim men are the Killing Crew. And there's something to do with the bank's new governor happening tonight. A finale, they're calling it."

"And how did you discover all this?"

"It's what we pieced together and information from another investigator." She told him about Charlie Mason. "His notes helped put it together. And we think we've got the Engineer."

He looked at her sharply. "Oh, and who's that?"

No way was she telling the reporter anything without Wolfe's approval. She shook her head.

He drove for a moment and the only sound was the Bentley's tyres on hard road.

Eventually, he said, "The key to this, and always is in my world, is the source of information."

She took another sip of water. "Why do you say that?"

"Think about it: the source of information that the Killing Crew existed and killed Jews."

"That you printed."

"Correct. You see, I know more of the story."

He asked if she wanted to hear it, and of course, she did. She wanted to learn if there were any discrepancies between what they and Levi knew.

He said that it had all started with the raid on the Anglo-Palestine Bank. Three soldiers had done it and the source claimed it had been the Irgun.

"I knew it wasn't," she said, and then regretted the interruption.

However, Levi carried on. He said that they hadn't got away with over a hundred thousand pounds, it had been much less. But they had taken a safe.

"You'll remember the safecracker who escaped from prison?"

She just nodded this time rather than break his flow.

"They got him out and he opened the safe. There was money inside, but it wasn't the cash that was interesting, it was the paperwork. There was something damning in there. It implicated a number of senior men in a crime."

"What crime?"

"I'll come to that."

He seemed calmer now, as though talking made him less nervous. He mentioned their leader, and Rom immediately thought "the Engineer"—SIR.

Levi said that the leader came up with a plan. They would punish the men named in the documents by making them pay. He had come up with the idea of the Killing Crew. It would be used to cover their tracks as well as blame rogue Irgun members for the raid. There were bank guards who had known the truth, and after being lulled into a sense of security by payments, they were killed. Not by snipers, but by the soldiers. They also killed one of the men listed in the documents to make sure they were taken seriously by the other four.

Rom thought about the photograph of the governor flanked by three guards. Had they all been killed?

Levi said, "Shomrim Security was a way of protecting their assets and being paid legitimately."

Rom could hold back no longer. "So the Engineer was your source! That's what you meant by the source of information being the key."

Levi said nothing, just focused on the bumpy road.

Rom took another sip of the water and closed her eyes in a long slow blink. If only she had some coffee. Suddenly she was feeling so tired. Her eyes heavy.

She turned to Levi.

He was looking at her with a curious expression. Then his face blurred.

"What?" she said, realizing he'd been talking.

"You're tired," he said. "Close your eyes, Sylvia."

She complied and felt warmth calm her breathing as she relaxed.

Levi was saying something else. What was it? Sorry? Why was he saying sorry?

"Sorry," he said again. "I have to do this for my wife and child."

# SIXTY-TWO

The road for Palmachim took me directly west. The sun was no longer on the horizon, which was now bruised crimson fading to pink. The map in my head said it was about a mile and a half.

However, after a mile, I saw a burning torch beside the road. It illuminated a handmade sign that read: Shuldik. I turned right along a stony track. More torches lit the way ahead, although it wasn't fully dark yet. There was probably another fifteen minutes of twilight before that.

The track turned west and I saw buildings ahead. There were torches around a courtyard, a house at the end of a cobblestone square, outbuildings left and right.

The Bentley was parked by a low stone building on the left. I approached with my heart pushing up into my throat.

Sylvia Rom wasn't inside the car.

She'd left the map in the hotel for me. She'd driven here with the reporter.

I stood on the jeep's seat, looked around and called, "Sylvia?"

I could smell the sea and chalk. I could hear a gull crying into the wind.

"Sylvia!"

"Don't move!" A man's voice boomed out across the courtyard.

I looked around and it took a second to spot the man in the loft gable of the house. There was a pulley above the space and I figured this was for hauling stuff up there. Maybe like a hayloft.

I peered at him. It was darker up there, but I could see it was Paul Sir, the reporter I'd known as Levi. He had his hands up, leaning on the frame, posed, like he was the lord of all he surveyed.

I jumped out of the jeep.

"Don't move, Carter!"

I stopped moving towards him.

"Why?"

"Because of the tripwires. I've rigged this, so keep your distance."

I raised my hands, indicating that I'd accept his word.

"Where's Sylvia Rom?"

"That's not the important question, Carter. Come on, you can do better than that!"

"You're the Engineer."

"Well, that's not a question, is it? And even if it were, you're still missing the point."

While he was talking, I was scanning the ground, trying to spot the tripwires. What had he rigged? In daylight, I might have seen them easily. The burning torches helped a little.

I saw flickering lines across the square. I could see some on my left and right, stopping me from going into the outbuildings. Why? Was Rom in one of them?

I said, "Tell me why. What's this all about, Sir? Is it about the bank raid?"

"Well done, Captain!"

"It wasn't Irgun, was it?"

"No, it was the British soldiers. They found documents in a safe they took. They couldn't get it open and broke a safecracker out of prison to help." He laughed. "You know, being on the inside, working for the British Army, helped. And then I created the Killing Crew to distract your lot. I was the source of my own stories." He laughed again, and I had the sense that he was probably mad.

I said, "You put a bomb under the building at Sarafand."

"Did anyone survive?"

"None of the Shomrim chaps or their prisoners."

"They were all guilty," he said, his voice dropping lower.

"Pardon?"

"They were guilty and I'm guilty."

Behind my back, I had my gun in my waist. Taking a step closer, I put my hands behind me. Trying to move casually.

"Stop!" he shouted.

I pulled my gun out but he beat me to it. I didn't see his hands move but a bullet ricocheted off the stones a yard ahead.

I froze.

"Step back."

I stepped back.

"I've explained everything. Go to the Bentley."

My initial thought was that he'd rigged the car. I'd open the door and it would blow.

"There's no bomb in there," he called. "Just a note. But before that, you'll want to save your secretary. Miss Rom is in the building behind the Bentley."

As I walked swiftly towards the Bentley, I scanned for wires. I'd stopped looking at Sir in the loft.

At first, I heard a *whoosh*. The sound made me dive for my Land Rover. My instinct told me he was shooting. But he wasn't. When I turned, the loft was on fire.

Sir hadn't moved, his hands were still on either side of the window, and he was watching me.

"Read the note!" he yelled.

I expected screams as the fire licked at him, but he didn't. But it only lasted a second because he was there and then he wasn't. The top of the house exploded. It wasn't as big a bang as at Sarafand, but big enough to knock me back. I felt the blast and then the heat.

My instinct told me to go towards the house. Could I save him? Did I want to save him?

But as I was processing these thoughts, the outbuilding on my right exploded. This one was a bigger boom.

# SIXTY-THREE

I expected the outbuilding on the left to explode at any moment. Levi had blown himself up, he'd blown up the men at Sarafand and now he was killing us.

He was a madman!

But even so, I stepped over a wire across the front of the outbuilding behind the cars. Was she in there? I grabbed a flaming torch and kicked open a barn door with my teeth clenched and breath held.

Was this the end?

The door crashed open. There was no explosion. Not yet anyway.

I took a breath and leaned in, using the torch, expecting to see barrels of explosives.

The room was empty.

Except for a bundle in the far corner.

Still expecting a booby trap, I hurried the twenty feet, scanning for wires. The hump on the floor was Rom, unconscious but alive.

I hoisted her onto my shoulder and hurried out, still half expecting the world to burst into flames with each step.

Then we were outside, and after getting some distance from the buildings, I laid her carefully on the ground. The outbuilding on the right was completely destroyed, flames already going out. Ahead, the main building spat and crackled but was still intact.

I thought I heard a car engine and looked down the track. The torches were burning out, but I could still see them along the farm track to the Palmachim road. There were no cars. The sound was there and gone, leaving me wondering if I'd imagined it. The effect of blasts can do that to your ears.

I got a water bottle from the jeep, and after splashing Rom's face, she came round enough to take a sip and then a gulp.

Rom insisted she was fine, although I could tell she'd been drugged. She was in no condition to drive, so I helped her into the passenger seat of the Land Rover.

While she waited, I opened the Bentley and found a note on the dashboard. It was addressed to me and Wolfe.

I handed it to Rom, told her there was a flashlight in the glove compartment, and let her read while I drove.

"It's a suicide note," she said. Then she told me it confirmed what Levi had said to her in the Bentley on the drive to the farmhouse.

"He was SIR," I explained when she paused. "Levi's real name was Paul Sir."

She said, "He told me we were meeting someone— the source. And that you'd be here. I knew it didn't ring true."

We were on the main coast road, my headlights all over the place, but that didn't matter. We were the only vehicle on the road.

I said, "What does he say about the documents in the safe?"

It was probably the effect of the drug she'd been given, but her speech was slow and awkward. However, she made sense and told me that the soldiers came to Levi because of the shocking thing they'd found. Nazi money was being used to fund the building of Jewish developments. There were five wealthy Jews involved in the scandal and the soldiers thought it should be made public.

"But he didn't make it public," I said.

"No, they used the information against the businessmen. He says here that he regrets it. They're all criminals."

I said, "We're going to Sarafand. That's where I left Wolfe."

She looked at me, her face full of concern.

"Is he hurt? Is that why he's not with you? Oh, I feel bad for not thinking."

"He's fine. I'll tell you about it later," I said. "But you'll see that Levi blew that up too. He killed four prisoners, presumably the wealthy men he mentions."

"They were Shomrim clients," she said. "They were milking them."

"Well, we killed the Shomrim chaps, but I suspect they were supposed to die in the explosion. I guess they thought something good was going to happen at 7 pm. Maybe the final publication of the story. Instead, it ended with a bang."

We turned east, across country towards the rail line and the garrison. Rom was reading the note again.

She said, "That explains why he said they were all guilty." She took a breath. "It's sad."

I waited for her to explain.

"He says that his wife found out and was leaving him. He killed his wife and his son before setting up the explosion at Sarafand."

"He was wracked with guilt," she said, before repeating what she'd already said. I let her talk.

"He'd decided that they all needed to be punished. They were all criminals: the British deserters and the Jewish investors. He had no faith in the law, so he'd concluded that they must all die." She stared out into the gathering darkness. "My God, he killed his wife and child!"

I said nothing and listened to the thump and rattle of the jeep on the rough terrain.

Rom said, "He told me we'd meet the source. But he was the source."

"Yes."

I turned into the garrison, went past the headquarters and parked well short of the bomb site.

When I stopped, she was looking at me. I could see she was struggling with something.

"He said I was brought along as a witness."

I nodded. It's been troubling me too. "Why involve us?"

"So that we'd know it was over?"

Why would that matter? Why did Levi take Rom to the farmhouse near Palmachim? I was also troubled by the engine sound I might have heard.

We got out.

"Where's Major Wolfe?" she asked suddenly. "What happened here?"

As we walked towards where the officers' club had been, I told her about the fighting and Nazeem's involvement.

"So where was Wolfe?"

"He'd been knocked out and left in another building."

"And he's all right?"

"He has a lump on his head, but that's it."

"And Nazeem?"

I'd forgotten to say that he'd been killed, and felt bad that I hadn't recognized his role. I'd done the man a disservice. After all, he'd come back to help us and died for a job that wasn't his.

Wolfe wasn't there. We walked all around and saw the deserter called Zach, who I'd shot first. Maybe if I hadn't lost control, hadn't shot him, maybe if we'd gone with the plan and got in and out faster, maybe Nazeem would still be alive. He wouldn't be lying in the dirt, blown half to bits.

But he wasn't in the dirt where I'd left him. Wolfe wasn't around, and I noticed that one of the Shomrim vehicles had gone.

Later, I learned that Wolfe had decided to take Nazeem home. He hadn't known Rom had been kidnapped. Nor did he know about Levi. He'd last sent me to make a call to the reporter. When I didn't return, he waited almost an hour before leaving. We must have just missed him.

"What now?" Rom asked as I drove out of the garrison.

"It's time we told the police."

# SIXTY-FOUR

We went to the police headquarters and I asked for Sub-Inspector Rosen. He wasn't available because he was out investigating a double murder that evening.

I left a cryptic message about the Killing Crew and meeting me at the farmhouse called Shuldik at seven in the morning. I marked it on a map for them.

Then Rom and I went to Wolfe's hotel expecting him to be there. He wasn't but we decided to wait.

By midnight, Rom was asleep on the bed and I was on the chair. I wanted to sleep but couldn't. My brain wouldn't let me. Maybe it was the excitement of the last few hours. Or maybe it was a puzzle piece that didn't fit.

By the time it got light, I was starting to make sense of it.

"You want to be a detective," I said when Rom stirred.

"I do."

"The key question you will learn to ask is why. Why has this happened? Why did he do it that way?"

"You mean Levi? Yes, why did he kill himself like that?"

"Or appear to," I said. I'd been looking through the briefcase for a newspaper clipping. I couldn't find it.

"You don't think he's dead?"

"It would be a good cover," I said, shutting the case. "Make it look like you blew yourself up—"

"—with us as witnesses!"

"So you think Levi is still alive?"

"Meet me back at the farmhouse," I said. And then I asked her to get hold of a newspaper article that bothered me. I felt the answer was in there. The clipping had been in Mason's file, but Levi must have taken it because the piece had gone. Its disappearance added to the likelihood I was right.

# SIXTY-FIVE

Dave Rosen ran his hands through hair that looked redder than usual in the light. Dawn filtered through the burnt-out farmhouse. He was already there with three police cars and armed men when I arrived.

I went up, and from the loft I watched them searching the grounds. No need for guns now, chaps. The action's over.

I could smell the man's flesh still heavy in the air. Flies were starting to gather.

"He's definitely dead!" Rosen said beside me.

"But he made a mistake."

Rosen suppressed a laugh. "Yes. It's a terrible way to go."

I had to agree. The body's bottom half was burnt to a cinder. The top was black. The hair and clothes were gone and his face had melted.

Even so, it still looked like Levi, the reporter.

"Shuldik," Rosen said, "The name of the farm. It's Yiddish for 'guilty of a dishonest act'. It fits with the suicide note."

I shook my head.

My initial theory was that it hadn't been Levi up here. Then I thought he'd created a literal smokescreen and done a Houdini vanishing act. I thought we wouldn't find his body. But it was him and he was dead.

One more theory.

I pointed to the arms. They had been spread wide as though imploring God or perhaps expressing his superiority. That had been the impression I'd got from down below. Now I could see why. His right wrist was tied to a nail at the top of the window frame. The left arm hung down now, but it was more burnt than the other. Where he would have been leaning against the frame, I saw another nail.

I said, "He expected all of this to burn."

Rosen looked at me, curious.

I pointed to the right wrist. "It's a handcuff," I said. "Both hands were tied."

"He made sure it happened. No backing out if you're handcuffed."

I shook my head. "Levi didn't do this to himself, Dave. He could tie one but not both of them."

"Bugger!" Rosen said, finally seeing it. "There was someone else here."

Outside, I could see dust on the road. A car travelling fast towards us.

"Ash, you're telling me that Levi wasn't the Engineer?"

I was already hurrying to the stone stairs at the back.

Rosen called, "If Levi wasn't the Engineer, do you know who was? Who did this?"

"Not yet," I shouted back.

He didn't follow, and when I was outside, I could see him with the body. Last night I hadn't seen Levi's face clearly. I saw Rosen run his hand through his hair again as he pondered the problem but it was still hard to see his features.

314

I jogged towards the road and the approaching car. It was a green Morris.

Good girl, I thought. She'd used her initiative and taken the secretary's car from outside Shomrim's office.

Rom skidded to a halt and got out.

"Sorry, it took me so long to get the clipping. I went to the *Press* and got another copy. Ironic."

There was a grin on her face as she handed me the newspaper cutting that I'd asked for. She also gave me a magnifying glass, although I didn't need it.

"It's what you thought?" she asked, trying to read my face.

"It is. I'll explain later. Go back to the hotel and wait for Wolfe. I'm going with Rosen."

I knew she was full of questions, but I left her and jogged back to the courtyard. Rosen was outside now and walking towards me.

"What?" he said.

"It's all an elaborate trick," I said. "Clever, but he made mistakes. Like you said, that's not the Engineer up there."

I handed him the newspaper clipping and pointed to the photograph. The old bank governor and security guards.

"What am I looking for?" the detective said, puzzled, but I was already heading for the Land Rover.

"Let's go," I said. "You drive, and I'll explain on the way."

Rosen barked out some instructions to his men before firing up the Land Rover. He was aiming for the main track, but I told him to go the other way.

He looked a question at me.

"There must be another track, and it'll confirm my theory." I pointed and he followed my direction.

"So who is it?" he said.

"We've time. I need to start at the beginning. Then I'll point out the clues."

I needed to be sure of this other track. No doubt Rosen was irritated by my delaying tactic, but he listened patiently as I talked. I told him everything that had happened—except for our run-in with the Slovak gang.

The track behind the farmhouse went north along the coast before cutting east. Eventually, we came out on the main coast road and turned towards Jaffa. We'd been travelling on the first track that I'd seen last night while searching for the farm.

"We're looking for someone with a connection to the original crime," I said.

"The bank raid?"

"The bank raid."

"So the killer is another reporter?"

"Close," I said. "Someone was feeding the reporter information from the start. He was the source. I believe he also gave Mason the name Sir. I think he broke into Mason's apartment in Jerusalem to give us the date. He may even have put the name on the calendar. I should have realized that Shomrim would have removed anything incriminating if it had been them."

We passed the road that would eventually lead to Sarafand Garrison. Rosen would have to visit the other bombsite later.

I continued: "We found a taxi receipt in the apartment. He should have removed it. I should have guessed the connection. Mason couldn't travel by train at the end so he took a Kesher Passenger Car."

I pointed to the newspaper clipping. It was the photograph that tied it all together. The old governor and three men behind. Three guards.

Two of the bank guards were now dead.

"Look closely at the one on the right," I said, holding out the magnifying glass.

"What about him?"

He struggled to steer and use the glass at the same time.

"Those teeth," I said, pointing to Snaggletooth. "That's the taxi driver. That's Levi's source."

# SIXTY-SIX

The taxi driver had taken me to Sarafand. He'd been outside Mason's apartment in Jerusalem. He hadn't necessarily been following; he was making sure we found the clues that would lead to Levi. He wanted a fall guy.

He also wanted a witness to the apparent confession and suicide of Saul Levi. But Levi must have been drugged when I saw him in the farmhouse loft. It wouldn't have been his voice talking to me, it would have been Snaggletooth's.

The explosions and saving Rom were to distract me as Snaggletooth made his escape. I thought I'd heard an engine, and there was a way back to the main road that was hidden behind the farm.

I figured Snaggletooth had been outside the garrison to make sure I went to the farm. He'd waited on the road in the blue car and pretended to be scared. He'd confirmed I was chasing Levi and heading for Palmachim.

After I'd gone, he'd undoubtedly raced after me. I'd been driving too fast to worry about someone in my dust. He'd have taken the first track and probably arrived at the farm only minutes before me. Although he would have already set it all up. Rom would have been tied up in the barn and Levi drugged and standing in the window.

As I talked I'd also remembered seeing the blue car outside the hotel when I'd returned. Snaggletooth hadn't taken Rom, he'd either been following them or watching for me.


Rosen planned to telephone all police stations and have the IDF checkpoints on the lookout for anyone matching the taxi driver's description.

Before doing that we decided to visit the bank in case they had a name for our taxi man. Rosen also wanted to warn them in case there was trouble today.

We discovered that the new bank governor was missing, and we had no luck with the photograph until an old-timer was brought forward to take a look. He remembered the raid and the deaths of the guards and said that Snaggletooth was called David Ettinger.

"Right," Rosen said. "I'll telephone about him from the Jaffa police station."

"Not yet," I said. "I have a hunch."

We got back in the car and I drove to the Passenger Car office.

"Let's go to Kesher's first. They'll have a name and his address."

"Likely phoney."

I thought he'd be right, but as we arrived at the Passenger Car office, I saw the drivers outside. Snaggletooth-Ettinger was there, sitting on the wall chatting without a care in the world. My hunch was right. Ettinger hadn't run yet. He was playing dumb. Carrying on as though nothing had happened.

I told Rosen to continue and drop me around a corner. When I walked back to the office, I saw Ettinger glance at me. He must have been considering his options, but he turned away and acted casual, talking to the man beside him.

"Oh hello," he said as I approached. "Did you find the reporter?"

He was good. I saw nothing in his face that hinted at what he'd done.

I nodded. "Just in time."

"Just in time?"

"He's badly injured but the fire didn't kill him."

One second, Ettinger seemed relaxed, the next he was on his feet, darting away.

Straight into the arms of SI Rosen.

Ettinger didn't confess. However, the police found Levi's car—a dark blue Fiat—close to Ettinger's home. Inside the house, they found two travel cases. One was packed for a long journey. The second was full of money and documents. *The* documents: contracts that proved five men were using money sourced from Nazi Germany.

Perhaps if they'd used the money for the public good it would have been ironically acceptable. But they hadn't. The five men had become wealthy on the back of the investments and building projects using the money. The Killing Crew, who became part of Shomrim Security, used that information to extort money from the investors, killing one of them early on as a message to the others.

The documents linked Ettinger to the crime, but he said he'd uncovered them during his part-time investigative work for Levi. Maybe he'd have gotten away with it, but the police found another address for him. And at that address, they found evidence that Ettinger was a bomb-maker. He'd rigged it up to explode, destroying the evidence, but a timer had failed and the police hadn't been fooled by a backup trip switch.

Two days later, Dave Rosen came to see me and explained that one of the bodies they'd found at Sarafand Garrison was the new bank governor. From the description, I realized this was the man Wolfe referred to as Fatty.

"He'd been executed," Rosen said.

"They wanted him to confess."

"Ettinger also needed him dead, we believe."

I was intrigued.

Rosen said, "Some of the paperwork in Ettinger's suitcase—from the bank raid—were promissory notes. We think Ettinger was afraid they'd become invalid if the new governor took over. Perhaps he could have cancelled them or changed the currency. We'll stop using Palestinian pounds eventually, but I'm told the government has higher priorities."

He also told me that they'd found Levi's wife and son poisoned. They also found a written confession by Levi, which corroborated what they knew and pointed the finger at Ettinger. Maybe he kept it as insurance or leverage against Ettinger. Whatever, it hadn't worked, but it did serve to add to the weight of evidence against the man we knew as the Engineer.

"It seems that he was responsible for another death," Rosen told me. "Remember Thomas Flynn?"

Of course I did. Thomas Flynn had been allegedly held for ransom by the Stern Gang. They were paid but killed him anyway. It had been the trigger for *Palestine Press* staff to change their names.

The Stern Gang always denied it.

Rosen said, "Levi says that it was Ettinger. He says Flynn was close to discovering the truth and Ettinger killed him, both to keep him quiet and as a warning to anyone else. I've no doubt Levi benefited financially from the relationship with Ettinger, but his confession claims a high degree of coercion."

We walked and chatted about other things. It wasn't like old times. Our relationship could never be what it was before—when we'd been on the same side.

"I thought you were involved," I confessed to my friend.

"What?" He was taken aback.

"You were always mysteriously absent. Like last night."

"Ah," he said.

I looked at him, curious. He had a twinkle in his eyes. "What?"

He bit his lip before speaking. "An affair, I'm afraid."

"Another man's wife."

He nodded.

"You don't change," I said.

We walked a few more paces. "And that was it. You suspected me because of that?"

"Much more," I said. "Ettinger gave us the name Sir and I wondered if it was SIR—the initials of Sub-Inspector Rosen."

"Hopefully this success will make me Inspector Rosen."

"Hopefully," I said.

"Don't think I'll forgive you though, Fred," he said, using his old nickname for me.

I laughed.

"Don't expect you to, Ginger."

# EPILOGUE

A female division of the Israeli police force was formed and Sylvia Rom was made a sergeant. But that was a few months away yet.

Bill Wolfe telephoned Bert Finney's parents. They'd already had the official notification of their son's death, but Wolfe provided a personal touch. I listened in and heard him say that Bert had played a major role in stopping war criminals. It would never be in the public domain. It was too sensitive for that. But Bert had been an asset to the team and a hero.

Wolfe hadn't needed to say that. He could be a difficult man to work with, but my respect for Bill Wolfe increased that day.

With nothing better to do, we cleaned up and supervised repairs to the SIB office. On the day it was finished we finally received new orders. We were going back to Cyprus. Back to play the waiting game until needed again.

We had three days before our boat out of Haifa.

After a workout at the gymnasium, I took a stroll through Jaffa. People were moving back into the premises. Port business was starting up again, although

I didn't see any Arabs returning. After all, they were still officially the enemy.

I walked along the street where I'd first met Hannah Münz—the girl with the baby—and saw her coming towards me. She wasn't crying this time, but she still appeared weary.

"How are you doing?" I asked.

"Surviving."

"Did you find work?"

"I did. There are cleaning jobs, but how can I work with a baby?"

"How much work can you get as a cleaner?"

She told me and gave me a handsome figure as her potential earnings. "But—"

I looked into the pram and the cute child smiled up at me. I wondered.

"Be here tomorrow at this time," I said. "I have an idea."

It didn't take much persuasion. I told Ruth Gotting the full story about the Killing Crew and the Engineer and Charlie Mason's role. I'd planned to update her anyway, but I now had a request. As a favour, I asked if Ruth would act as a childminder for a few weeks while Hannah Münz established herself as a cleaner.

After I told her about Hannah's plight, Ruth was delighted by the suggestion. She said it would give her more of a purpose and she would only charge for any out-of-pocket expenses.

Erika, my landlady was also delighted by the news.

We played cards and I told her the story of the bank raid and documents that had been found by the soldiers.

"So they never got all that money?"

"Not much. Not until the bank guard persuaded them to use the information and effectively blackmail the businessmen."

"How did he get involved?"

"The detective thinks he was the inside man. So he was always involved. He was the mastermind, it seems. He told the reporter it was Irgun."

"I knew it wasn't!"

"He also created the myth about the Killing Crew."

She nodded. "Now you've solved this major crime, what's next for the intrepid Ash Carter?"

And so I told her about our orders. We'd be leaving in three days.

"Two nights," she said.

"My room will be available. Could I keep paying for it?"

She looked at me quizzically and I explained my idea. I would pay for two months and let Hannah Münz have the room. After that, Hannah would have to pay for herself. What I didn't say was that the remaining Slovak debt collector money would be paying for it.

Erika seemed upset. She took a sip of her brandy and said nothing.

"Erika?"

"Yes," she said finally. "She can have the room, but that rate will get her four months."

I laughed because that meant I had been paying double the going rate. Then I stopped because she still looked sad.

"What is it?" I asked.

"You're getting soft. That's bad."

"Bad?"

"Bad for me. You're rather nice for an Englishman. You've got the looks and a heart."

I said nothing.

"I suppose for a moment I hoped you'd be back. You know, that you wanted the keep the room on for when you returned."

"I don't know when or if I'm coming back," I said.

"And I don't think I'll ever forgive the British."

I understood. There was a great deal of pain on both sides.

We packed away the cards and cleared the drinks.

We were in the hall when she spoke again as though we'd not stopped. "And as for a relationship... Did you mean what you said a week ago?"

I looked at her, uncertain of what she meant.

"You said, when I smiled... you called me a beautiful woman."

*Ah.* I nodded. "You are."

"I can't forgive the British," she said and touched my hand. "You know that."

"I wouldn't expect you to."

Her hand was still in mine, her other opened her bedroom door.

"So you'll be gone after two more nights."

She stepped through and then waited. Still holding my hand, our arms outstretched. Her eyes were warm and inviting.

"Two nights," she said softly, and gave a little pull. "Perhaps it'll be an incentive for you to come back soon."

I moved towards her.

We went inside and shut the door.

# Acknowledgements

In addition to the authors mentioned in my note, I am grateful to Eric Stanford-Jones for personal information concerning the Palestine Police Force which included photographs of his father, Charles William Robert (Bob) Jones who served in 2152 B/C Security Section, Palestine Police HQ, Haifa.

Richard Sheehan once again did a great job, providing insight during the editing process. I must also thank my unofficial editing team of Maureen Bailey, Pete Tonkin and Richard Lipscombe. In addition, I should like to thank John Christiansen for his advice on military matters, and Jonathan Dunsky, author of the Adam Lapid mysteries, for historical corrections. I should also mention Phil Ellis, SIB Branch Secretary, who kindly answered my random questions.

A special word of thanks must also go to Jonathan Abratt, my friend and man on the ground in Tel Aviv. As always, any mistakes are mine and not theirs.

Finally, I should like to thank you, the reader for your support.

# THE SINGAPORE
## ASH CARTER THRILLERS

murraybaileybooks.com

## IF YOU ENJOYED THIS BOOK

Feedback helps me understand what works, what doesn't and what readers want more of. It also brings a book to life.

Online reviews are also very important in encouraging others to try my books. I don't have the financial clout of a big publisher. I can't take out newspaper ads or run poster campaigns.

But what I do have is an enthusiastic and committed bunch of readers.

Honest reviews are a powerful tool. I'd be very grateful if you could spend a couple of minutes leaving a review, however short, on sites like Amazon and Goodreads.

If you would like to contact me, I'm always happy to receive direct feedback so please feel free to use the email address below.

Thank you
Murray

murray@murraybaileybooks.com

Printed in Great Britain
by Amazon

80893263R00195